FINALLY
SEEN

Published by Knights Of
Knights Of Ltd, Registered Offices:
119 Marylebone Road, London, NW1 5PU

www.knightsof.media
Published in the UK, 2023
First published in the US by Simon & Schuster, 2023
001

Written by Kelly Yang

Set in Adobe Garamond Pro
Typeset design by Sophie McDonnell
Typeset by Sophie McDonnell
Printed and bound in the UK

A CIP catalogue record for this book will be
available from the British Library

ISBN: 9781913311872

Chapter 1

I listen to the quiet hum of the plane and the not-so-quiet flutter of my heart in my chest. *This is it.* Another six hours and I will finally see my parents and my sister again! I try to picture Mum's and Dad's faces when I land. Except I keep picturing Marge and Homer Simpson. Only Asian. With shorter hair. And a less smart Lisa. (Hopefully.)

I guess that's what happens when you haven't seen your family in five years (and you've watched a *lot* of subtitled *Simpsons*). I was starting to give up on the whole going-to-America thing, until my Mum called six weeks ago.

"Lao Lao told me you're doing your middle school applications," Mum said. "And you're writing an essay on your parents being in America?"

I nodded, coiling the phone cord around my fingers.

"Is that not a good topic?" I asked.

"No . . ." she said, "it's just . . . what are you going to say?"

I shrugged. I like writing, but not as much as I like drawing pictures. But art's a sure way to get kicked out of any school in Beijing, let alone Beijing Normal Middle School #3, where I was applying. It was my aunt Jing's middle school. She now has a fancy tech job in Shenzhen. She says there's no future for artists in China. Beijing Normal would get the art out of me . . . and turn me into a steady workhorse. Just like her.

"Well?" Mum asked.

I felt a rush of heat spread across my forehead. Here was my chance to tell her how I really felt about being left behind all these years. I was only five years old when she left. I thought she was going on a *work* trip. I didn't even understand. Most of all, how could she take Millie, my baby sister, and not me? My sister got to grow up with my parents. Me? I grew up with postcards from my parents.

But as usual, my voice was locked in the chamber

of my throat.

There are things I don't want to tell anyone, well, except Lao Lao.

My grandmother, Lao Lao, is my moon and my Wilson. Like the volleyball in *Cast Away* (another movie I binged), she is my companion in my waiting city. That's what Beijing feels like, just me and Lao Lao waiting. It used to be me, Lao Lao, and Lao Ye. But last year, when Lao Ye passed away . . . our trio of tea leaves went down to two. Now I am Lao Lao's human alarm clock (I wake her up every day at 6 a.m.), dumpling steamer, pu'er brewer, flower waterer, and medicine fetcher.

I know how much she needs me. I'm all she's got left. Which is why some feelings are too hard to even tell her.

Instead, I catch them and tuck them behind my cheek.

Lao Lao says that's the way to succeed in China.

Every morning, Lao Lao reminds me: go to school, make your parents proud, and watch your words, lest they label you a bad apple. She grew up in the era of the Cultural Revolution, and her father was thrown in jail for being a "bad apple." Even though that was a long time ago, the memory of it never really left. She's always telling me to sew up half my mouth. I imagine an invisible thread running along my mouth, my lips stitched like a sock.

But the thing about some feelings is . . . they just won't go away. Instead, they form a tight ball at the base of my throat. Where they sit and they wait, planning their escape from the thread. And one day, just when you least expect it, they shoot out like a rocket.

That's exactly what happened that rainy Beijing spring day when Mum called.

"Do you really want to go to Beijing Normal #3?" Mum asked.

I looked over at my lao lao, craning her head eagerly to catch snippets of our conversation. She put her knitting needles down, massaging her hand. Her arthritis had gotten so much worse since Lao Ye passed, she could hardly keep knitting. The doctors in China had warned her that this day would come. They told her to do more acupuncture, to get out and exercise. But Lao Lao was born in the Year of the Ox. She does not like anyone telling her what to do.

I turned away from Lao Lao, held the phone close

to my face, and cupped a hand around my mouth.

"No," I whispered. "I want to go to school in America. Please, Mama. I want to come."

And with that, I chose my future over my past.

*

A hand on my arm pushes me awake.

"Lina Gao?" the flight attendant asks. I rub my eyes awake. She smiles and says to me in Chinese, "We're moving you up to first class. So you can get out first when we land!"

I blink in confusion. I reach for my sketch pad. I was in the middle of working on a sketch of Lao Lao gardening, but as I look up, my eyes nearly pop when I see the flight tracker on the screen. We're almost *there!*

"Your escort will be waiting as soon as we get to LAX to take you to your parents."

I leap up from my seat. *Let's gooooo!!!*

I follow the flight attendant up the long aisle to first class, staring at all the people stretched out in *beds* with their noise-canceling headphones and candyfloss slippers. These are airplane *apartments.*

I take a seat in one of the cabins and reach for the

fancy first-class cotton slippers. I'm so saving these for Lao Lao. I wonder if she likes her new nursing home.

I feel a tug of guilt thinking about it, but Aunt Jing said it was necessary. She and Uncle Hu both live in Shenzhen, which is about twelve hundred miles away from Beijing, and they both have 9-9-6 tech jobs. A 9-9-6 job means you work from 9 a.m. to 9 p.m. six days a week. They're the envy of the country, because they make the most money. But it also means there's no *way* my aunt can be a tea brewer for my lao lao.

So they took me and Lao Lao to visit the nursing home. I remember the floors were very shiny, almost like you could go roller skating on them. I pictured a bunch of elderly folks roller skating, and then had to bite on my cheeks to stop myself from giggling. Because it wasn't funny.

The rooms were bright, with big windows that allowed the team of nurses to look in at all times. Aunt Jing said she got Lao Lao the biggest room of all – a private room. It was the nicest room in the entire nursing home. But to Lao Lao, it was like living inside a fishbowl. She didn't like the idea *at all*.

"No way!" she said, stomping her walking cane down on the ground. "Not happening! I am a free spirit — I need to be able to roam around the park and go to see my friends!"

"They can come see you!" Aunt Jing insisted. "That's why we're putting you into a retirement home in Beijing — so your friends can come visit. Anytime!"

Lao Lao has two good park friends: Chen Nai Nai, a grandma who loves to dance, and Wang Nai Nai, whose daughter is also in America. I've never seen either of them come to our house, though.

"Why can't I just stay by myself?" Lao Lao asked, peeking at my aunt.

"Because, Ma, your arthritis and osteoporosis, it's all getting worse. And now that Dad's gone . . . Frankly, you should have gone into a retirement community a long time ago," Aunt Jing said. "But you had Lina —"

"And I loved every minute of it, sweet child," Lao Lao said, patting my hand.

I felt a tear escape. This was all my fault.

"No, don't you cry," Lao Lao told me. She nodded to my aunt, and with a shaking hand, she signed the papers.

I put my hand to the airplane window and whisper

with all my heart:

"I'm so sorry, Lao Lao. I promise I will find a way to bring you over. I will find a way to get you out of the waiting city, too."

"Fifteen minutes to landing!" the captain announces on the speaker.

I immediately grab the stash of free goodies next to the candyfloss slippers. I stuff as many as I can into my backpack. Socks, sleeping masks, you name it. I add the stash to my collection of Chinese snacks I've brought over for my (almost) new family. I've packed wheat flour cake, hawthorn flakes, pumpkin chips, and White Rabbit sweets for them, hoping the sweets will fill them with sweet guilt for leaving me behind.

I gaze out the window at the wispy clouds. The Los Angeles houses sprawl across the land, stretching all the way to the shimmering blue sea! I've never seen the ocean before. Before Lao Ye passed, we talked about going to Beidaihe, the closest beach to Beijing. But it was always too hard, with Lao Ye's work and health. He was a magazine editor. Even after he "retired" he kept going into the office. He said working was the best way to stay young, but Lao Lao secretly suspected it was so he could keep eating lunch at his favourite fried dumpling place next to his office.

My lao ye had heart disease and diabetes. He used to joke that at his age, heart disease and diabetes were like stamps in a passport – signs of a life well lived.

I wish Lao Ye had had actual stamps in his passport, though, and more time to get them. But at seventy-two, he had a stroke in the taxi on his way home from work.

We didn't believe it even when we were sitting in the hospital waiting area. Lao Lao and I were still talking about going to the beach and pushing Lao Ye to actually retire after this. When the doctor delivered the news, all I remember is my grandma falling to the ground, pounding the cold stone floor, crying, "You get back here, you old goat! Don't you dare leave me!"

But her beloved goat was already gone.

Lao Lao's voice comes burrowing into my head as the plane starts to descend.

This is different. Remember, we may be six thousand miles apart, but I'm right there in your heart. Anytime you want to talk to me, just put your hand over your chest and I'll feel it, sweet child.

As the turbulence jiggles my butt, I open my mouth, like I'm about to eat a gigantic baozi, the tears running down my cheeks. *This is it, Lao Lao! I made it!!!*

We touch down at 9:58 a.m. As the plane taxis, a flight attendant comes up to me. "Are you ready?"

"I'm ready!" I announce.

Chapter 2

I scamper after my escort, who kindly helps me with my carry-on suitcase. She's a fast-walking Chinese lady named Miss Chen, with a walkie-talkie and a giant stack of documents, leading me through immigration. The immigration officer takes one look at my passport and stamps it with his big rubber stamp.

As we wait for my bags, Miss Chen chats with me in Mandarin.

"You excited? I hope your parents are here already, we got in an hour early."

"I'm sure they'll be here!" I say to her, rising to my tippy toes with excitement. I can hardly wait to walk out those double doors to see them.

I scan the conveyer belt for my luggage. Lao Lao

made me bring over three full suitcases of stuff. One of them is an entire suitcase of sweaters she knitted for me and Millie – even though Mum kept telling her it's warm in LA.

"Did you go on a trip to visit your relatives?" Miss Chen asks.

I open my mouth to say *No, this IS the trip* – but I nod instead. Probably easier.

"You have any brothers or sisters?" she asks.

"I have one sister," I tell her. "She's seven."

"Oh, that must be fun! You two love playing together?"

I cross my fingers behind my back. *Sure hope so!*

As I wait, I tell Miss Chen all the things I know about my family by heart, from reading their many letters. I tell her my dad is a scientist. A microbiologist, to be exact. My mother works at a big fancy salon. We live in a beautiful pale blue two-story house with a white fence in Los Ramos, California. A house that's taken my parents some time to finally find. It's just forty miles from Los Angeles.

I talk of my family's accomplishments, as if they're mine.

"Wow," she says. "Sounds like they've really achieved the American dream." I smile.

Every movie and TV show I watch is always talking about the American dream. I'm still not sure exactly what it means, but I think it means something like this:

1. To be able to buy any kind of Frappuccino you want.
2. To have a nice home and fill your bed with *a lot* of pillows, like you have a thousand heads.
3. To say *I love you,* all the time, to your family. And not be embarrassed.

I like number three the most. I don't remember when Mum and I stopped saying it on the phone. Maybe Mum didn't want my little sister Millie to be jealous. Or she didn't think I needed to hear it.

But I did.

The truth is, my time in the waiting city wasn't just all dumplings and tea. It was hard, too. I'm not going to tell Mum now that I'm back because what's the point? But I hope I hear Mum say *I love you* again. All the time. And not just because it's the American thing to say.

Chapter 3

Lina? Is that you? Lina?" a voice calls out in Mandarin when Miss Chen and I finally push through the double doors with my luggage.

I see a Chinese woman with long, wavy hair. A man standing next to her is snapping pictures. She runs up to me, crying and sobbing so uncontrollably, I take a step back. The little girl standing next to her looks just as confused as I am.

It's only when the man says, "It *is* you, sunflower!" that it hits me. This is them. My parents!

I recognise them from the pictures!

I stand there, emotion choking me as I replay Dad's nickname for me on my tongue.

Mum kneels in front of me on the stone airport floor and wraps me in a warm hug. I close my eyes and breathe her in. She smells like warm congee on a rainy day.

"Mama!" I cry.

Dad adds his arms around us and Millie jumps in too, and we're a wet sandwich. We stay like this, cocooned in our little world. And I know I made the right choice. The future is infinitely better than the past.

When we finally pull away, I smile at my little sister. She looks just like me. But cuter. I try not to think about how much cuter. (Like, a *lot*.) She still has all her baby fat and her eyes shine brightly above her dimpled cheeks. She looks like some sort of perfect Pixar character.

"Is China enormous? Do you like my earrings? Mum let me get my ears pierced for my birthday and I have to keep these in for six weeks, but then I can change them! Do you have a TikTok account?" she asks in Chinese.

I am relieved she knows Chinese, and I shake my head. My new sister's mind is like a space cruiser from *Star Wars* – traveling at light speed. Her rapid tongue shifts between Chinese and English words whenever she gets stuck. At my old school, I studied

English too. But hearing *her* speak English . . . my tongue shrinks in intimidation.

"No, we don't have TikTok," I reply in Chinese. "We have something called Douyin, though."

Millie repeats it. "Well, do you have *that?*"

I shake my head. Lao Lao had very specific rules against social media. Especially after some kids in my class started calling me *Lina, Lina left behind. Out of sight, out of mind! She's such a bore, even her parents don't want her anymore!* My ears turn bright red at the memory.

Luckily, Millie is too busy dancing to notice. She prances around my luggage cart as we push it toward the exit. Mum suddenly stops.

"Are you hungry?" Mum asks. "Thirsty?"

"I could use some water," I say.

Mum looks to Dad, who says regretfully, "I forgot the water bottles at Pete's."

Mum fumbles through her purse and pulls out a five-dollar bill. She hands it to me and tells me to go and buy something from the café in the airport. "Millie, why don't you go with her?" Mum says.

My sister dances ahead toward the café. I get in line and stare at the enormous menu of drink options.

There are so many words I don't understand, like *Blends* and *Smoothies* and *Kombucha*. They all sound so delicious, and terrifying at the same time. I turn to my sister, but I'm too embarrassed to ask.

When it's my turn, the server asks me what I want.

"Water," I say, with as much confidence as I can.

"Sparkling or still?" she asks.

Uh-oh. *Is she asking me if I still want it?*

"Yes, I do," I tell her.

"Nooooo." Millie jumps in and says in Chinese, "She wants to know what *kind* of water."

There are kinds?

"Water kind!" I tell her. Obviously. I look at my sister. She smacks her forehead, like there's a huge fly on her brow. I squirm, embarrassed. I should never have opened my mouth and said I was thirsty.

"She means still," Millie says. "How much is that?"

"We only have Fiji. That'll be four seventy-five plus tax," the server says.

"Do you have Dasani? Or Arrowhead, maybe?" Millie rattles off brands I've never heard of. The server shakes her head. Millie peers down at the five dollars in my hand. "You know what, can she just have a cup with ice?"

17

Before I know it, the server hands me an empty cup with ice. I stare at it, confused. *That's* it? Am I just supposed to eat this ice?

But Millie's already bounced back to my parents, who praise her for her quick thinking.

"Good call. They're always overcharging at these airport places! We can fill the cup up with water when we pass a water fountain!" Mum reaches out a hand and smooths Millie's hair.

I follow my family, chewing nervously on the ice cubes.

To think that in Beijing I was able to converse effortlessly with Lao Lao's doctors on the phone and take down complex medicine combinations. Here, I can't even order a water without my little sister.

I wonder how I'm ever going to be the big sister.

Chapter 4

Dad plays tour guide, chatting away in Chinese as he drives. I'm so glad we speak Chinese as a family, aside from the occasional English word Millie sprinkles in. I'm in the back of our Honda Civic, with Millie, trying not to spill my cup of ice water.

Mum found a fountain for me to fill it, and I drink hungrily from it. I glance down at the duct tape holding together the backseat of the Honda Civic.

"To your left is the Westside," Dad explains on the freeway. "It's where the beach is. And actually, if you take the beach motorway all the way up, you'll end up in Ventura County, where we live!"

"Can we go there sometime?" I ask, putting my ice water down on the hot seat. I sit up. "Oh, please!

I love the beach! I saw the ocean from the plane – it looks so blue!"

Mum and Dad exchange a glance. "We'll see. Your dad usually has to work," Mum says.

"Even on the weekends?" I ask, picking at the duct tape on the seat with my finger.

Millie gawks at my hand, like *What are you doing?* I instantly stop tugging at the tape. Note to self: Don't destroy our car.

"Weeds and insects don't understand weekends, unfortunately," Dad sighs.

I furrow my eyebrows. *Insects?*

"Dad works on an organic farm!" Millie says, bouncing in her seat.

Millie seems to always be moving. If she were in China, the teachers would definitely label her a zuo bu zhu, or can't-sit-still kid. Definitely not the best kind of apple, but still redeemable with a little work and discipline. First, the teachers would try to scare the bouncing bean out of her. And if that didn't work, they'd call up her parents and demand she be taken off all sugar.

But Millie reaches into her pocket and gleefully tosses orange Tic Tacs in her mouth, bouncing so hard I can hear the duct tape go *squish-squish-squish*. I look at my parents, but they don't seem to mind. It really is a totally different country. "Yes, an organic farm! It's pretty amazing. Actually, it's also a regenerative farm," Dad says proudly.

"Wait, I thought you were a scientist," I say, looking at my parents, puzzled. "That's what you wrote in all your letters. A microbiologist!"

"I am," Dad says. "That's what I studied in graduate school, when I first came to America. Now I work on a farm for Pete Burton. He's one of the first organic regenerative farmers in Winfield."

"What kind of stuff do you grow?" I ask.

"Carrots, tomatoes, beans, you name it."

So Dad's a legit farmer. Why didn't he just say so in his letters?

I think of the farmers Lao Lao and I met in Bei Gao Li Village. It's out in the countryside, about three hours from Beijing. Twice a year, Lao Lao and I used to go and volunteer there. It was the only time she left Lao Ye at home. And even after he passed, when walking started getting painful for her, she insisted we go.

We had some of our best memories in Bei Gao

Li Village. It used to be a farming village. But over the years, as the locusts ravaged the land and the droughts sucked the soil dry, folks went in search of new opportunities in Shenzhen and Shanghai, leaving behind young children with grandparents.

Bei Gao Li became a waiting village.

I think that's why Lao Lao always took me there. I smile a bit, thinking of little Tao, a five-year-old boy with a teddy bear he carried around everywhere. Little Tao would run around, helping Lao Lao pass out her homemade pork buns.

At the thought of pork buns, my tummy rumbles. Mum must have heard it because she turns and asks, "You hungry?"

This time, I shake my head. I don't dare risk going into a restaurant and making a fool of myself ordering again, just to come out with a bowl of napkins.

"I'll make us some lunch when we get home," Mum says. "Just as soon as the bombs harden."

Did she say *bombs?!* My heart lurches. Who *are* my parents??

"Maybe you can help!" Mum says. "The more hands, the faster it'll be."

"Yeah, it's fun!" Millie adds.

She's making bombs too??

I put a hand to my forehead, horrified that I left my lao lao in a nursing home to join a family of carrot-chomping criminals.

"Uhhhhh . . . I don't know," I say, chewing on my lip. "I'm not really good with explosives."

"Explosives, what are you talking about? We're making *bath* bombs," Mum says.

I stare at her.

"It's like a soap, for the bath," Millie says. "And they smell really nice! You'll see when you get home."

"Ooooooooohhhh," I say, sighing in relief. How did I forget? American homes have bathtubs! I imagine myself soaking in a warm, soothing bath, surrounded by candles, in our beautiful American home.

I close my eyes for just a second, the word *home* tickling at my lashes. It feels almost too good to be true.

Chapter 5

I drift asleep in the car, dreaming of Lao Lao. If Beijing is a waiting place, my dreams are like meeting places.

In my dream, the two of us are running around the fields of Bei Gao Li Village. We're playing the Eagle and the Chicks, my favourite Chinese playground game. In my dream, Lao Ye's still alive and Lao Lao's chasing me, her arms stretched as she laughs and tries to catch me. Lao Lao's the eagle, trying to chase us "chicks."

There's a long trail of village children behind me. We make a giddy, squealing dragon as we run around the field, dodging Lao Lao.

Every time a kid runs near Lao Lao, she tries to hug them in her arms, her silvery hair glistening in the wind. But she's too slow. Finally, she sits down on the green field to catch her breath, and I sit down next to her.

I put my head on her shoulder and twirl a blade of grass around my finger.

"I'm getting too old for this game," she says, patting my head. "You guys keep playing without me."

"No you're not," I insist. I try to pull her up to standing but she won't budge.

The other village kids are waving me over, shouting, "C'mon, c'mon! Lina jie jie, we want to keep playing!"

I look at them and gaze back at my lao lao, torn between joining them in their screaming, giggling fun and staying here with my grandmother.

"Go on," Lao Lao urges. "Have fun! Your friends are all playing!"

In my dream, I do not choose my friends. I sit right by Lao Lao, shoulder to shoulder until the sun sets. It feels like the right choice.

Until I wake up and I realise, it's not the one I actually made.

Chapter 6

Two big eyeballs blink down at me from the top bunk. I scream, which prompts Millie to scream back.

"She's awake!!!" Millie shouts.

I look around, disoriented for a minute. My parents must have carried me in while I was sleeping. Millie jumps off the bunk and tries to pull me to standing.

"Do you like our room?" she asks. She pounces from one corner to the next, like a proud tiger cub showing me her cave. The room is bare and small, but the sun reflecting off the apartment wall next door tints the space light pink.

"I do," I tell my sister.

Millie walks over to my suitcases and examines them curiously.

"Here," I say to her, reaching over and unzipping

one of them. I pull out the big bag of Chinese sweets and hand it to her.

"YESSSSSS!" she squeals. "I love sweets."

She grabs hawthorn flakes, Meiji biscuits, and rabbit sweets and rips them all open. I laugh at her enthusiasm. She takes five rabbit sweets and stuffs them all in her mouth.

"What is this?" she mumbles, chewing.

"Rabbit sweet!" I tell her.

She immediately spits it out into the trash can. "These are made from rabbits?" she asks, making a face.

"No! They're just called rabbit sweets because they're creamy."

"But rabbits aren't creamy," she says, confused.

"You know what – never mind. Just try it. They're really good."

I get out another piece, urging her to try it. I unwrap it for her. Lao Lao and I went around to five different stores, which was not easy with Lao Lao's arthritis. Millie has to give the sweet chewy vanilla sweet a chance – it'll melt her mind!

"No thanks, I'm good," she says.

I frown at Millie, trying to brush off her rejection.

Whatever.

Millie walks over to the closet and opens the mirrored doors. "This is our closet. You can unpack and put your stuff in here!"

I stare at "our" closet. The whole space is packed with Millie's clothes, crinkled-up posters, and stuffed animals. I don't know where I'm supposed to put my clothes – tape them up to the back of the door?

Mum walks in.

"Are you settling in all right?" she asks.

"Uh, where do I put my clothes?" I ask her, pointing to my three stuffed suitcases.

Mum glances at the packed closet and then scolds Millie. "I thought we talked about this. You were supposed to put all your stuffies in a bag and gift them to the little kids in the apartment building, to make more space!"

"But Unicorny and Deery will be so sad to leave," Millie protests. "And so will Liony and Piggy, and Mousy. And don't forget Rabbity!"

Rabbity? Okay, we have got to come up with some better names. Millie grabs each stuffed animal from the closet and holds them tight in her arms.

Mum sighs. "We'll talk about this later. Let's eat

first! I made some lunch while you napped." At the mention of lunch, Millie drops her animals and bolts out of our room.

I follow her down a long corridor. There are framed family pictures hanging in the hallway, and I peek curiously at them.

I see baby Millie trying to walk at the park. My parents holding her at the zoo. My dad in a Texas cowboy hat holding hands with my Mum. Mum and Millie jumping on a sandcastle at the beach.

They look like the perfect family . . . but I'm not in any of them. I plunge my eyes to the ground.

I feel the temperature rise as I try to shake the feeling of being completely left out. *Why am I not in any of the pictures?* Lao Lao and I sent them so many over the years. There was the one of me at the Bird's Nest and at the Beijing Zoo, when my grandfather was still alive. I even remember Mum writing back, *Wow! Lina's so tall now!*

So what happened? Did she run out of frames? She could have just used tape! As my mind runs through millions of other possible adhesives, a powerful scent wafts up my nose – lavender. I look up. There are bath bombs everywhere in the living room – on every corner, every surface, every square inch of the carpet.

"Whoa!" I exclaim. Mum and Millie weren't kidding about their fizzy hobby. "You guys must take a *lot* of baths!"

"Oh, they're not for us," Mum says, picking one up and carefully wrapping it in paper. I notice that Dad's not home. It's just Mum and Millie.

"We don't even have a bathtub!" Millie adds.

I knit my eyebrows. *Then . . . ?*

"We're selling them!" Mum announces. "Twenty dollars a box on Etsy!"

I've heard before of people selling things on the internet in China. One of my classmates' moms sold pencil pouches on Alibaba, but she had tons of employees working for her. Is Mum doing this all out of our home? And wait, whatever happened to the spacious two-story home with a garden they wrote about in their letters? I look around.

This apartment, crammed full of plastic buckets of Epsom salts, is decidedly single story. Was *anything* they said in the letters true?

Mum quickly moves aside the blankets and pillows on top of a thin yoga mat on the floor. I stare at the mat – is that where my parents sleep? Mum sees the

shock on my face. "I know this isn't what you imagined
. . . but your dad and I . . . we're working hard."

My face heats in embarrassment. "No, it's fine!"
I quickly say. I've been here two seconds and I'm
already making my Mum feel bad. I leap past the
buckets of Epsom salts toward the bath bomb
moulds on the kitchen table. "How can I help?"

Mum gives me a smile.

"You can help by moving those bombs outside so
I can get lunch on the table. We're having stir-fried
aubergine!"

The name of one of my favourite dishes puts a
big old grin on my face. How I've missed stir-fries!
Lao Lao used to make the best ones, my favourite
being chicken and mushrooms. But with her arthritis, she hasn't been able to cook as much as before.
We've been living on steamed dumplings that I'd
defrost from the grocery store. My heart leaps at
the prospect of stir-fried aubergine.

Home may not look the same as I imagined – or
even smell the same – but I'm glad it'll still taste the
same in my belly.

I think.

Chapter 7

"How long have you guys been doing this?" I ask Millie as we set down the last of the bath bombs in the courtyard.

The sparkles from the powdery balls sit on my fingers They look pretty under the sun.

"Ever since they announced the rent Morse code's due." Millie says "rent Morse code" in English.

"Rent *what?*" I ask, confused.

A Black man watering his hanging flowers at the apartment next door chimes in. "Y'all talking about the rent moratorium?" he asks.

Doors open and a couple of other neighbours gather.

"What have you heard, Joe?" a Latinx woman walking a small terrier asks.

Millie and I both bend down to pet her adorable dog.

"State says it expires in six weeks. After that, landlords be coming around here, demanding their back rent. And if you can't pay up, they gonna evict you," Joe says.

Mum steps out of our apartment.

"It ain't fair! So many of us lost our jobs during the pandemic," a worker in blue overalls says. "We're just getting back on our feet. Now we gotta come up with six months of back rent?"

"Down at the dry cleaners, we're *still* not at the same volume as before," a woman adds.

Mum shakes her head.

Joe gestures with his hands to stay calm.

"So long as we applied for rent relief, should be all right," he says.

"But that takes forever and a day!" the overalls man says. The neighbours jointly sigh. "I applied back when I lost my truck. Still waiting for my relief cheque."

"Should have known better than to count on the US government," the lady with the dog says. "Been in this country nine years, never asked the government for a cent. And the one time I do, we waiting like grass for rain. And now with groceries up thirty dollars a week . . ."

Are groceries more expensive here, too? Lao Lao was complaining about the price of cooking oil right before I left. (The only thing she appreciated about moving into the nursing home is she wouldn't have to worry about groceries anymore.)

"The cheque will be here. They may be slow as molasses, but it'll be here, and so long as we apply before the deadline, the landlords can't evict us," Joe says. "Come six weeks from now, mark my words, they'll be here swarming like flies!"

I look over at Mum, who looks like she's about to pass out. She quickly takes my hand and Millie's and tells us to come on home.

My mind is full of questions as I walk into the apartment. *What's back rent? And do we owe that too,* I wonder as I slide into the plastic kitchen chair. Is that why we can't buy more frames for my photo in the hallway? But I'm temporarily distracted by the sweet, tangy aroma of stir-fried aubergine.

"Where's Dad?" I ask, picking up my chopsticks. The aubergine melts in my mouth. It tastes just like my lao lao's – soft and sweet, with just enough kick. It'd be even better without the tiny bits of parsley.

"He had to go back to work," Mum says, handing me a spoon and a bowl of egg drop soup. I sip the soup. "It's farmers' market day. We're lucky he could come with us to the airport."

Lucky to come pick up his daughter, after five years apart? Whoa.

"Dad's *always* working," Millie says, reaching for the aubergine. I watch her expertly pick up the delicate vegetables with her steel fork. She doesn't even bother with chopsticks. She really is an American.

"True, but he also brings us lots of vegetables," Mum says, pointing at the heads of fresh lettuce and little bunches of radishes on the counter. "And that's important, at a time like this."

Millie nods as she eats. Mum picks out all the little bits of parsley from the aubergine dish for my sister. I wonder if I should tell Mum I don't like parsley either. I decide I haven't earned the right to change her dishes. Not yet.

"Because of the back rent?" I study Mum's eyes. "What were they talking about out there?"

Mum hesitates. I wish she'd just tell me, now that I'm here. I want to know every detail of our life. The *real* details, not just the version she writes in letters.

"During the pandemic, times were hard," Mum says. "A lot of people lost their jobs, including me."

"Mum used to paint nails!" Millie declares.

At least *that* part about Mum working in a salon was true from the letters. But I'm sad to hear Mum lost her job.

"I was lucky enough to get a job at the only Chinese nail salon in Winfield. The owner hired me even though I'm only on your dad's student visa," Mum says. Her face falls. "But during the pandemic, the salon went out of business."

"Can't you get another job?" I ask her.

"Not without a green card," Mum says with a sigh. "Which is how I started selling bath bombs online. To pay for the back rent . . ."

I swallow hard. So we *do* owe back rent.

"*But also* to launch my new career," Mum says emphatically. "As an entrepreneur! Being in charge of my own destiny! And the great thing is, this is something we can do together."

"I'm Mum's head of product design," Millie brags.

I feel a twinge of jealousy that my sister's beat me to that role. "What about me?" I ask.

"You can be . . . in charge of issuing receipts or something."

I make a face. Do I look like a fifty-year-old accountant? "We'll figure it out, we only started a few weeks ago! But look!" Mum says, whipping out her phone to show me the Etsy app. "Got ten more orders, just today!"

"But what about what Joe said about the rent relief program?" I ask. I didn't understand every word, but I distinctly remember hearing the word *relief*. It made me think of an episode in *The Simpsons* when Marge Simpson gushed, "What a relief!" when the doctors saved Homer after a cart of bobbleheads fell on top of his head.

"Yeah, Mum, maybe we should apply too!" Millie says encouragingly.

"It's . . . complicated," Mum says regretfully. "We're not the same as everyone else."

She doesn't explain how. Instead, she tells us to focus on the goal – selling as many bath bombs as we can for the next six weeks. "If we put all our effort into it, we'll make the back rent money in no time and launch the greatest bath products company America has ever seen! Who's with me?"

I throw my hand up, almost knocking over my bowl of rice. Mum can count on me. I'd say I have a pretty good record in achieving the impossible!

I'm here, aren't I?

Chapter 8

After lunch, while my sister and Mum mix more dry ingredients for the bath bombs, I sit at the kitchen table designing the receipt. It's a donkey-butt job, but I'm determined to impress Mum. So I focus on designing the logo that goes on top of the receipt. Since Mum and Millie have only been doing this a few weeks and have been preoccupied making the bath bombs different scents and colours, they haven't gotten around to designing a logo yet.

I work all afternoon at the kitchen table, sketching in my notebook as the golden California sun filters in through the honeycomb-screen window. As Mum and Millie mix ingredients, Mum tells me why she picked bath bombs in the first place.

"I just love the way they can transport you with

just a scent. For instance, Osmanthus. One whiff and I am back in Guilin during the annual sweet Osmanthus bloom. It's where your dad and I went on our honeymoon."

I smile.

"Or the plum blossom. We used to take you girls every year to the Summer Palace in Beijing. Do you remember that?" Mum asks.

I nod eagerly, even though I don't remember it. But I want to remember.

"Of course!" I say.

"We would go boating on the Kunming Lake together," Mum says.

"It was such a beautiful lake." I close my eyes, imagining.

"And we'd look up at the clouds and try to make pictures together," Mum continues.

"The clouds looked like long feathers," I say dreamily.

"I don't remember that," Millie says.

"How can you not remember? It was so lovely." I grin, glad I can finally beat her at something family-related. Even if it's just a pretend win. I walk over and show Mum my logo design. I drew a pink bath bomb with little bubbles surrounding it. I drew our initials, *QML*, in cursive through the ball. "Do you like the *Q*?"

Millie wipes the baking soda off her hands onto her apron and walks over to peek at it.

"Mum's not *Q*," Millie says. "She's *J. J* for *Jane*."

I turn to Mum. When did she become Jane?

"Jane's just easier than Qian," Mum explains.

"Easier for who?" I ask. I can't believe it. All this time, I've been climbing up the steps to the Temple of Heaven to wish my parents health and good luck, with Lao Lao in tow, and I've been praying for the wrong name!

"For the customers I used to do the nails of, at the salon," Mum says. "When they heard Qian, they thought, *She's totally new. She doesn't know how to do gel or dip powder or rhinestone cuticle art.* So I had to switch to Jane."

I stare at Mum, shocked that she would swap her beautiful Chinese name that Lao Lao lovingly gave her – which means "trailblazer" – for nail gel. I mean seriously.

But mostly I want to ask her, *What about me?* I'm new. What are people going to think of me and

41

my Chinese name?

"I think it'll be better if we make the *M* like a heart," Millie says, plopping down at the kitchen table. She turns to a clean page in my sketchbook and starts drawing a *new* logo.

I look over nervously. When it comes to my sketchbook, I guess you can say I'm pretty protective. That's because for five long years, it's been my constant companion. There are things that only those pages know about me – tears that shade the drawings as much as the watercolours, wishes that fill the space as much as words.

And right now, Millie's veering dangerously close to messing all that up. As she scribbles furiously in her big, messy handwriting, I react instinctively.

I lunge over and grab my sketchbook away.

"Hey!" Millie shrieks.

"That's mine," I tell her. "You can't use it."

"I just want to draw this one thing–" Millie protests.

"Well, you can't! Not in this book," I tell her, holding the sketchbook tight to my chest. I give off serious *don't test me* vibes.

Millie looks at Mum. But Mum sits there, hands covered in citric acid, unsure of which daughter to side with. Finally, Millie turns and stomps to her room.

And I feel terrible. Like a rotten sister who came all the way over from the other side of the world just to give her little sister a hard time over paper.

That is not who I am.

I know that's not who I am.

But as I open up the sketchbook and lovingly stroke my picture of Lao Lao gardening that I drew on the plane, I breathe a sigh of relief that Millie's sharp pencil did not jab it.

I also know . . . my lao lao would *not* be happy with me.

Chapter 9

"Lao Lao!" I say into Mum's phone. I finally get to call my grandmother. It's our late afternoon, but it's morning in China. Beijing is fifteen hours ahead of us. I imagine Lao Lao on the other end, waking up next to her juniper bonsai tree that I got her right before I left, in her private room.

"Lina!" Lao Lao exclaims. I wish I could see her, but Lao Lao doesn't believe in smartphones. Never has. Still, her enthusiasm comes across in waves. "Oh, how I miss you! How was your flight? Tell me everything! How's your Mum? Was that first hug spectacular or what? How's Millie?"

"She's . . . fine." I hug my sketchbook and glance over at our room. Millie's in there with the door closed, still sulking. Which is just as well. I don't want her to listen in on my private conversation with Lao Lao. I sit down on the thick hallway carpet, trying not to gaze at the pictures of not-me.

"What's wrong?" Lao Lao asks.

Leave it to Lao Lao to figure out something's wrong without even seeing my face. I picture her sitting up in bed, reaching for her bamboo comb. It's a ritual of ours. She'd comb my hair while I told her all my problems. *Let's brush out the stress,* she'd say.

Now the problems lather in a thick goop on top of my head.

"Nothing . . . I'm just tired," I tell Lao Lao. "How's the retirement home? Are you settling in okay?"

"Oh, Lina, you should see this place. They got rules for everything! Last night, I was trying to call your aunt, and my neighbour next door complained to the nurses that I was talking too loud. Can you believe it? I got in *trouble,* like a little kid!"

I can't imagine Lao Lao getting in trouble with anyone. She's the nicest person I know. She's always going out of her way to help her neighbours, picking up extra bundles of green onions or a couple of cucumbers for Li Tai Tai, because she knows Li Tai Tai is on a tight pension.

"Can Aunt Jing help?" I ask.

"She'll only make things worse. She'll call up all huffing and puffing, like it's one of her big important conference calls. They'll promise the moon and the stars. Then the minute she hangs up, everyone will laugh at me."

"Oh, Lao Lao," I say. I want so badly to reach into the phone and give my grandmother a hug.

"That's not even the worst of it. You know my bonsai tree? One of the nurses said juniper needs a lot of sun or it will die. Before I knew it, they moved it outside. Now I can't even admire it every day."

"Mumu's gone?" I ask.

I jump up at the injustice, ready to go over there and kick some bonsai butt! Then I remember Lao Lao's on the other side of the world. I sit back down.

With a quiet sigh, Lao Lao confesses, "Mostly, I just miss you."

A tear rolls down and I wipe it. I'm glad Mum's out, doing laundry in the apartment building laundry room, and not here to see me. I push my palm deep into the thick carpet and watch the imprint disappear. "I miss you too."

"Ever since your lao ye passed, the time has gone by a

46

lot faster with you around. I guess I'm not used to feeling like an empty old seashell drifting in the ocean."

"Well, you're not the only one." I take a deep breath. I tell Lao Lao about my embarrassing water-ordering episode. The fact that I got into a stupid fight with Millie, and my Mum probably thinks I've got "issues." "Now Millie'll never tell me the way to my parents' hearts!"

"You don't need her to tell you," Lao Lao says. "You already know the way to their hearts."

I shake my head into the phone, my tears collecting. *No I don't!* I didn't even know Mum's name until today. Five years is an impossibly long time – how am I ever going to make it up? "You just have to keep trying. As for Millie, you're sisters.

You don't think your mama and your aunt Jing fought? They were like two squabbling phoenixes . . . but you know something?"

"What?"

"They always made up," Lao Lao says. I dab my eye and glance at the bedroom door. "All it takes is one person to try."

"Thanks, Lao Lao," I tell her, standing up. I look at the time on the top of Mum's phone. She said to keep the call under five minutes, since it's expensive dialling a landline internationally. "I gotta go. I hope things get better for you at the retirement home."

"I'll be right here in my room, if you need to talk more," Lao Lao offers.

"Aren't you gonna go play cards or something with the other residents?" I ask.

"They're all partnered up already. They don't need another mah jong player or bridge gal!" she says with a heavy sigh.

"You don't know that! Have you even tried talking to them?" I ask.

"I can just tell," Lao Lao says. "I get that vibe walking around here."

"But you gotta keep trying, remember?" I remind her.

There's a long pause on the phone. I wait on the line for her to answer. Finally, Lao Lao says, "Okay . . . for you, I'll keep trying."

I smile. I'm glad we seashells can pep each other up, even from six thousand miles away. On that note, I put the phone down and walk up to the closed bedroom door.

Here goes.

Chapter 10

Millie's lying on her stomach on her top bunk, drawing when I walk in.

"Hey," I say quietly, sitting down on my bunk. I put my sketchbook under my pillow. "Whatcha drawing?"

"Logos. I've got eight. Five I think are fire and three that are just so-so," she says. She shows me her crayon logos and adds, "I used *my* paper this time."

Ouch. I suppose I deserved that.

"I'm sorry," I tell my sister. "I shouldn't have yelled at you about my sketchbook. I didn't mean to freak you out."

The apology feels gummy and weird but I push it through my lips. When I glance back at Millie, I feel lighter.

Millie shrugs, climbing down from her bunk. I'm relieved she's not still furious with me. She walks over to a small white laptop and starts punching on the keys.

I watch from behind her as she shows me our Etsy shop on her Chromebook. I look at the beautiful photos of glistening bath bombs. Underneath the photos, there're about five long sentences of description. I try to read the words, but there are too many I don't understand. Words like *shimmer* and *lustrous* and *fizzy* and *hand-crafted*.

"Did you write all that?" I ask Millie.

My sister nods.

She puts the laptop up on her dresser, next to her BEST SPELLER and BEST READING certificates. She sure has *a lot* of awards.

Back in Beijing, I never won any award. That's because Lao Lao could never afford to load me up with after-school tutors, which was the prerequisite to do well in math. The kids who won awards were known as the walking calculators. Me? I was a walking rock. The only time I came close to winning an award was for Chinese. I wrote an essay about running away to America.

In my story, I snuck into someone's bag at the airport and wrapped my legs around me like a pretzel the whole flight. My teacher said she liked my descriptions. She nominated me for the class prize.

I never told Lao Lao, though. I knew she'd be proud of me. My lao ye, too, being a magazine editor. But I didn't want them to be sad because of what I wrote.

I didn't want them to know I dreamed of running away.

I point to Millie's certificate. "You good speller?" I say to her in English.

She nods. "Once I got a medal for winning the spelling bee! But the medal was made out of plastic, and it got really really hot where we lived. And it melted."

I nod along, pretending I, too, have had that exact problem. English used to be mandatory in Chinese schools. But that all changed when the government decided to prioritise Chinese. Now all that time and effort I spent on Chinese, all the thousands of words and ancient poems I memorised . . . I wonder what's going to happen to them. Did they melt, too, in the plane when I crossed the ocean?

I want to ask Millie, *Is it hard? Learning English?*

But my pride catches the words just in time.

Instead, I start unpacking my suitcase. I pull out a picture of Lao Lao and me at the park.

"Is that . . . ?" Millie asks, reaching over and touching Lao Lao's face with her fingers.

"That's Lao Lao." I beam proudly.

"I thought she can't walk anymore!" Millie says.

"She can . . . It's just hard." I think of our slow laps around the park after school, her hand holding on to my arm, one step at a time. We'd make up stories for every bird we passed. I hope the nurses are going to keep doing that with her. I hate that I don't know for sure.

"Hey, let's send her one," I tell Millie in Chinese, pointing to the bath bombs on our Etsy page. "Cheer her up!"

Millie gives me a funny look. "Lao Lao likes baths?"

"No, but it doesn't matter. She'll still get a kick out of it."

"But we'll waste one!"

It makes me sad when Millie says this. To her, Lao Lao is just some old lady in a photo. I reach down and pull some mittens out of my luggage.

"Here, she made these for you." I hand the knitted

wool mittens to her.

Millie holds them to her chest. "She did?" She puts them on, then jumps into a dance in front of the mirrored closet doors. As her arms lock and her legs bounce, I'm impressed. My sister has *moves*. "How'd she know my size?"

I giggle at her enthusiasm.

"She guessed."

"Wow, she's a pretty good guesser. These fit!" she says. "I can't wait to show Hazel! She's going to lose her mind!"

"Who's Hazel?" I ask.

"Just the coolest girl in my year," she says. "She and her friends are called the Starbursts."

Millie explains it's an American sweet. She reaches into her backpack in the closet and gives me one. It tastes just like a White Rabbit sweet, only fruitier. As I chew, my sister explains that Hazel's Starbursts are already TikTok famous.

"They have a TikTok account with eight thousand followers. That's because Hazel's Mum is a hair influencer. I only have five followers," Millie says, flashing her fingers.

"What's a hair influencer?" I ask Millie.

Millie looks at me like *Duh.* "Someone who has great hair!"

That's a job?? America is such a weird place.

"Anyway, I've been trying to be friends with her. Maybe now with these" – she does jazz hands with her woolly fingers – "I'll finally be a Starburst!"

Millie takes my picture of Lao Lao and puts it up on our dresser. "I guess we can spare a bath bomb for Lao Lao." She pinches her fingers together. "A small one."

"She'd really like that," I tell Millie.

"But *only* if we use my logo."

Oh come on. I open my mouth to protest – I *know* I can come up with something a hundred times better than her crayon scribbles – but I catch the words just in time. Maybe this is my chance to be the bigger sister. For Lao Lao.

"Okay, fine," I mutter.

Chapter 11

"What do you mean you want to ship bath bombs to Lao Lao?" Mum asks. We're inside Second Chance Clothes, a thrift store in Winfield, the next town over.

It's Sunday morning. Dad and Millie went to the Chinese grocery store to get rice. Mum's holding up a pair of shorts to my waist.

I try to stand still as I tell her about my last phone conversation with Lao Lao.

"She's feeling real sad, Mum," I tell her. "They took away her bonsai tree and the other residents won't play with her!"

Mum shifts through the shorts on the rack. "She's probably just getting settled in. It's a big place. She'll find her people." She holds up a pair of denim shorts. "What about these?"

I stare at the floor while she measures me with her eyes.

"Don't you feel guilty leaving her there?" I ask.

I lift my eyes to Mum. She hugs the shorts to her chest but doesn't say anything.

Long, suspenseful minutes pass. I'm hopeful we're finally going to have a real conversation, about why she left me and why she never came back.

But Mum just announces, "You know what we need? T-shirts." She starts heading down the aisle. I scurry after her.

"Did you hear what I said?" I ask.

"I heard you," she says, shifting through the T-shirt rack.

"And?"

"You like tie-dye?" she asks, moving the hangers at lightning-fast speed.

At the sound of the metal hooks dragging along the steel rods, I put my hand out to stop her endless hanger shifting. I couldn't care less about the T-shirts and the denim shorts (though they do look pretty cool). I want some answers. I've waited long enough. Does my Mum really feel *nothing* leaving my lao

lao in China? Why didn't she at least come home for Lao Ye's funeral? Was she even sad?

"Look, I know it's hard. But sending her bath bombs isn't the answer," she finally says. "If we send them to her, she's going to want to know why we're making them. Then I'll have to explain. And that'll worry her. I'd rather she just live the rest of her years peacefully in the Imagination Hotel."

I hang back, quiet, as Mum turns to the shirts again.

Is that where Mum thinks I've been living for the last five years – some luxurious five-star Imagination Hotel? Because I have news for her. I have not been living in the Imagination Hotel. I have been living in the Reality Freezer.

*

Later, I'm sitting outside on the curb in front of Second Chance, hugging the plastic bag full of used clothes Mum bought me, while she checks the parking meter. I gaze up at the storefront sign.

SECOND CHANCE.

I used to think that my coming here was a second chance for me to get to know my family. But now I wonder . . . do they even want to know *me?* What

I've been through, all the moments big and small that carried me through these last five years? Even if they didn't frame it on the wall, just to *know* in their hearts – or do they just want to lounge around in some plushy Imagination Hotel?

I hug the plastic bag tighter. We didn't end up buying the shorts, because they were fifteen dollars. Mum says that's a *lot* for used clothes. She says everything's gone up in price in America. Something called inflation.

At least I got a great pair of watermelon shorts. I wonder what Lao Lao would say about them. She loves watermelon. Shorts? Not so much.

"Good girls wear long trouser," she said. *"Shorts attract too much attention."*

"From who?" I asked.

"Bees, mosquitoes, boys," she tsk-tsked.

I turned bright red, even though I didn't really know why. "You're growing up fast," *Lao Lao said.* "Boys will come knocking soon. I'll try my best to chase them off with my fly slapper. But it'll be up to you to shoo them away."

I told Lao Lao she didn't need to worry about that. The boys in my class wanted nothing to do with me . . . except give me hand farts. (A hand fart is when you fart in your hand and make someone smell it, which was what they were constantly doing to me in class.)

"C'mere, I got something left over for you, Lina!" they'd taunt me.

"Who you calling 'left over'? The only thing left over is your BO when you walk into a room!" I'd shout.

I'm not proud of the way I talked to the boys in my class, but it was the only thing I could do to survive.

I shudder at the memory.

"We still have twenty minutes left," Mum says, coming over. "You want to walk around a little?"

I get up slowly.

Two American girls walk by us. I stare at their shiny blonde hair, bouncing from side to side. One has on a pair of red heart-shaped glasses. The other has a pink purse the shape of a cupcake. They walk into an ice cream store.

Mum must have followed my gaze because she asks me, "You want to go in there?"

I nod eagerly.

"Maybe they have a kids' cone or a free sample," she says. She glances down at her purse hesitantly.

"I guess we can take a look."

As we step into Cindy's Ice Cream, the sugary toasty smell of fresh waffle cones hits my nose. My knees go weak. I stare at the gigantic menu of flavours – there are enough to make my head spin around the globe twice.

"What should I get, Jessica? The Almond Caramel Swirl or the Brownies and Cream?" the cupcake purse girl asks her friend.

Heart-glasses girl shrugs.

The cupcake purse steps up to the counter. "Can I get two free samples?"

"Absolutely!" the staff member behind the counter says.

Mum pokes me with a smile. I watch in disbelief as the server hands the girl two *free* small sample cups of the ice cream to taste. You can get FREE ice cream in this country?!

I dash to the counter. "Can I free too?" I ask.

I hear a giggle behind me. I turn around to see heart-glasses girl laughing. Is she laughing at me? Did I say something wrong? Mum gives them some serious side-eye.

"What flavour?" the shop person asks me.

I glance at all the options and try my best to pronounce the flavour from the big board. I'm determined not to screw up like with the water in the airport. I'm going to get it right this time.

"Chocolate Sheet Cake," I say, except I pronounce *sheet*, well, not "sheet." The girls start laughing hysterically.

"We don't have that one, unfortunately," the shop person says. "Would you like to try something else?"

"Yes. Something else." I nod. That sounds like a great flavour.

Mum puts a hand on my shoulder. "Lina, let's go," she says.

"No! I haven't gotten the ice cream yet," I protest in Chinese, wriggling my hand free. Can't she see – I'm *this* close! If I leave now, all the snickers will be for nothing.

"Stop," she says in English. It's weird hearing her speak English. I fall quiet. Her eyes beg me, *Let's go*. And I follow reluctantly, dodging the burning stares from the snickering girls, who watch me and my Mum with glee. All this without even a taste of Something Else.

Once outside, Mum speed-walks away from the

shop, holding my hand tight. "I didn't like the way those girls were acting," she says, reverting back to Chinese.

"I didn't either. But I really wanted that ice cream!" I follow her, craning my neck to look back at the store.

She stops when we're finally a good distance away and looks into my eyes. "Sometimes you have to do the hard thing and remove yourself from a bad situation. Even if it means parting with what you want most. Do you understand that?"

There's an urgency in her eyes that shines bright. And I realise, maybe it's not about the ice cream.

"You're the daughter of first-generation immigrants. Do you know what that means?" Mum asks.

I shake my head.

"It means your blood is made of iron will and determination. Your backbone is built from the sacrifices and impossible decisions of all those who walked before you. You have a duty to them to protect your heart. Never let yourself be treated that way, over ice cream. It isn't worth it. You understand?"

With moist eyes, I finally nod. "Yes, ma'am."

"C'mon now," she says, taking my hand. "Let's

go home."

I swing my plastic bag as I follow Mum. Even though I did not get to taste Something Else today, my belly is filled with a flavour even more satisfying – the hope that maybe my coming here really does mean something to Mama.

Chapter 12

Dad calls Mum on her phone as we're driving home. He tells her to pick Millie up from Pete's.

"I thought you were at the Chinese grocery store," Mum says.

"There was a plumbing emergency," Dad says with a sigh. "Just come."

Fifteen minutes later, we arrive. Pete's house is an impressive white farmhouse, sitting in front of a gigantic spread of land. Mum says it's a little over two acres. Tall eucalyptus trees and rose gardens line his lush front lawn.

Mum gets out of the car and heads up the stone steps to the big house.

"Be real polite to Pete," she says. "He's . . . a character."

Mum knocks on his door. A tall white man in dirty overalls, with a walking cane, answers. "Took you long enough!" he hollers at her. "This isn't day care!"

Mum's face flushes. I see my sister Millie inside the kitchen. She runs over. "Mama!" she calls out, hugging Mum.

"I'm sorry. I got here soon as I can," Mum says to Pete in English. "What happened?"

"Wwoofers messed up the plumbing again, that's what happened," he says, shaking his head. He lets us into the house and walks toward the back porch. He stomps down the stairs. I look out the double glass doors at the gorgeous expanse of green.

Pete's organic farm is *massive*. There are plants and vegetables as far as the eye can see. To the side of the plants, there's a tiny home on wheels. It looks like a trailer, the kind I've only ever seen in American movies. I spot Dad kneeling on the ground next to it, trying to turn off a pipe.

"Dad!" I cry.

I follow Pete out the back, running down the stairs toward Dad. Millie beats me to him. Dad temporarily stops his pipe fixing to give her a high five, snap, fist bump, elbow tap, and finally a hug.

I stare at the two of them doing their thing.

Whoa.

How long did it take them to come up with that? I bake in the heat, counting *five* gestures, when all this time in Beijing I couldn't even get *one.* I try to hide my embarrassed face. I wish I had a large sun hat like the lady's Pete's arguing with.

"How many times I gotta tell you? You gotta go easy on the toilet paper!" Pete says.

"We didn't do anything to it!" the woman says. "It just stopped working."

"It's that daughter of yours. Carla must have tried to flush a crayon, or some nonsense," Pete huffs.

"Hey!" a girl exclaims, walking out of the tiny home. She's a Latinx girl in a baseball hat and glasses, about my age. She looks up from the book she's holding – *The Science of Regenerative Farming* – and assures Pete, "I would never put anything in the toilet that wasn't completely compostable. There's something wrong with the plumbing. Remember the time water started coming *up* from the sink –"

"You're lucky you even have this tiny home. I could Airbnb this thing and make a fortune, and have you two sleeping in the garage."

"Pretty sure that's against Wwoof rules," Carla informs him.

Pete swats the comment away. "'Stead of lecturing me about the rules, why don't you earn your keep around here? I see a big patch of weeds over there with your name on it."

Carla glances at her Mum, who nods to her. She sighs, puts her book down, and starts walking to the fields.

I follow her.

When I finally catch up with Carla, by the beans section, I extend a hand.

"Hi! I'm Lina," I tell her.

"She's my sister!" Millie announces, trailing behind me.

"Carla Isabella Muñoz." She shakes my hand. She plops down and starts yanking on the little stubborn weeds that dot the garden. Millie and I both sit down too, and help. Millie's little fingers tug and pull expertly. Clearly she's had more experience than me.

"What year you?" I ask Carla.

Millie leans over and whispers, "It's what year

are you."

Carla shrugs like it's no biggie. "Fifth," she replies. "But I'm homeschooled."

I put a dirt-soiled hand to my chest. "I fifth too," I say. I ignore the grammar-anxious looks from my sister. I'm excited to make my first friend in America, and to be able to carry on a conversation with her. I point at the tiny home. "You live there a long time?"

"*Too* long." Carla explains, "My Mum and I are volunteers with Wwoof."

"Woof?" I ask, puzzled. Is that a secret wolf pack?

"It's this volunteer organisation for organic farmers. My Mum and I, we've been Wwoofing since I was eight," she says.

I am not sure what *volunteer* means. Millie explains in Chinese that it means they work for free. My eyebrows jump. Never in all my years of watching American movies have I ever seen anyone working for free. What do they do for clothes and other essentials?

Carla must have caught my confusion. "We're *supposed* to volunteer just a few hours a day, in exchange for free room and board. That's how it is usually." She gives me a bright smile. "And it's fun!

I've milked goats, learned Italian. We've gotten to travel the world!"

Millie translates for me. When I hear that Carla's been around the world, I ask Millie to ask her what's her favourite place.

"Nazaré, Portugal! Thompson Falls, Montana! To tell you the truth, *anywhere* but here," she says.

"Why?" I ask.

I follow her gaze to Pete, sitting on his deck, surveying his land, clutching his cane like a wooden scepter. "He may *look* like an organic farmer, but the pesticide he spews some-times . . ."

I look at Carla funny.

"Millie! Lina! Come on, we gotta run!" Mum says in Chinese.

Pete scolds Mum. "Quit yakking in Chinese! Speak *English*."

"See what I mean?" Carla asks.

I jump up and dust the dirt off my trousers, my ears burning. I try to think of some nice parting words for Carla, but in the end can only manage, "Good talk. Bye!"

"See you around!" Carla calls back, not taking her eyes off the weeds.

Chapter 13

It's not until that night, when Dad finally comes home, that I think of Carla's statement again. Sweat stains hug the pit of Dad's arms, like two giant atlases. I try not to look at them, or at his knees, caked in dirt. Did he spend all day kneeling on the ground, I wonder? I *hope* Pete at least paid him.

"Daddy!" Millie cries, looking up from making her TikTok with Mum's phone. She runs over. This time, I look away as they do their complicated routine of high fives and fist bumps. I count the seconds until I can safely look up again.

"What took you so long? Did you fix the plumbing?" Mum asks.

"Oh, I fixed that hours ago," he says. "But then I had to turn to the soybeans, and the mulch, the seeds that needed to be transferred into the ground, and the compost. You know Pete."

"I know," Mum says, shaking her head. She holds up boxes of bath bombs to show Dad. "Well, we finished filling all the orders."

"That's great!" he says.

"You like our logo? We made it together," I tell him. "Me and Millie."

Proudly, I show Dad our logo – *JML*. I took Millie's crayon *M* and reshaped the *J* and the *L*, so now they look symmetrical on both sides.

"Looks amazing," he says, closing his eyes and smelling the gloriously scented bath bombs. They turned out so beautiful, I wanted to eat them. But Mum said that would not be good. "When are you going to mail them?"

"Tomorrow, after I drop off the girls at school," Mum says.

I bite my lip at the mention of school. Back in Beijing, each new term brought on a whole new level of anxiety. There were the teasing from the boys and the rejection from the girls. The side-eyes from the teacher for having to print out every permission slip for Lao Lao, because she didn't have email. Don't even get me started on the avalanche of homework!

"Do I have to go so soon?" I ask.

"It's going to be great!" Mum says while Dad goes to get cleaned up. She and Millie sit cross-legged on the floor, dividing Millie's pencils and erasers into two sets – one for her and one for me. "You'll see – American school is not like in China. It's fun, right, Millie?"

I glance over at my sister hoarding all the nice colouring pencils for herself. Mum tries to take a few.

"She doesn't need *Crayola* pencils," Millie says. "She doesn't even know what they are."

"Yes I do!" I tell her. Truth be told, I do not, but still, I want them.

"There's no need to fight," Mum says. "We have plenty of pencils."

Mum goes to the kitchen drawer and pulls out five more colouring pencils. Unlike the bright, colourful Crayola ones, these are unbranded and worn out.

"Look, these are perfectly fine. I used them when I was trying to babysit, after I lost my job," she says. I stare at the pencils. They look like a giant baby chewed them.

Mum hands them to me sheepishly. I stuff them in my backpack and turn away from her, before she can see the hurt in my eyes. Why can't she give Millie these? It's bad enough I had to stay behind in China, now I have to take the crummier pencils, too?

Dad walks out in his pajamas and takes a seat on the side of the couch that doesn't have springs poking through. I walk over and sit down next to him. Dad reaches up with his hand and strokes my hair. It feels nice.

"What's *pesticide?*" I ask Dad.

"It's bug spray. Full of chemicals. It's terrible for humans," he says, putting his tired feet up. "That's why Pete never uses it. Once you spray it, it gets into the soil, into the rivers, the groundwater, into us."

Mum disappears into the kitchen and returns with a mug of hot tea and a freshly steamed zhongzi she made from sticky rice.

"But it's hard farming without pesticide," Dad says as he eats. "Which is why Carla's Mum and I have to work so hard."

"Does Pete really not pay Carla's Mum?" I ask.

Dad responds with a long sigh. "She's a Wwoofer, so technically she's volunteering in exchange for free room and board," he says. "But if you ask me, she and her daughter ought to get paid. They're up at the crack of dawn, working. Every day."

"Doesn't Carla have to go to school?" I ask.

"Carla's homeschooled," Dad says.

I turn to Mum, immediately thinking *Can I be homeschooled?* But Mum nixes this idea with a shake of her head.

"Uh-uh. I got way too much to do around here," Mum says, pointing to the bath bombs. "We have *six weeks* to come up with the back rent money. Otherwise, we're looking at pitching a tent in Pete's field."

I look worriedly at Dad, who adds, "She's kidding."

"Besides, you get to go to a great school in Winfield. That's the one nice thing Pete's done for you. Because his farm's in Winfield and your dad works for him, Pete helped us apply for an interdistrict transfer permit so you girls can go to a good school in Winfield," Mum says.

"That's not the *only* nice thing," Dad adds. He puts his zhongzi down for a second. "He's helping us get a green card."

"What's a green card?" I ask.

"It's a card that lets us stay."

"Wait, we can't stay?" I ask.

"Well, we can, but . . . it's hard," Mum replies, with a glance at Dad.

"Technically, when I first came over to this country, we were on a student visa," Dad explains. "But there are lots of limitations. Pete's gonna change all that. He's already got his lawyers working on it."

"It's been a year, though. Do you think we should be concerned that it's taking forever?" Mum asks him.

"These things take time. I trust Pete," Dad says. "He might be harsh, but he gets things done. We just gotta wait, and not rock the boat. Even a single misstep can get us denied."

Mum reaches for another bath bomb box and starts folding it. Now I understand why she'd rather sleep in a giant bucket of baking soda than ask for rent relief.

I hope we get our leafy card soon.

Chapter 14

Later that night, I'm standing in front of the closet mirror, practicing giving myself a high five. I just want to see what it feels like, to do this with Dad. I grin at myself, then smack the mirror hard with my hand.

As my hand lands on the cool surface, Millie walks in.

"Uhhh . . . what are you doing?" she asks.

"Nothing." I yank my hand down. I stand frozen, eyeballs looking to the ceiling.

"Were you just giving the mirror a high five?" she asks quietly.

"No!" I insist. "Why would I do that?"

I pretend to be totally weirded out by that suggestion. Millie shrugs, *Whatever,* as she climbs into her bunk. I crawl into my bed too and bury my humiliated head in my sheets. Thank God I didn't start with a mirror *hug* – that would have been awkward.

Mum comes into our room to say good night. She tucks Millie in and talks to every one of her stuffed animals. I wait and wait, wondering when she'll finally get to me. When at last she sits down on the bottom bunk, she puts her hands over mine.

"I don't want you to be scared," she says. "After listening to what your dad said."

"I'm not," I tell her. I clutch the blankets tighter.

Mum reaches for the light and switches it off. I think she's about to leave, but she comes back over to my bed. "Close your eyes," she says.

I close one eye and peek at her with the other. In the silvery light, I see Mum flutter her own eyelids shut.

"I want you to imagine us in five years. Doing anything we want and everything we dream of. If you could live anywhere, where would you girls want to live?" she asks.

I think it's a trick question, so I answer, "I'm fine here, Mama."

"No, baby," she says. "Dream big."

I close my eyes firmly this time and imagine myself drawing in the sand with my finger. The waves lap in front of me, little baby waves, like the ones in my Mum's long black hair.

"At the beach," I say to Mum.

"With a dog," Millie adds from the top bunk.

I smile, hearing the gentle barks of our eager puppy as it comes running out of the house to join us. I hear Lao Lao's warm laugh behind Patches. "The little critter's escaped again!" she cries. "Watch out, here he comes!"

"And Lao Lao's there too!" I tell Mum. "She's running down the beach after our dog!"

Millie starts giggling, imagining the image.

"And now Patches has sprayed her full of water!" I continue. "Oh, that dog's in for it!"

Mum laughs. "Where are me and Dad? Are we playing with you two?"

"Yeah! Dad's in the ocean swimming," Millie says.

"No, surfing!" I add.

"Yeah, surfing!" Millie agrees excitedly. "It's Sunday and he doesn't have to work all day at Pete's farm anymore because we have our green card now."

"And I'm drawing a picture of him," I tell Mum.

"Oooh, is it going to be a watercolour or a pencil drawing?" Mum asks.

"Whatever it is, it's going to be with Crayola supplies," I tell her boldly. I open one eye to make sure she heard. Millie, too.

"And when you're done, we'll celebrate with watermelon," Mum declares. "Because my bath bombs have officially made it into Target! The first bath bomb brand by an Asian American woman!"

My eyes open wide. "You think we can really get there, Mama?" I ask.

"Only one way to find out," she answers, kissing my forehead. "Gotta dream big, right, girls?"

I smile. Mum bids us a good night and walks out of the room. She lingers in the hallway for a second, and I'm tempted to blurt out, *I love you.*

But she closes the door before I can.

I tell myself I'll have another chance tomorrow. I turn to Millie and ask, "Does Mum do that every night?"

"Check into the Imagination Hotel? Only on special nights," Millie says, yawning. She sticks her head down from her bunk. "She used to be an

Imagineer in China, you know."

I'd heard that Mum worked at the old Panda Amusement Park in Beijing before it closed. My aunt said it used to be popular, before Shanghai Disney opened. Now everybody in China flocks to eat seventeen-dollar Mickey-shaped Popsicles.

"What does an Imagineer do?" I ask my sister.

"They design rides!" Millie says.

"She *designed* rides?? I thought she just did the ticket sales!" I cry. How could Lao Lao casually gloss over a detail like this?

"No, she showed me once this ride she designed – it sounded cooler than Space Mountain at Disneyland. I mean I've never *been* to Disneyland, but my friends have and I know all about it!"

"So why doesn't she just get a job working there?" I ask.

Millie reaches down with her hand and makes a card rectangle shape with her fingers.

Oh yeah, the green card.

I watch the shadows of the trees dance through the window and sigh.

"Hey, Millie." I hesitate before asking her, "When you guys checked into the Imagination Hotel, before

I got here . . . was I there too?"

"Are you kidding? That was the whole point of checking in. So Mama could say, *Lina this,* and, *Lina that!*" Millie whispers to her mattress, "You know how hard it is to live up to an invisible sister?"

I'm stunned. A smile stretches across my face in the dark.

"Well, I'm not invisible anymore," I tell Millie.

I stare at my handprint on the mirror from my self-five in the silvery light – proof that we may not have the card yet. But one wish's already come true from the Imagination Hotel.

Chapter 15

In the car on the way to school the next morning, Millie tells me all about her teachers.

"They're so nice," she says, talking animatedly with her mittens. She's wearing the ones Lao Lao knitted for her, even though it's 26 degrees out. "They let us sit on bean-bags. And read whatever we want! And draw! And we all get Chromebooks! The school lunches are so good and they're *free!*"

I look up from my watermelon shorts. "Do they have ice cream?"

"No, but they have cookies and fruit. Pizza, hot dogs, and my favourite – enchiladas."

"Enchiwhat-now?"

"It's this cheese thing."

As Mum drives, I imagine myself eating cheesy

hot dogs on beanbags at my new school.

"Don't forget," Mum reminds us as she turns toward the school. "We're not supposed to be at this school. Your zoned school is the one over on Las Amidias, by the landfill. We're here on a permit. So what does that mean?"

"Act invisible, don't create trouble," Millie mutters. I give her a funny look. Act *invisible*?

"Exactly," Mum says. "The district can pull your permit if they don't like you. So mind your teachers and don't be sassy, you hear?"

"Yes, Mama," Millie and I reply.

I want to tell Mum she doesn't need to worry. I've been trained well by Lao Lao. I know all about sewing my mouth half shut with the invisible thread.

As Mum pulls into the parking lot, I check my backpack to see if everything's in there. To my surprise, I spy half a dozen Crayola pencils. She must have taken some from Millie's bag in the middle of the night! I grin as I zip my backpack up.

I look up to see the stunning architecture. This school looks like a museum, even nicer than Springfield Elementary! The arts building is a glass-dome. Carved onto the side of the building are the words **DREAM, IMAGINE, BE KIND, BELIEVE.**

I breathe in the words, putting a hand over my heart so Lao Lao can feel them too.

"Told ya it was beautiful!" Millie grins. A proud sign declares Winfield Elementary a California Distinguished School. I'm not sure what *Distinguished* means, but it sure sounds fancy. Millie takes my hand in her mittened one and opens the car door. "C'mon, I'll show you around!"

I follow Millie over to the playground. My jaw drops.

There are swings, a climbing wall, and the longest slide I've ever seen. I bend down to touch the soft, rubbery ground. Back in Beijing, my old school playground was on hard cement. I scraped my knee once, jumping from the swings. And we were considered *lucky*. Some schools didn't even have playgrounds.

"Hi, Hazel!" Millie calls out to a girl walking with her friends. The girl turns and glances at Millie. She's wearing a super-short top and jeans with stars on them. Her tanned tummy sits proudly exposed.

I can almost hear my lao lao's voice in my head, *Aiya! Girls can't go to school like that! What's her*

Mum thinking?

"Hey," Hazel says. "Nice gloves. Where'd you get them?"

Millie hands them over to Hazel. I watch as Hazel tries them on. "From Janie and Jack," Millie says.

I look over, confused. I may not know much English but I know my lao lao's name is definitely *not* Janie or Jack.

"Did you have a good weekend?" Millie asks. "My sister and I, we did a bath bomb. Right, Lina? It's this amazing new brand on Etsy, called JML. You should try it! Makes your skin so soft."

Wait . . . is she advertising our bath bombs on the playground??

I have to admit my little sister is a terrifying genius.

The bell rings and Millie and Hazel scurry to class. I look at Mum as she hurries over from the far side of the parking lot.

"Sorry, I couldn't find a spot!" Mum says, catching her breath. I gaze over at the row of empty spots, right in front.

"Oh, those are reserved for the school's biggest donors," Mum says, following my gaze. "They're called the Blue Patrons!"

She points to the big signs that say **RESERVED FOR THE SCOTT FAMILY – DO NOT PARK!**, **RESERVED FOR THE TAYLOR FAMILY – DO NOT PARK!**, and **RESERVED FOR THE CASEY FAMILY – DO NOT PARK!**

There sure are a lot of important people at this school.

"You ready to meet your new teacher?" Mum asks me. Inhaling deeply, I nod.

"Her name is Mrs. Carter."

Car-ter, I repeat under my breath as I follow my Mum toward the classrooms. I stop for a second to admire the arts center.

"Incredible, isn't it? The PTA raised over two million dollars to build this," Mum says. My heart fills with gratitude as I look over at the **DREAM, IMAGINE, BE KIND, BELIEVE** sign once again.

Maybe here, away from the stress of having to memorise hundreds of ancient Chinese poems, I'll finally be able to stretch my arms as an artist and draw my dreams to reality.

Chapter 16

I try to collect myself outside 5A, a handsome red-and-white classroom, just to the right of the arts building.

"If you don't understand the English, just raise your hand. The teacher will help you," Mum says.

I nod.

"Oh, and at lunch, if you don't like something, just dip it in ketchup —"

I give Mum a look. I may be new to America, but I'm not new to lunch. "I'll be fine."

Mrs. Carter opens the door. She's a Black woman with warm, inviting brown eyes that remind me of my lao lao's. They dance back at me. "You must be Lina!" She holds her hand out.

Timidly, I shake it. She's wearing a bright solar

system dress and I smile at all the planets.

"You like my dress?" she asks.

I nod shyly.

"Makes me feel like I'm a walking astronomy lesson! Come on in!"

I wave goodbye to Mum. My teacher seems so nice. Walking inside, I beam at my new classmates. They sit in pairs at tables that face a Smartboard. Most of the kids are white. A few are Latinx, and I'm the only Asian kid. I slide into an empty table in the back, trying to dodge all the curious glances.

"Oh, not there," Mrs. Carter says. "Up at the front, next to Finn!"

I look up and see a white boy in glasses up by the front, with a mop of brown hair and his nose stuck inside a book. He puts his book down and gazes at the empty seat next to him.

I walk over and slide into the seat.

"I'm Finn," he introduces himself, holding out his hand. I notice the tiny freckles on his pale skin as he smiles. He's wearing some sort of sports uniform. RAMS, it says, on his shirt and on his shorts.

I reach out my own hand. As I touch Finn's hand, I hear a snicker from behind me. I look back. My

eyes land on a pair of heart-shaped glasses.

It's the girl from the ice cream shop – the one who laughed at my English! She's in my class??

Oh, that's just perfect.

I instantly yank my hand back, feeling the flush of my cheeks as I stare ahead. I dodge Finn's gaze. He's probably wondering why I didn't shake his hand, but I am determined not to give heart-glasses *any* more reason to make fun of me.

Judging by the grin on her face as she watches me and Finn, though, she already has a few ideas.

Chapter 17

"Let's give a warm Winfield welcome to our new student, Lina Gao!" Mrs. Carter says.

The room collectively bellows, "Welcome, Lina!"

"Lina, why don't you stand and tell us a little about yourself? You just moved here from China, right?" the teacher asks.

I get up hesitantly. "Yes."

"Are those watermelons on your shorts?" a boy asks, snickering.

I look down, instantly realizing my watermelon shorts might look a little babyish to my classmates. I squirm, regretting my decision not to wear plain trousers.

"Do you know kung fu?" someone else asks.

"Just because she's from China? Really?" Finn calls

back, turning around. I give him an appreciative smile. I don't know this Finn, but so far, I sort of like him.

Almost immediately after Finn says that, the boys in the back start hooting "Oooooo!" followed by "Finn has a crush on the new girl!"

Finn's face turns beet red. "I do not! Shut up!" he exclaims. I plunge down onto my seat, shrinking into the size of a gum wad and covering as many watermelons as I can with my hands.

Mrs. Carter tells the back-row tables sharply to cut it out. "I do apologise," she says to me. "And welcome. We're so glad to have you. Now, class, we'll be starting our language arts unit this morning with a special Book Tasting. As you all know, the book fair is coming up and this year, with the help of our Blue Patrons, our PTA has generously raised funds to invite a big author to come and speak to us at the school!"

"Woo!" my classmates cheer.

I peek back and see heart-eyes throwing her hand up in the air.

"I already told my Mum last night who she should invite," heart-eyes says. "Tony Walsh, the author of the Royal Pets series."

"Boring!" a voice calls out.

Jessica jerks her head back, offended at the outburst. "How can you call the Royal Pets series boring? It's about Pomeranians in the royal family! Do you know the pressure to take a poop under the public eye??"

"Thank you, Jessica, for that . . . visual," Mrs. Carter says. "We'll certainly take it into consideration!"

"Well, it's as good as done," Jessica informs Mrs. Carter. "My Mum's a Blue Patron. So . . ."

Wait, Jessica's Mum's a Blue Patron? I think back to the reserved parking spots in front of the school.

"And we thank her for her generous donation to our school. But we still need to vote on it *as a school*." Mrs. Carter passes out a bunch of papers that say *Menu*. I reach for one eagerly, expecting to order pizza. Instead, it asks me a bunch of questions about the book. "Lina, I see you're already way ahead of us – why don't you read the menu for us?"

I freeze. The room falls quiet as everyone waits for me to start reading. As my heart hammers in my chest, I tell myself it's just like in China, when I had to stand up and recite a Tang dynasty poem.

"Welcome to Mrs. Carter's Book Tasting," I start reading shakily. "The wool point of this Book Taste –"

A giggle starts from behind me. I stop reading. Did I mess up a word already?

"Whole," Finn whispers. "Keep going – you're doing good!"

"Whole point is make informed onion on the book."

My classmates cackle when I say *onion*. It's only a second later that I realise my mistake – the word was *opinion*, not an edible bulb.

As my class roars with laughter, I sink down in my seat. I wish I could melt into my table. In China, it was never this bad. Even if I forgot an entire poem, or if I showed up to school in my *underpants*, it would not be this bad.

I look up at Mrs. Carter, who smiles and nods encouragingly, like I'm doing just fine. For her, I make myself press on.

"First rule of Book Tasting. Keep an open m-m–" I struggle to pronounce *mind. Is it* mind *or* mend?

Jessica throws her whole upper body onto her table dramatically. "Oh my God, we're going to be here *alllllllll day!*"

When she says that, I feel the invisible thread

stitch across my lips and pull tight. I glance over at Mrs. Carter. *Help!*

"Jessica, why don't you read for a little while?" she suggests.

"Thank you," Jessica says, with a long, annoyed look at me. At five times my speed, Jessica takes over reading big words I'll probably never understand, let alone know how to use.

I sit down and scrunch into a ball at my desk, relieved I don't have to keep talking. No matter what Mrs. Carter says, I'm not reading again. It's way too humiliating. I think of Apu, the Indian-American shopkeeper in *The Simpsons*, and how he was always the butt of the joke because he spoke accented English, and I shrivel up. Being "bad at English" seems like the worst kind of apple you can be here.

And until I know for sure that's not going to be my fate, I vow never to speak in class again.

Chapter 18

Thankfully, Mum's too distracted by a custom order request we received from a customer named FunkyVeganMama to dig into me about my first day when I get home.

"How'd it go today?" she asks, distractedly clicking on graduation hat moulds on Etsy.

"Fine," I say.

"Did you make friends?"

"Yup!" I lie.

"How was the food?" she asks, glancing over.

I nod enthusiastically. The enchilada turned out to be pretty good. And they gave me so many cookies and sliced apples, enough to feed a family of four in Bei Gao Li Village! I don't mention the fact that there was nowhere to sit and no one to sit *with*.

I finally ate on the grass, under a tall eucalyptus tree, far, far away from the lunch tables.

It was the most delicious, lonely lunch I've ever had. "That's great! What do you two think of this request?

FunkyVeganMama's offering us twenty dollars to make her daughter a custom bath bomb – in the shape of a graduation hat," Mum says. "I found a mould online for twenty dollars!"

"Oooh! We can make the tassel gold!" Millie says.

"But it won't get here until next week," Mum says, frowning.

"And twenty dollars is a lot," I say. "Won't that eat into our profit?"

I may not know much English, but thankfully I could keep up in math. All those mountains of homework I had to do in China paid off. Today in class I got a 92 percent on my math test. That's compared to a 22 percent on the vocabulary quiz, and a pitiful 5 percent on the spelling test. I don't even want to *think* about the Book Tasting homework sitting in my backpack.

"We could reuse it?" Mum suggests. "The next time someone else has a graduation hat order . . .

we'll be all set."

If someone else orders one. If they don't, we'll be out twenty dollars, plus the cost of making the bath bomb. I twist my body, glancing over at the powdery white balls on the kitchen table. They look like tiny white canvases to me. Suddenly, I have an idea.

"What if we just paint a graduation hat on them?" I ask.

"Paint them?" Mum asks. "With what?"

"There's gotta be some kind of paint that'll work," I say, reaching for Mum's phone to look this up.

But Millie grabs the phone before me.

"I'm head of product design," she reminds me. I roll my eyes.

She takes the phone, her fingers typing effortlessly on the screen. I marvel at my sister's speedy search skills, the fact that she knows all the right words.

After just forty-five seconds of searching, she announces that it's not possible to paint on a bath bomb. The paint will simply mix and react with the citric acid.

"Let me see that," I say, reaching for the phone.

Millie tries to hold Mum's phone away. "What for? I've already looked!" she says. We wrestle for the phone.

When I can't pry it away from my sister's sticky fingers, I shoot Mum a desperate look.

"Let your sister have a turn," Mum says.

"I'm just going to Baidu it from my own computer," I inform Millie, patting my new school Chromebook in my backpack. It was by far the highlight of my day – getting a Chromebook. If only Lao Lao had one too.

Millie hands over the phone. "It's called *Google*."

I roll my eyes, swiping into Mum's phone. As I'm tapping into every app, I can hear Millie urging Mum to get the graduation mould, not waste another second!

"With expedited shipping, it could get here earlier!" Millie says.

"Expedited shipping will cost even more, though." Mum grimaces.

"Look!" I declare, holding up the phone. I show Mum and my sister beautifully painted bath bombs on something called Pinterest. "It can totally be done! We just need something called mica."

Mum gets up. She and my sister crane their necks as I show them a video of a woman painting a gorgeous metallic butterfly onto a pale pink bath bomb. We all stare at the kaleidoscope of colours.

"Mica it is!" Mum grabs her keys. "Let's go to Michaels!"

*

Michaels, as it turns out, is heaven on earth. It's a huge arts and crafts store the size of a Beijing hutong! As Mum goes to find the salesclerk with her plain bath bombs in tow, my sister and I linger in the paintbrush section.

"Do you realise what this means? If this works, I can paint *all kinds* of designs on the bombs!" I tell Millie, reaching for the paintbrushes. I can already picture it in my head – I can paint birthday cakes, wedding rings, people's initials! This is even more exciting than Bart Simpson accidentally discovering a comet!

But Millie's still sour on the idea.

"What if it stains? Then people will complain about their bathtubs," she says.

I frown, tired of Millie's shade. I decide to confront my sister.

"Why you always gotta be breaking my noodles?"

I ask her. "I'm not breaking your noodles."

"Yes you are."

"I don't even know what that means," she says.

It means don't you think you've had it your way for long enough? The words sit on the edge of my tongue as I watch Millie, rocking to a song in her head, swaying her hips, touching everything on the shelves. A woman walks by and says, "Work it, girl, you got moves!" To which Millie hollers back with a smile, "Thanks! I'm @milliegao8 on TikTok!"

As she chats with the lady, still dancing, I stare at her total lack of self-consciousness. And the fact that she can just talk. Millie doesn't need to think and translate in her head. She just *talks.*

I think of this morning in class and reach for my lips. I tug them apart with my fingers, just to make sure they're not permanently sewn. *I'll get there.*

As Millie's yakking and dancing, I suddenly notice her hands are bare. What happened to her mittens?

"Millie!" I call out. "Your mittens! Did you lose them?"

I start searching the aisles frantically.

"No, Hazel has them," Millie tells me.

"Wait, you *gave* them to her?" I ask.

"I *lent* them! Relax!"

But I am not relaxed. I am fuming. Lao Lao worked on them for a whole month. She continued to knit even when her hands hurt and her eyes were getting blurry. I put my hands on Millie's arms and try to get the importance of those gloves through to her. "They are precious. Lao Lao may never make another pair! Do you understand?"

"All right! Geez!" Millie exclaims in English, wriggling away from me.

A few people look over and stare at us. Mum walks over with a bunch of mica paints and asks what's going on. Millie hisses in English, "Lina was just being a *drama queen.*"

I wish I had an equally powerful comeback phrase for Millie in English. But I do not yet know enough English.

Instead, I stick my tongue out at her. Which is definitely not as satisfying, but at least it's the same in every language – *Millie's being an armpit.*

Chapter 19

In the car, on the way to Pete's, I protect the precious mica from my sister with my hand – in case she tries to lend *that* to Hazel too. The mica turned out to be quite expensive, ten dollars for three colours. We had no money left for the new brushes, which were five dollars a brush at Michaels, so we're counting on Pete to have some lying around his garage.

As it turns out, he does have some. But he wants to charge us four dollars a brush for them.

"Four dollars?" Mum asks. "C'mon, Pete, I'm trying to make money for back rent. It's due less than six weeks! I already spend ten dollars on paint!"

"You want to fulfill your order or not?" Pete asks.

Mum gazes hesitantly at her thin wallet. I

immediately jump in with an idea.

"Mum! Tell Pete we'll work – me and Millie. We'll help Carla for a free brush!" I blurt out in Chinese.

Mum doesn't translate this right away, but Millie tells him what I said. Pete considers the offer. No doubt, he's doing the math in his head. Two farmhands for four hours, versus two brushes at four dollars. Finally, he nods.

I grab the mica from Mum, and the brushes from Pete's hand, and run out the back and onto the field.

*

Sandwiched between the tall leaves of the leek plants, I paint in the sun, while Millie and Carla cover me.

"How's it looking? You done yet?" Millie asks me.

"Last part," I say, inhaling deeply. I've already painted the black hat. Now, deep in concentration, I dip the paintbrush in gold mica for the tassel. Millie helped make the special solution with rubbing alcohol, which Carla had in her tiny home.

Millie and Carla watch as I work. When I finish, Carla starts gushing.

"Oh, that's so good!" she exclaims. I give her

a grateful smile.

"You think so?" I ask in English.

"Let's show Mum! We're *out of here!*" Millie squeals, jumping up. She reaches for my bath bomb and takes off sprinting.

I watch as Millie stops to say bye to Dad. The two of them do their elaborate high-five routine again. I try to decide if the left-out vinegary feeling feels any better as I watch them today. Carla interrupts my thoughts with a compliment.

"You're a really good artist," she says. I blush.

"Thanks."

"Did you learn to draw like that at Winfield?" she asks. "I hear it's a nice school."

I shake my head. "Not nice school," I tell her. For some reason, when I talk to her in English, my invisible thread disappears and all my feelings come out, no problem. I don't feel scared or nervous.

"Why not?" she asks.

I search around for the words. It's like pulling the weeds from deep in the soil. Finally, I say, "Other kids not nice. Not like you."

Carla wipes the sweat from her brow and gazes at me in the late-afternoon sun.

"What are they like?" she asks.

I think of the disgust on Jessica's face as she complained that I was reading too slow.

"They not like me," I tell her. "Because my English bad."

"Your English is not bad," she says. "Come here. Let me show you something." She gets up and holds out her hand. I take it hesitantly. She pulls me up and leads me to the greenhouse. I peer at the little seeds growing in delicate cups. "Do you know the key to transporting seedlings?"

I peer at the tiny, fragile seedlings and shake my head. "Gotta be extra delicate," she says. "And real patient. It takes them a while to find their footing in their new home. But once they do, they shoot up like a beanstalk."

Carla reaches under one of the tables and produces a gigantic stalk of celery. She takes a bite and throws it to me. I laugh and take a bite too.

"Give yourself time," she says. "You've just been transplanted. You'll find your root system again."

"Thanks," I say to her. "You very smart."

She gives me a toothy grin. "My Mum says it's because I'm always reading about plants. Guess I'm an old fern!"

I smile. I ask Carla why she doesn't go to regular school. I'd sure like her sitting behind me rather than Jessica Reads-Too-Fast.

"My Mum says it's so she can teach me more in science."

Carla shrugs. She lingers. "But I think it's because we're always moving."

"Why you always moving?" I ask. It fills me with hope that I can actually follow along with this conversation.

"Ever since my dad died, we just don't want to stay in one place . . . ," she says in a small voice. "Otherwise we'll feel sad."

When Carla says that, I feel a tug at my heart. I want to give her a hug. I want to tell her I know her grief. I went through it with my lao ye and now I'm headed there again. It's like I'm in a big waiting room, one I hope I never leave. But Lao Lao's getting older and older, and there's nothing I can do to slow it down.

And now I've run away from the only home I've ever known, which has made things worse for Lao Lao. And that makes me feel like a coward.

But I don't say all that. Instead, I take a seedling and gesture to Carla, *Can I?*

We walk over to the soil together and, as gently as possible, transplant it into the dirt. We're careful not to touch or damage the root system. Then we pat the soil with all our best wishes and hope for the seedling.

And for a brief second, I feel a little less alone.

Chapter 20

Mum shows me the message from the customer on my way to school. Last night, after the paint dried, she took a picture of my bath bomb and Millie's (she insisted on painting some too) and sent it to FunkyVeganMama.

"Look at that! She loves it!" Mum announces. "Read it out loud! Go on!"

I glance hesitantly over at my sister, but she looks just as eager to hear what the customer said about our painted bombs as I am. In my shaky English, I start reading.

"Hi, JML. These look beautiful," I read. "I would like them very much for my dater's graduton."

"Daughter's graduation," Mum helps me.

"Oh, sorry." I blush.

"Nothing to feel sorry about, keep reading!" Mum encourages.

"She is turning eighteen next month and going to Cal Poly. I am so proud of her. She is the light of my life."

I finish reading and turn to my sister, who claps her hands together and does a happy dance. "We killed it! KA-CHING!"

I can't help but laugh, even though I'm still a pea mad at her for lending Lao Lao's mittens out.

"You think we're going to get more?" Millie asks Mum.

"Well, now that we have our resident artist, I hope so." Mum beams at me.

Millie clears her throat.

"I'm sorry, resident *artists*," Mum corrects with a smile.

Despite the correction, I feel myself glowing from ear to ear at the confirmation that I am *not* completely useless in this country. I can do this! I can help my family not just in the Imagination Hotel but in real life, too!

Getting out of the car, I vow to try hard today at school and not let Jessica or anyone else get to me.

Unfortunately, when I walk into class, the first thing Mrs. Carter asks for is our Book Tasting homework.

Uh-oh.

In my eagerness to paint more glittery bath bombs when we got home, I completely forgot to do my homework.

"Oh no . . . ," I mutter from my desk.

Finn turns to me. He's in a new Rams shirt – this one looks about two sizes too big on him. He gets out his homework from a plastic Rams folder. "What's wrong?" he asks.

I glance down at my backpack. "I not do."

"It's okay!" Finn says, glancing over to see if Mrs. Carter's looking. "Just pull it out now and I'll help you do it. Real fast." He turns his body to block the view from the front of the room and I dig into my backpack. Jessica's prying eyes stare curiously at us.

"What are you guys doing?" she asks.

"Nothing, mind your own business," Finn tells her.

I grab my homework and we turn back, whispering between ourselves and huddling close so no one can see.

"What's *rating?*" I whisper.

"Like . . . if you go to a restaurant," Finn whispers back. It takes me a minute to register *restaurant*, and Finn blurts out *"fan guan"*.

My pupils widen. "You know Chinese??" I ask. Unfortunately, I forget to whisper, and Mrs. Carter looks over.

Finn blushes. "Some. I had a Chinese au pair when I was little," he says.

"You did? Oh, that's perfect!" Mrs. Carter cries. "Finn, I want to see you at recess, after I've had a chance to talk to Lina!"

Chapter 21

As the rest of my classmates pile out for recess and Finn waits awkwardly outside the classroom door, I walk up to Mrs. Carter's desk. I try to guess Mrs. Carter's awesome idea, taking inspiration from every episode of *The Simpsons* I've ever watched.

She's decided to have a school play and she wants to cast me as Mulan.

Better yet, she wants to take us on a class field trip to Beijing!

Or maybe she found out I make bath bombs and wants me to paint a custom one with her favourite book on it. But she can't decide which one is her favourite, so she orders five hundred bath bombs. And we no longer owe any more back rent. I'm still smiling about the last one when Mrs. Carter reaches for my vocabulary quiz and spelling test from yesterday – the ones with a big red 22% and a cringey 5%. The smile on my face dissolves faster than baking soda.

"So, Lina, I was looking through your tests from yesterday," Mrs. Carter says.

Here we go. I'm getting kicked out, I know I am. The tears start welling in my eyes as I think about my mother's fingers caked in baking soda, and all the weeds Dad had to pull and the mulch he had to lay down to get me into this school.

"Oh no no no," Mrs. Carter says, grabbing a tissue when she sees my moist eyes. "You're fine! I'm sorry if I'm making you worried. You just need a little help with vocabulary and reading, that's all! I had a chat with the district, and guess what? They're sending over a special teacher for you!"

I peek at her from behind my tissue. A special teacher?

"Her name is Mrs. Ortiz. She's our English Language Learner instructor. I wrote all this to your Mum in an email, and she just emailed me back and said she's fine with it!" Mrs. Carter says. "And the best part is, you'll be working with Mrs. Ortiz one-on-one!"

I don't know what *one-on-one* means but if it'll rescue me from embarrassing read-alouds with my impatient classmates, I'll try it.

"Anyway, you'll start on Friday," Mrs. Carter says. "In the meantime, now that we know Finn understands Chinese, he can help you!"

I glance over at Finn, still standing outside the door.

"It's not easy starting at a new school . . . and learning a new language," she says. "But I want you to know, I'm so happy that you're here. You're going to do wonderful things in our school. And in this country. I'm absolutely positively sure of it."

I smile at Mrs. Carter, grateful for her kind words. I walk out to recess with an extra bounce in my step, excited by the prospect of my new teacher *and* my very own personal translator!

Chapter 22

With Finn as my translator, I figure I can kick back and take it easy in class the next few days. The heavy weight of figuring out all of Mrs. Carter's instructions will finally be lifted and I'll be able to float effortlessly by, nodding along with all my classmates.

But on Wednesday, when Mrs. Carter asks Finn to translate a worksheet on recycling, I realise there's a problem.

Instead of translating *fizzy drink can* as "yi la guar," he translates it as "noodles." And he calls plastic bottles "spring rolls." That's when I realise that most of Finn's Chinese is limited to Chinese dishes he and his family like to order from takeout restaurants.

Not wanting to embarrass him, I smile and

nod politely.

Unfortunately, Finn takes this as a sign that his Chinese is *perfect*, and he throws himself even *more* into the job of being my official spokesperson.

When Mrs. Carter asks me if I know one of the top-five carbon emissions, I strongly consider saying cars, but then I glance over at Jessica and tense up. I whisper "cars" to Finn in Chinese instead.

He turns to the class and proudly translates "Chicken!"

My entire class gawks at me. *Chicken?!*

Mrs. Carter makes a regretful noise through her teeth. "No, Lina, I'm afraid chickens are not a source of carbon emissions. The biggest contributor is burning coal, which still happens in developing countries."

I turn to Finn, annoyed. "Why'd you say that?" I ask him in Chinese.

He blinks at me, genuinely confused. "Do you want soup?"

UGH!

For the rest of science class, I put my head down on the table. As Mrs. Carter praises Finn on his impressive bilingual skills, I think of all the things

I want to say, if I could actually speak for myself.

*

Mum picks me and Millie up after school excited for an update on my new ELL teacher.

"Did she come yet?" Mum asks.

"Friday. Until then, I have to deal with Finn."

"How's that going?" she asks.

"He only knows menus," I tell Mum, getting in the car. "Everything out of my mouth is an answer. Everything out of his mouth is a food. It's making me look totally dumb in class *and* it's making me super hungry!"

"Well, good news – Dad brought home some fresh cucumbers! I'll stir-fry up some cucumber and egg when we get home!"

At the thought of cucumber and egg, my tummy fills with nostalgia. "Can we call Lao Lao?" I ask, reaching for Mum's phone.

Mum glances at her watch and calculates the time in China with her fingers. "I guess so. It's early morning her time. Make it quick, though. Long distance to China costs –"

"I know, I know," I say, taking the phone and

dialling. I push 01186 for China. Millie bounces excitedly next to me.

"Can I speak to her?" Millie asks, reaching over with her mittened hand. I'm glad to see she's got them back.

"Put her on speaker," Mum says.

I press speaker on Mum's phone. Lao Lao answers on the third ring.

"Wei?" she says.

"Lao Lao!" we greet her.

"Hold on, I gotta get my sweater on. It's freezing cold in the rooms here," she says. We wait for her to get her sweater. Finally, she comes back on. "Dang it, this sweater. I can't get my hand in the sleeve!"

I can hear her groaning and sighing as she struggles, and I want to jump into the phone to help her. In Beijing, whenever Lao Lao had trouble getting dressed, I'd always give her a helping hand.

"Just take it nice and slow, Ma," Mum says, pulling over. "Can the nurses help? You want me to call them?"

"No. I don't want to call them for every little thing," Lao Lao says.

"But, Ma, that's what they're there for –"

"They'll just get irritated and move me to the

section of folks on watch twenty-four seven, who aren't allowed to do anything without five pounds of paperwork."

"I promise that's not going to happen . . . ," Mum assures Lao Lao.

"You don't know that! You don't know anything about this place! You've never even *been* here," Lao Lao snaps in frustration. A long empty minute passes. "I'm sorry. I just feel . . . so far away from all my lovelies." Softly, Lao Lao starts to cry.

"Oh, Lao Lao," I say, the tears pooling in my own eyes.

"We miss you, Lao Lao," Millie chimes in. "I love your mittens! Thank you for making them!"

"You're so welcome, sweetie. I've got to go," Lao Lao says. "I'll catch a cold if I stay on for too long without my sweater."

"Course, Ma . . . we miss you," Mum says, her voice cracking slightly.

"Hang in there, seashell," I add.

"You too, seashell," Lao Lao replies as she hangs up.

I put a hand to my heart, and I picture her putting a shivering hand to hers. I hope it warms her, just a little.

Chapter 23

"We've got to get Pete to hurry up with our green card." Mum calls Dad on the phone as soon as we get back to the apartment. "I have to go home and see my Mum – she sounds miserable in that nursing home all by herself!"

My hopes shoot up. I would *love* to take a family trip to Beijing! Millie looks similarly stoked.

"I know, but we can't rush him. He's already working on it," Dad says on speaker.

"Can't we just go down to immigration and explain the situation?" Mum asks, swiping over to Google Maps on her phone and looking up how far it is.

"No. Pete specifically said not to do that. Everything's going through his lawyer's office," Dad says. "Besides, we don't even know what our case number is. It's all being handled by Mr. Westlake, his lawyer."

"Well, can we go and talk to this Westlake guy?" Mum asks.

"If you want to pay three hundred fifty dollars an hour!" Dad says. "We don't have that kind of money. We can barely cough up the back rent!"

Mum lets out a heavy sigh.

"Pete's calling for me. I gotta go," Dad says. "It'll be all right."

Mum hangs up the phone and sinks into a kitchen chair. I know how she feels . . . like it's absolutely impossible to reunite with her Mum. But I know from experience that where there's a will, there's a way.

I walk over to her and, gently, put my hands over her eyes. It's my turn to check us into the Imagination Hotel.

"Imagine we email every single customer on Etsy, and we tell them that for a limited time only, we'll make a bath bomb especially for *them*. Any drawing or message they want. Something unique they can send to their friends . . ."

A small smile forms on Mum's lips.

"We can't email *every* customer on Etsy —" Millie

starts to say.

"But imagine we can!" I cut in. "The orders start flooding in. People want to send these as gifts to their friends."

"For their neighbours!" Millie adds.

"For their moms," Mum finishes, her eyes flashing wide. She claps her hands. "Let's get to work!"

I grin at my sister, running over to Mum's laptop and tapping the keys awake. After hearing the conversation between Mum and Dad, I know this isn't just about back rent, or launching a small business. It's a road map to seeing Lao Lao again!

"Here, Millie, write a cool message and we can start sending it to all our customers!" I point to the laptop.

Millie grins, taking the laptop from me.

"Actually, why don't you write it, and Millie can help?" Mum suggests.

"Me?" I ask, panicking. "But my English is horrible!"

"All the more reason to practice!" Mum responds with a smile.

Chapter 24

Dear customer,

We excited to call you SPECIAL bath bomb. Buy for your friends. We paint any message on our bomb! Message can be, I love you. You beautiful. Congratuation! Or if an enemy, can be: you rotten squid egg. Your eyeball is hairy. Anything. You think, I draw. VERY BUBBLE way to make someone feel special.

Special offer end soon. ORDER NOW!

It takes me most of the afternoon to write the message.

When I'm done, I hand it over to Millie nervously.

"*Call* you SPECIAL bath bomb??" she asks, covering her mouth with her hand.

I yank the laptop away, hot with humiliation.

I should have known better than to show her. I pound on the delete button until all my words are wiped clean. What was Mum thinking, asking me to do this?

"WAIT!" Millie says, reaching for the laptop. "We just need to edit it!"

I shake my head firmly. No amount of editing can save my embarrassing words.

"Some of it was good! I liked the 'hairy eyeball' part!" Millie says.

I glance over hesitantly.

"And bubble way to feel special – that's kind of creative!" Millie says.

I study her eyes to see if she's just saying that out of pity.

But Millie's already hard at work, tapping control Z over and over again, until all my words reappear. She shows me how to use spell check, which corrects all my spelling mistakes. There sure are a lot of tools for English learners like me!

"You should have seen my first TikTok. CRINGE! But now I can totally rock it. Mistakes are how we *grow*," Millie says.

I watch as my sister spruces up my writing. She changes "Dear customer" to "Hi there!" Together, we come up with a great hook. When we're all done, I stand back to admire my letter.

Mum walks over and reads the message.

"Wow. Did Lina write that?" she asks.

"Yup!" Millie says.

My eyes flash with surprise as Mum gives us her enthusiastic approval to start sending. As we push send on the first message, Millie reaches over and gives me a high five. As her small hand touches mine, my fingertips jump. My first high five with my sister! I'll have to admit, it feels a hundred times better than high-fiving the mirror. A spark of pride shoots through me. Maybe I am not hopeless with this new language.

And maybe my sister isn't a total armpit.

*

On Friday, there's a knock on the door just as our next Book Tasting is about to start. A smiling Latinx woman enters. She has big hoop earrings that jingle when she walks. I try to sketch them in my head.

"Mrs. Ortiz!" Mrs. Carter greets her. "Lina's right here."

She's Mrs. Ortiz?

"Hi!" Mrs. Ortiz smiles at me. "I'm excited to work with you! Won't you follow me?"

Finn turns to me to translate, but I'm already reaching for my stuff and standing up. As I walk out with Mrs. Ortiz, the other kids stare at me. *Why's she going? Is she in trouble?* I ignore the whispers as I follow my new teacher out.

"So," Mrs. Ortiz says in English, leading me down the hall. "Mrs. Carter says you just came over from China."

I nod.

"I still remember when I first came to the United States from Guatemala with my parents," she says, her earrings bouncing as she walks. "I was six years old. I'll never forget that first year in America, not knowing English. I didn't even know the word *girl!* Which made it very hard for me to find the bathroom."

Really? I want to ask how did she find the bathroom, then? But I hold my tongue.

"But you want to know something? I had an amazing ESL teacher," she says. "She took my hands and traced them on a piece of paper. And taught me the word *hand*. Then she took my feet and traced them, too!"

I looked down at Mrs. Ortiz's feet in her open-toed sandals. And at my own toes squished inside my sneakers, which I am fairly confident are more stinky.

"The point is, one word at a time, I learned English," Mrs. Ortiz says, opening the door to an empty classroom in the back of the arts building. "And that's exactly what we're going to do together. Now, I want you to know, the point of ESL is not to erase your other language. But to learn to hold both in your mouth . . . if you want to."

She waits for me to reply. I decide to break my no-speaking-at-school rule, just this one time. For Mrs. Ortiz.

"I want," I say in a tiny voice.

"All right then!" She turns the lights on in my new classroom. To my surprise, it is *filled* with art supplies, from floor to ceiling!

Mrs. Ortiz chuckles. "You like art? Me too! I'll make you a deal If there are ever any parts you're not sure about as we're working, you can draw it . . . How's that?"

I smile back at her. That sounds like a fine deal to me.

Chapter 25

It's nearly eleven when we start to pack up. I've learned five new vocabulary words, thanks to Mrs. Ortiz patiently helping me fill out the ALL ABOUT ME worksheet. Who knew *pop* could mean so many things – Dad, fizzy drink, music, and Popsicle? For hobbies, she let me draw bath bombs and two seashells.

"You're a fast learner, Lina! And clearly a very gifted artist!" I smile.

She nods to the seashells on my papers as I pack them into my backpack. "I love the beach too! Have you been to Oxnard yet?" she asks.

I shake my head. "Not yet."

"Oh, you should go!" she says. "Maybe this weekend. With your parents?"

"My dad works on weekend. And my Mum, too."

"I understand exactly," she says. "My parents worked hard too. My dad had a small business, selling watches down at the swap meet. Weekends were the busiest time for us!"

"My Mum, too! She sell bombs!" I say proudly.

Mrs. Ortiz looks at me, slightly alarmed.

Realizing my mistake, I quickly add, "Bath!" and point to the little soapy balls on my paper. "We sell bath bombs online. I paint them."

"That's lovely!" Mrs. Ortiz tells me. "A mother-daughter small business." Her eyes widen. "Oh, I know the perfect book for you! Come with me!"

I follow Mrs. Ortiz out of the arts building and down the hall to the library. Walking inside, I am transplanted to a reading oasis. Light streams in from the windows on all sides. There are comfy little reading nooks everywhere and even a reading tree house! Mrs. Hollins, the librarian, waves at us and walks over from shelving the books.

"Hi, Ana! I thought you were over at the middle school! How are things going?" Mrs. Hollins greets Mrs. Ortiz.

"Going well! This is Lina. She's my new student,

and you know the book I think would be perfect for her? *Flea Shop* by Catherine Wang!"

"Oh, I *love* that book! And you're in luck, someone just returned it – I'll go get it!" Mrs. Hollins turns and walks over to the returned-books pile.

While we wait, I gaze at the colourful signs for the upcoming book fair. The bulletin boards are decorated with gold and blue ribbons, our school's colours, and the big bold letters at the top say **BOOKS ARE SLIDING DOORS AND MIRRORS!**

Mrs. Hollins walks back with my book. She hands it to me. To my surprise, it's a thick book, not a little picture book, which was what I *thought* she was going to give me. As I thumb through it, I realise that there are comics inside!

"We call this a graphic novel," Mrs. Ortiz tells me. "I think you'll really like it. It's about a ten-year-old girl who moves to the US and helps her parents manage a flea market shop!"

"It has so much heart!" Mrs. Hollins adds, putting a hand to her chest. "And humor! I laughed and cried!"

I flip the pages, mesmerised by the format. It's like watching a movie in a book! Now when I get stuck on a word, the picture clues me in!

"So have they decided who to invite to the book fair yet?" Mrs. Ortiz asks Mrs. Hollins as we walk over to the checkout station together. I read as we walk.

"Not yet. There's some talk about Tony Walsh, the guy who writes the Royal Pets series," Mrs. Hollins says, making a face.

Mrs. Ortiz rolls her eyes.

"No offense to royal Pomeranians, but I hope we invite someone the kids can relate to. Who can get the kids excited about books again! Ever since the pandemic, it's been such a tough battle getting them to read," the librarian says.

"The reading slide is very real, that's for sure," Mrs. Ortiz says as she holds out her hand for *Flea Shop* so she can check it out for me.

I wait anxiously, bouncing on my feet, for her to check it out.

When I get it back, I turn the pages madly, looking for the spot where I left off. I laugh out loud at the line *Uhhh, flight attendant? Can I have an extra cookie? I'm about to move to a new country where I know zero people. And soon I won't even be able to ask for another cookie, because I know zero English.*

I gaze apologetically at Mrs. Hollins, because I'm not sure if she has a no-laughing-out-loud policy in her library. But her face blooms brighter than Pete's azaleas.

Chapter 26

"Mum!" I jump in the car. "You're not gonna believe it! My new teacher Mrs. Ortiz is amazing! She took me to a special classroom! Oh, and I got this great book – it's so good, I'm already at chapter nine!"

And the amazing thing is I understand about 75 percent of it!

"That's wonderful," Mum says, gesturing for me to hurry up and get in. Excitedly, she tells me her own great news. "We have *fifty* orders for the custom bath bombs! They just came in! And they need to be FedExed to a bridal party right away!"

"Oh my God!" I jump in the car. "Do we even have that much baking soda at home? Or paint?"

"That's why we're going to the store! Millie, hurry up and get in!" Mum says.

I look over at my sister, dragging herself along the pavement with a frown.

"What's wrong, Millie?" I ask.

She shakes her head, not wanting to say. Instead, she gazes over at Hazel, who's getting into her Mum's Porsche SUV. As Hazel waves to her Starburst friends, Millie gets in and slams the car door with a bang.

On the way to Michaels, I get it out of Millie what happened. Hazel's having a sleepover and she's not invited.

"I really thought I was her friend. That's why I lent her the special mittens from Lao Lao! But she said she only wants to invite her Starbursts, plus a couple friends she's going to sleepover camp with."

"What's sleepover camp?" I ask.

"It's this super-fun summer camp in Winfield," Millie says.

Mum adds, "Super *expensive*."

"They have waterslides and go-karts," Millie says. "And horseback riding and gold mining!"

"Well, we have bath bombs!" I try to cheer Millie up.

"We can't even use them," she says, pouting.

134

She searches mournfully in her backpack for some Starbursts, but there are only wrappers. She takes them and smells the wrappers.

I reach into my own backpack and pull out my copy of *Flea Shop*. Maybe some of the jokes inside will pull her out of her rut. But Millie pushes the book away.

"I don't want a book." Millie reaches for Mum's phone. She checks her latest TikTok. Five views. Millie frowns and gives Mum her phone back.

"This isn't just a book," I tell her. "This is *us*."

Mum glances at the book in the rearview mirror as I explain.

"You think that just because Hazel goes to fancy sleepaway camp, that's cool. Guess what? In this book, the girl and her parents live inside a flea shop! Every weekend, they have to go searching at garage sales, looking for valuable junk!"

Millie doesn't say anything. But she gazes curiously at the smiling Chinese American girl on the cover.

"That sounds pretty cool to me," Mum chimes in. I show her the cover in the mirror so she can see. As soon as Mum sees it, she gasps. "Oh my God! Is that *you* on the cover, Millie?" I pretend to be

135

equally shocked.

"Millie Gao, when were you going to tell me?" Mum asks. That gets a giggle out of Millie. She reaches for my book and beams proudly at the picture of her look-alike on the cover.

"I see what happened – all that time you were in your room crying and pretending to be all upset about Hazel, you were secretly writing this book!" Mum gasps. "And now you're a huge literary star! With a million readers!"

"And a movie deal!" I grin. Leave it to Mum to Imagination Hotel Millie's way out of her ridiculous woes.

Millie laughs, hiding her embarrassed face. But I can tell she's tickled pleased.

"And for the premiere of your new movie, you've invited everyone you used to go to school with. Including Hazel . . . ," Mum continues.

"By this time, she's no longer talking to *any* of her sleepover friends . . . ," I add.

Millie throws her head back and laughs. She bounces excitedly in her seat.

"And she looks inside her gift bag," Millie adds. "And she sees her custom bath bomb, which says,

'Who's the real Starburst now?'"

I put my hands together and make an explosion gesture.

Millie points straight ahead at the street, toward Michaels. "Hit the gas, Mum!"

Chapter 27

By Sunday morning, we've finished mixing the bath bomb mixture and putting it into moulds. There's just one problem – getting them to harden in time. Usually, we let the bombs harden overnight in the moulds. But seeing as how we need to FedEx them Monday morning and we haven't even painted them yet, I get the idea to freeze the moulds.

"Freeze them?" Mum asks. "We've never tried that. I suppose it could work!"

We start taking out all the frozen dumplings from our freezer and squeezing in our moulds.

But fifty bombs is a lot, and we soon run out of space. Millie and I go around asking the neighbours if they've got freezer space to spare. Luckily, Rosa, the lady with the adorable terrier, says she has some room in her taco truck fridge!

As we follow her to the taco truck with our precious bombs, she tells us today's her lucky day.

"My rent relief cheque finally came in!" she says. "Now I can stop worrying about the landlord demanding all his back rent!"

She shows us the pale-green cheque with swirly lines. Our pupils widen as we stare at all those 000s. *Whoa.* My stomach sours with envy.

"You guys get yours yet?" Rosa asks.

We shake our heads.

"We can't apply because we have no green card," Millie says. "That's why we're selling bath bombs."

"You can apply without a green card. Get it in before the deadline's up!" Rosa insists. "I know plenty of folks applying! All you have to prove is you were impacted by the pandemic, which you were. I saw your mama crying when her nail salon went under. That poor girl. She was walking up and down this courtyard, asking if she could do our nails. She deserves this cheque as much as the rest of us."

Hearing Rosa describe Mama, my heart aches. I can't imagine what it must have felt like for her – but she never once mentioned it in any of her letters.

I wish she'd told me.

We thank Rosa and race home to tell Mum about the relief checks. But Mum doesn't believe it.

"What if it backfires on us?" she asks.

"But what if it doesn't?" I ask. My eyes jump from the baking soda to the citric acid in our living room, just buckets and buckets and buckets, filling the air with white dust.

"You don't think they take notes on who's getting the relief cheque? They're taking notes, trust me. They *always* take notes. And then when we get in there for our green card interview, this will come back to haunt us."

"But it would be so much easier!"

"Let me explain something to you," Mum says. "We're immigrants, which means if there's ever a choice between something easy and something hard, we pick the something hard."

I swallow hard.

"Forever?" I ask.

Mum doesn't answer. The gravity of her words sits in the air. I reach for my *Flea Shop* book, wishing I could ask the author. *Surely not forever . . . right?*

"Let's just worry about finishing this bath bomb

order," Mum says. "Eyes on our own lane and everything will work –"

Mum doesn't get to finish her sentence because Millie opens up our small freezer door.

"Ummm, you guys? You might want to see this!"

Chapter 28

We stare at our precious, crumbling bath bombs. In our haste to get everything into the moulds, we didn't mix it up well enough. It wouldn't have been such a problem if we'd let the bombs sit out to dry, but my wise idea of putting them in the freezer made them all crack and crumble. All our lovely creations are ruined!

My sister picks up the little crusty pieces from the bottom of the freezer.

"Can we repack them?" Millie asks, trying to reshape the crumbles into a little ball in her hand. But the edges stick out in awkward jabs.

After about five tries, Mum shakes her head. "We're just going to have to remake them."

"But we spent seventy-five dollars on the

materials!" I cry.

Millie bites her lip as she looks at me. She doesn't have to say the words. I hang my head as I walk past the me-less pictures to our room. *This is all my fault.*

*

I load the laundry machine that night, sighing. I feel worse than Lisa Simpson accidentally destroying Springfield's oldest tree. The least I can do is make it up to Mum by doing laundry. I smash up some more of our ruined bath bombs and put them into the machine. At least we can use the scraps of bath bomb for laundry detergent. I press start.

I climb on top of the machine and read. The whir of the washing machine helps cover up the pounding guilt in my heart.

We spent the entire afternoon getting tiny little pieces of bath bomb out of Rosa's taco truck fridge. And because I couldn't paint on any good bombs, the mica that I'd already mixed was all wasted too.

I fight the tears in my eyes. The one thing keeping me from jumping inside the washing machine and wringing myself dry is reading *Flea Shop*.

I'm so engrossed reading the part about the mean girls in Cat's class making fun of Cat's eyes, I almost fall off the washing machine. Cat's so utterly depressed when it happens, she accidentally uses an ancient letter opener as a knife to make a peanut butter sandwich. And let's just say, the sandwich does not turn out well.

What happens to Cat makes my blood boil. I think about how this whole week, Jessica's been making fun of me – starting in the ice cream shop. I reach for some of the crumbling bomb and mush it up in my fingers. I hop off the machine and walk to the laundry room sink, add some water, and watch it fizz in my hand. It's oddly satisfying. Closing my eyes, I try to imagine what it's like taking an actual bath, soaking in the bubbly, calming scented water.

So deep am I in my imagining that I don't hear Dad walk in.

"Hey, sweetie," he says gently.

I jump and bolt for the sink, rinsing my hand. "I'm sorry! I was just–"

"You don't need to apologise," he says. "I heard about the bath bombs. I'm sorry." He points at the small bowl of crumbles I'm using as laundry detergent. "May I?"

I nod.

He walks over, grabs a pinch, and adds water. As the baking soda starts to crackle, he pats the foamy, colourful suds onto his face!

"I've always wanted to shave with this," he says, reaching for an imaginary razor. I laugh as Dad "shaves."

When he finishes, he washes off the foam and turns to me. "Hey, you want to go for a drive?" he asks.

I nod eagerly.

I haven't really spent any time with Dad yet, since he's always working for Pete or bone-tired from all that weeding and harvesting. As I head out of the laundry room, I wonder if it's the colourful shave that gave him a boost of energy.

Either way, I'll take it!

Chapter 29

Dad drives up a long, curvy mountain road under the moonlit stars. I peer out the window at the glimmering city lights to our left and long stretches of farmland to our right.

"Where are we going?" I ask him.

"Centurion Peak," he replies. "Sits right between Santa Paula and Ojai. Beautiful up there – one of my favourite spots. You'll see."

I breathe in the fresh mountain air, feeling mildly bad that he's being so nice to me, considering what I've done. I pick at the bath bomb crumbles under my fingernails.

"I'm sorry," I say in a small voice. "I really thought it would work. I made a mistake."

Dad looks at me. His forehead is smooth in the

moonlight, not full of valleys and peaks like during the day. "Let me tell you something about mistakes. A professor of mine once told me a mistake is progress you can't see. Every time you make a mistake, you're learning. You're growing. And if you want to find a *new* path, you've got to be willing to make lots of mistakes."

I give him a small smile.

"What class did this professor teach?" I ask him. "Microbiology," he says. "He was my PhD advisor at California Golden University, when I first came here. I helped him with his research."

"What were you guys researching?" I ask.

"How to convert algae into biofuel. The algae had to be watched around the clock. There were two of us minding the lab. The other guy was also from China. His name was Tai Li Hong. From Shenyang," he says. "Guess how long he'd been working for Dr. Stone?"

"How long?"

"*Thirteen* years. That's thirteen years of running his experiments, getting his coffee, even walking his dog. Poor Tai was tired. A typical PhD takes about seven or eight years. He was there *way* too long. So one day he goes into Dr. Stone's office and he tells him, *I have to graduate.* He missed his wife, missed his daughter – mind you, the whole time he's still on a student visa. When Dr. Stone says no, Tai loses it. He comes into the lab crying, hysterical. He takes his hand and in one fell swoop, he breaks all the glass bottles on the counter."

I gasp.

Dad drives around another curve and puts his blinker on. He turns into a small parking lot at the top of the mountain, but I'm too riveted by the story to get out.

"I told him if he left the lab right now, and didn't break another beaker, I wouldn't tell Dr. Stone it was him," Dad says. "So he did."

"Did he get in trouble?"

Dad opens his car door. I follow him out to a stone bench. The view from the top of the mountain makes me catch my breath. I stare out at the sea of lights, dancing like fireflies, as I wait for Dad to continue the story.

"Eventually. Not at first, though, because I didn't tell Dr. Stone it was him – that was my mistake. But he found out anyway. I should have known that the university has cameras in every room." Dad turns to me. "When Dr. Stone found out, boy, was he furious. Tai was toast. Blacklisted from every university."

"What does it mean, 'blacklisted'?" I ask Dad.

"It means no university would touch him now." Dad swallows hard. "Then Dr. Stone told me I couldn't stay on either. I hadn't been honest with him."

I look over and see the sadness reflected in his eyes.

"He said Tai and I must have been in cahoots because we're both Chinese. And that he couldn't trust me anymore." Dad looks down at his coarse, cracked hands. "One thing I'll say about Pete. He's always trusted me, and me him."

He looks up and gives me a smile. Now I understand why his new job means so much to him.

A breeze glides between us and I shiver slightly. Dad puts his jacket around me and hugs me tight. Nestled in his warm jacket, I listen as he points out all the landmarks and sights.

"And the ocean's just beyond there," he says. "If you keep following that motorway, you'll get to it. It's too bad you can't see it tonight because it's so dark."

I follow his finger. It's so nice spending time with Dad, learning about his past, that I don't even care if we can't see the beach. I fill in the image of it in my head, drawing in the crashing waves and the soft sand with my imagination.

Turning to Dad, I hesitate before holding my hand up midair. I've never initiated a high five before in my life. It's scary, and if I'm being completely honest, doing it in the low light of a dark mountain is probably not the best place. But nudged by the wind, I take my chance.

To my surprise, Dad beams as he slaps the palm of my hand. The hearty sound of our two hands rings in my ears long after we descend the mountain.

Our high five may not be anywhere near as long and complicated as his and Millie's.

But it's the start of everything.

Chapter 30

"What'd you think of the book so far?" Mrs. Ortiz asks me when I get to school on Monday. We're in the special classroom again.

I nod enthusiastically, getting it out of my backpack. "I like!" I tell Mrs. Ortiz.

"What was your favourite part?" she asks.

I flip to the page where Cat is frustrated working in the flea shop after school every day. She calls her grandma back in China, who takes her on a walking tour around Shanghai, so Cat can be "outside having fun."

There are some words I don't understand, but I can decode it from the pictures. It's kind of like with Chinese characters. If you know the radical, you can guess the meaning.

"Wonderful reading!" Mrs. Ortiz compliments me. "Now tell me why you like this scene."

"I like because . . . my grandmother," I say to her.

"Is she in China?"

I nod.

"You must really miss her."

I nod extra hard.

"Maybe you can go on a walking tour with her too, sometime!" Mrs. Ortiz suggests.

I shake my head. That's not possible. Even if Lao Lao were allowed out of her nursing home *and* somehow got a smartphone, she can't walk as easily as she used to. She needs a person to help her walk. And that person can't be inside a phone.

"She . . . not move well." I point to my legs and hands.

"I'm sorry to hear that," Mrs. Ortiz says. "Were you two close?"

I nod, feeling the emotions swell inside me. Slowly, I push the words out.

"She take care of me since I little. Now, she all alone." I put my hand to my chest. "It hurt here sometimes."

Mrs. Ortiz holds out her arms to offer me a hug,

and I walk inside. She's probably the first teacher I've ever been this honest with . . . and it feels good, even in my limited English. "You know, I also had to leave my grandmother in Guatemala when I first came over. Back in those days, we couldn't even call. So I would talk to my abuela in my heart."

I reach for a tissue and dry my eyes. I peer at her. "You did that too?"

"And you know what? Years later, she told me she heard everything I said!"

I don't know how to convey to Mrs. Ortiz how terrified I am that there won't be "years later." What if our bath bomb plan fails and we can't make it back? Just thinking that makes me itchy with anxiety.

"Why don't we write her a letter?" Mrs. Ortiz suggests, taking out a piece of paper. "You can write it in English or in Chinese. Remember, *both* languages are equally valid."

Slowly, I reach for the pencil and start writing in Chinese. . . .

Dear Lao Lao,

I hope you are not still cold in your room, and that you have made friends and they are treating you nice.

I miss you. Mum, Millie, and I, we're working on a plan to try to come back and see you. I know it's not easy being in the nursing home by yourself.

I'm sorry I left you. If I had known you were going to have such a hard time in the nursing home –

I pause.

Mrs. Ortiz looks over. "What's wrong?" she asks.

She tries to decode my Chinese characters, not understanding.

I stare at the impossible sentence, not knowing how to continue. It would be so easy to write *if I had known . . . I wouldn't have left.*

Then I think of yesterday on the mountain with my dad, the joy of our first high five together, the magical check-ins to the Imagination Hotel with Mum, and even cheering Millie up about her obnoxious friend . . . and I know in my heart,

I wouldn't miss it for the world.

Once again, I feel the tide of guilt rising inside me, even as Mrs. Ortiz tells me how proud my grandmother is of me – she is sure of it.

Me? I'm not so sure. But I decorate my letter with extra hearts, hoping they'll cover up my feelings like a warm fuzzy mitten over a shivering, worried hand.

Chapter 31

Walking back inside my regular classroom, I see Finn waving at me from our desk. It's another day of Rams gear for him, but the look on his face says there's something special going on.

"Hurry! We're doing self-portraits!" he says.

I glance at all my classmates reaching for colouring pencils and markers and I get excited. I take a huge piece of paper and rush back to my desk. As Finn explains to me in his restaurant Chinese how to draw a self-portrait, I resist the urge to silence him with a hand – *I got this*.

"Mrs. Carter?" Jessica asks, raising her hand. "Do you have a thinner paintbrush? I think I want to go for a Van Gogh-esque self-portrait."

"Well, that is certainly an impressive endeavor,"

Mrs. Carter praises Jessica, handing her a thin paintbrush.

Jessica beams. "I wasn't voted most talented artist in the yearbook last year for nothing!"

I crack my knuckles and get to work. Most talented artist? Not for long!

*

Forty-five minutes later, I'm putting the final touches to my airplane when Finn looks over and whispers.

"That's a great airplane . . . but you're supposed to draw a self-portrait, not an airplane."

He starts looking around for an eraser big enough to erase my colossal mistake, when I tap him on the shoulder and point to me in one of the windows.

It *is* a self-portrait of me, at my rawest, most vulnerable moment.

"Ooohhh," Finn says, gazing curiously at my eager, worried, thrilled, and scared eyes. "Is this when you first came to America?"

I nod.

"How did you feel?" Finn asks.

I try to think of the words. Instead, I reach for

another piece of paper. Quickly, I sketch a person about to go bungee jumping.

Finn watches as I draw, spellbound. When I'm done, he nods zealously, fully understanding. Next, I sketch me with my stomach in knots. Literal knots. Finn laughs.

"All right, kids, do we have anyone who wants to share their artwork?" Mrs. Carter asks.

Finn shoots his hand up in the air. "Mrs. Carter! Lina drew something that's *fire!*"

My face flushes deep red. *Why did Finn have to tell the whole class?*

As Mrs. Carter walks over, I plunge my face down on my table and cover my whole head with my arms. But to my surprise, she gasps and says, "This is *lovely!* Is this you on the plane ride over?"

"Yeah! And she was nervous and felt like her stomach was in knots!" Finn blurts out to the class.

I open one eye and peek out from under my arms as Mrs. Carter holds up my airplane self-portrait for the entire class to see.

"Lina, this is masterful work. I love the details and shading on the airplane flying against the setting sun. And the emotions on your face –

just exquisite!"

"You can barely see her face!" Jessica protests. "It's supposed to be a *self*-portrait, not an ad for Delta –"

Mrs. Carter hushes Jessica up with some serious side-eye. She turns and smiles at me.

"Lina, would you like to tell us any more about that day, or how you drew your gorgeous piece?" Mrs. Carter asks.

I wish I could borrow someone else's mouth – for just a minute. I want so badly to describe the emotions swirling through me as we touched down, not knowing whether my family would still recognise me. Still get me. Still like me.

But as I look out at my picky classmates, ready to pounce on my English and catch the slightest mistake, I feel the invisible thread closing in again. I shake my head at Mrs. Carter. I'd better not say anything.

Mrs. Carter takes my self-portrait and walks it over to her whiteboard with magnets. She hangs it up, and to my surprise, she writes *Most Talented Emerging Artist* next to my work.

Not even Jessica's furious scowl from behind me can stop me from glowing.

Chapter 32

I'm still grinning and thinking about my Most Talented Emerging Artist award at lunch on Tuesday. Is it an award? I'm going to tell Lao Lao it's an award, I decide. Maybe I can send her my picture along with my letter from today, and it'll cheer her up.

Mrs. Corso, the cafeteria server, puts a giant raw potato on a stick on my tray. I look up at the sign. **CORN DOGS**, it says. Which is weird, because it does not look like corn.

It looks like a raw potato.

I start imagining all the different ways I can draw on my raw potato with the mustard and the ketchup they give me.

I walk through the cafeteria with my food and

my copy of *Flea Shop*, looking around briefly for Finn. That was nice what he did yesterday. I'm glad he understands me a little more, through my art. Maybe I do have a friend in school, despite having no place to sit in the cafeteria.

Unable to locate Finn, I head straight for my favourite tree. Under the breezy eucalyptus, I get to work decorating my raw potato.

With deep swirls of ketchup and mustard, I paint my lush sunset. As I'm dotting my potato with daffodils, I accidentally get some ketchup on my shirt.

Noooo! I just did laundry on Sunday! I jump up and hurry to the bathroom with my book.

*

Thankfully, I manage to get most of the ketchup off my shirt, but now there's a huge wet stain the shape of the Forbidden City in the center of my stomach. It looks like I peed my belly button. As I'm grabbing paper towels, I see Jessica come out of the middle stall. She walks out with a purple marker in her hand.

Her face turns slightly red when she sees me. She

quickly dashes out of the bathroom, without a word or even washing her hands.

Do I smell or something? I lift my arm up, but I don't smell anything. Just to be safe, I grab some more paper towels and wash my neck.

When I'm all done, I walk into the middle stall to use the bathroom. As I'm sitting on the toilet, I look up at the door, and that's when I see it.

I wonder why she doesn't talk.
Her English is trash, that's why.
I bet Mrs. Carter only gave her the Best Emerging Artist thing because she felt sorry for her.
It's a pity award – for sure.

I stare at the last line, in bold purple marker. My skin turns scorching hot. My hands shake.

And here I thought I was starting to actually fit in.

Chapter 33

I tear out of the bathroom, clutching my book and a big old piece of paper towel, which I hold over my shirt. I run down the hall, straight past the **DREAM, IMAGINE, BE KIND, BELIEVE**, blinking back the pain.

I try to shake the image of Jessica scribbling gleefully with her purple marker behind the bathroom door. The words hurt so bad, it makes me want to run straight out the school gate and all the way home.

Maybe if I beg Mum hard enough, she'll let me homeschool myself, or maybe I can join Carla! I can help her and Dad with the farming. It'll certainly be better than dealing with Jessica! As I'm planning my future homeschool schedule,

I squirm and wriggle, eyes scanning for another bathroom. I really have to go. But the worst part is . . . *where* do I even go??

I spot the library and dash over. The sign on the door says **CLOSED DURING LUNCH**. Still, I take a chance. Pushing inside the double glass doors, I rush over to the staff bathroom to the left of the magazines.

Mrs. Hollins looks up from her desk. She's eating a sandwich. I gaze at her apologetically and do a little awkward wave as I slink into the bathroom.

The inside of the library staff bathroom smells like lavender. I dive into one of the stalls and am relieved to see that the doors are pristine.

No writing here.

As I walk out, Mrs. Hollins makes her way over. "Hi, Lina," she says. "How are you liking *Flea Shop*?"

I hug it tighter, nodding. I need Cat Wang now, more than ever, especially after what just happened in the bathroom. She's the only one who understands! I hope Mrs. Hollins doesn't make me return it.

"Oh, good," she says. "Say, I heard from Mrs. Carter today that you're a great artist. Would you like to help me with an art project? I'm making some posters for the library!"

She points to her desk; on top rests a poster she's making, entitled *If You Like This Book . . . Read This Next!*

I follow her over. I see she has about twelve small printouts of book covers. I reach for one, called *Fumble.*

"Put that one right here," she says, pointing to the left-hand column. I do as I'm told, gluing and pasting. It feels nice to be able to help Mrs. Hollins and not think about the bathroom wall.

She hands me a cover of another graphic novel, *Sunny Side Up,* and I stare curiously at the cover.

"Oh, you'll like this one, too," Mrs. Hollins says. "It's about this girl Sunny who goes to live with her grandpa one summer."

My eyeballs must have grown to the size of the poster, because she chuckles.

"That happen to you, too? Me too. I went to live with my grandparents one summer in London," she says. "My parents were moving houses. I was terribly homesick the first week, until I discovered Yorkshire pudding."

She waggles her eyebrows and even though I

don't know what Yorkshire pudding is, I decide in my mind that it tastes something like tang hulu, which is absolutely delicious. Sweet and crunchy, and warm in your belly . . . like the feeling of connecting with Mrs. Hollins over our joint experience. I guess that's the power of books.

"Hey, Lina. I want you to know that you can come in here anytime you want." Mrs. Hollins looks into my eyes. "Even during lunch, so long as you promise not to get ketchup on the books."

It takes every effort not to throw my arms around her. Instead, I reach out a hand and we shake on it.

Deal.

Chapter 34

I decide not to tell Mum about the bathroom wall later that day, or about the Most Talented Emerging Artist thing.

I really want to, but if I tell her about the Talented Artist thing, she might make a big deal out of it, and I could let it slip that it wasn't all good.

I hate that Jessica and her horrible wall comment ruined my good news. But at least now I have a bathroom I can *count on*. And I get to read more graphic novels – I'm super curious about the *Sunny Side Up* book! Mrs. Hollins says another student will be returning it soon.

As I slide into the backseat of our car, Mum greets me with the latest about Lao Lao.

"Good news! I got the nurses to move Lao Lao's

phone closer to her bed and put a heater in her room!" Mum says.

"Great! So we can call her now?" I ask, reaching for Mum's phone.

But Mum shakes her head with a regretful sigh. "I'm afraid I already spent ten dollars talking internationally to the nurses. We gotta wait a few days."

"Where are we going?" Millie asks, noticing that we're not turning the usual way.

"To Pete's," Mum says. "We need him to give us an advance on Dad's salary. I told the bride about our mistake, and guess what? She and her husband still want the custom bombs for the wedding party gift bag, coming up in three weeks!"

"That's great!" Millie exclaims.

"I know! But we need more materials!" Mum says, making a sharp right onto the main street. "Hopefully I'll be able to work something out with Pete!"

*

When we get to Pete's, we find him knee-deep in rotten fruit and vegetables, making compost and lecturing Carla's Mum.

"Now why would you take all the roots out?" Pete asks Mrs. Muñoz. "The roots feed the worms. The worms feed the soil. The soil feeds us. Without the soil, we're goners! We only have five generations of usable topsoil left in the world – once that's gone, the world becomes a dust bowl. Soil's our best shot at reversing the devastation to the planet – I thought you knew this! You were *supposed* to be a sustainable-farming expert!"

"I am!" Mrs. Muñoz insists.

I look over at Carla, who's glaring at Pete as she spreads compost.

"Well, obviously you're not. Or you wouldn't have made such a rookie mistake," Pete says, fuming. His voice is bordering on yelling now. "Do you know what happens when we run out of topsoil?"

"I get it. You don't have to scream," Mrs. Muñoz says, trying to calm Pete.

"No, you're not getting it. *The earth is dying!*" Dad walks over with his wheelbarrow.

"When the last topsoil runs out, we'll have to farm with chemicals. Which are going to run into our lakes and groundwater, causing cancer and God knows what else. So don't tell me to keep my voice down."

Pete grabs a fistful of dirt. "This is going to be all of us, if you don't do your job."

I gasp at Pete's ominous suggestion as he throws his fistful of dirt hard against the wind. Some dirt lands on Mrs. Muñoz's trousers, and she wipes them, blinking rapidly.

"We understand," Dad says quickly. He puts a hand on Mrs. Muñoz's shoulder. "I show you how to keep roots."

Pete turns to Mum. "What do you want?" Mum freezes and glances over at Dad, who gives her a *not now* shake. But Pete's eyes burrow into Mum like a worm into topsoil. "Spit it out."

"I . . . just . . . wondering can you give us advance for salary. I need money —"

"Join the club." Pete gestures at his farm. "I got eighteen bunches of carrots that won't make it till the next farmers' market, ten bushels of cucumbers. Thirty baskets of strawberries! And don't even get me started on the dill. So don't come crying to me about money. You need money, take out a loan."

"But without green card, no bank will give me loan," Mum says. "Or decent job. Please, Pete, we need money for back rent. It's due in five weeks!"

"I always told you it was a stupid idea to move out in the first place," Pete says, raising his voice so Carla and her Mum can overhear. "You should have just stayed here on the farm!"

Wait, what?? I look at my sister. We *lived* here?

"The girls are happy where we are," Mum says. "We just need small advance. Just tiny, so we can get by –"

"And who's going to give *me* an advance?" Pete looks up at the cloudless sky. "The rain gods? The bees being destroyed by the commercial farms up north? The Winfield Organic Farmers Association, with all their red tape and steep fees, saying my two-acre farm is too small to be certified organic?"

"You know . . . maybe you try to sell to Asian supermarket," Mum suggests, thinking out loud, glancing at the ripe carrots in the corner. "They won't care if not certified organic."

That finally gets a small smile out of Pete. "Tell you what. You manage to sell my vegetables to the Asian supermarket, and I'll give you your advance."

Mum does a little jump in the sun. She grabs the carrots and bolts toward the main house, ready to start selling!

171

Chapter 35

That afternoon, Mum makes calls from the main house to all the Asian supermarkets in the area. Pete's too busy trying to keep a family of robins from gobbling up his ripe strawberries to tell me and Millie what to do, so we scurry over to Carla's tiny home, where we send out cute designs to keep our customers interested.

"This woman wants to know if we can make a dog-friendly bath bomb," Millie says, tapping on her Chromebook to research ingredients. "It's her poodle Buttercup's fifth birthday!"

"Awww . . . ," Carla says. "Maybe we can make one that smells like peanut butter!"

I add peanut butter to the list of supplies we need to get, when we finally get the money.

"Or steak," Millie suggests.

I chuckle. "Good one," I tell her in Chinese.

Millie smiles. I brainstorm puppy designs to put on the bath bomb, grabbing my sketchbook. I head outside because it's getting too stuffy inside. Carla's tiny home is the size of our small, narrow hallway, with only enough space for a bunk bed, a small fridge, and a bathroom, but no shower.

There's a small outdoor shower, with a large bucket on the top. It looks like something from a water park. Is that where Carla and her Mum take a shower?

I wonder if Mum and Dad and Millie all lived inside the tiny home too. No wonder Millie's spelling medal melted. It must have been *boiling* inside during the summers, all of them crammed in here, stuffed tighter than a corn dog!

Speaking of dogs, I sit down on the step and start sketching. Carla comes out and sees the puppy I'm drawing.

"That's so cute!" she says. "I wish I could draw like that!"

I flash her a smile in the sun. I rip off a new page. "I teach you," I tell her. Slowly, I show her how to draw a dog.

As she shades in her dog's floppy ears, she grins at me. "That's so cool. I used to do all sorts of art with my Mum." Her face falls a little. "But now Pete has her working all the time."

I gaze out at Mrs. Muñoz and Dad hunched over in the field. I remember what Dad said about how Mrs. Muñoz and Carla get up at the crack of dawn, and ought to be paid. It makes me clutch my pencil even tighter when I think about how Pete yelled at Mrs. Muñoz.

"You know the thing that hurts the most?" Carla asks, picking at the grass beneath our feet. "He doesn't have to remind us that eventually we all become dirt. We know that." Her eyes fill as she scoops up a handful of soil. "It's why we're here."

I pause my drawing and put my arms around Carla's shoulders. I hold her as the dirt falls from her hand, and tell her about my lao ye. Graves are very expensive in China and my lao lao didn't have enough money for a plot of land, so we scattered Lao Ye over his favourite river in Shunyi. The whole time, my eyes were glued to the street, waiting, hoping my Mum would show up. I think I cried harder for

Mum not coming than I did for Lao Ye.

Carla says she's sorry. "I know how hard it is . . . people are always telling you to move on. But . . . it's more like a Boomerang on Instagram. You go forward two steps, then you go back one step," she says, gazing over at her Mum toiling in the hot heat. "My Mum loves those plants. But abusing that love . . . it's not the organic way."

I nod, agreeing fully. Hesitantly, I turn to her and tell her about my own unfair teardown. It wasn't as loud. But it's still loud in my mind.

Carla jumps up when she hears. "They wrote that it's a *pity award?*" she asks.

I nod.

"Don't believe it for a second!" she says, pointing to my sketchpad. "You got that award because you're amazing and talented. I hope you bury those words deep and fill it up with compost, so something more beautiful and deserving can grow!"

"Thanks," I tell Carla. "And I hope you and Mum art class again."

Carla grins at me. "Well, until we do . . ." She picks up two sticks and hands me one. She starts drawing a puppy in the soil.

I grin and kneel in the dirt. It's surprisingly soft and fluffy, almost like our bath bomb mixture. I draw a ball for the puppy and a little girl. Millie comes out and when she sees the art class, she wants in too. That afternoon, I teach Millie and Carla, doodling in the dirt.

Pete's right. The soil feeds the soul. So does opening up to a friend.

Chapter 36

"So, did you make any progress with the Asian supermarkets?" I ask Mum on the way home. We pass by a sprawling metropolis of tents, next to the landfill in Los Ramos. I'm so distracted by the sight of so many campers, I almost don't hear Mum.

"Yes, I did," she replies. "Tomorrow I'm going to drive over to Van Nuys to talk to the manager of 99 Ranch."

"Mum? Why are those people going camping by the landfill?" I ask, pointing to the men and women sitting by the tents.

"They're not 'going camping'. They live there," Millie tells me.

I turn to my sister. *She's joking, right?* But the look on her face says she's serious. In China, sometimes I saw construction workers sleeping near construction sites, but nothing like this. I wonder how all these people in tents got here. *Did it start with back rent for them, too?* The thought chills the air in my lungs.

"Don't worry," Mum says, reading my mind. "We'll be fine. I'm going to talk to the 99 Ranch manager, and we'll get back to fulfilling orders again in no time! You girls think you can walk over to Pete's after school tomorrow?"

"Sure!" Millie says.

As Mum drives away from the landfill, Millie tells her about the dog bath bomb request. Millie proudly tells Mum that as head of product design, she's compiled a list of all the dog-friendly ingredients, while I hold up my sketchbook to show her my awesome pooch design.

"I love it!" Mum chuckles. With a twinkle in her eyes, she leads us on another imagining. "Just think, soon that's going to be us washing Patches!"

My sister and I sit back as we check into our favourite hotel again.

"And he'll be splashing around our big bathtub," Millie adds. "Can you take a bath with a dog?"

"Sure you can!" Mum says. "If the bath is big enough!"

"As big as the one in Hazel's house?" Millie asks. "*If* I had gotten invited, I was gonna bring her some bath bombs so I could finally try them."

"You can try them at home!" Mum says brightly.

"The sink doesn't count . . . ," my sister replies with a little frown.

Taking a bath in the sink *would* be pretty hard. Arguably even harder than the outside shower next to Carla's tiny home. In a small voice, I ask Mum, "Did we used to live in the tiny home at Pete's?"

Mum falls quiet. I glance over at Millie, who nods.

"Why didn't you tell me about that?" I ask. I think back to all the musical birthday cards that sang "Happy Birthday." I would have much preferred to hear the truth than a battery-operated song. "*I* thought you guys lived in a light blue house with a white fence."

"Oh, that's just a house we saw when we were driving around. It looked pretty!" Millie informs me.

Looked *pretty*? That's why she sewed her mouth half shut, even with family?

"We didn't want to worry you, or Lao Lao," Mum

says. "She had enough already on her mind with Lao Ye and her own health. What she didn't know couldn't hurt her."

But it hurt me *not to know*, I want to say. Instead, I blink back the pain.

"Anyway, we're out now. Which is why it's so important we make the back rent, so we *stay* out. And we have a chance at a better life."

"What's a better life?" I ask.

I settle back, expecting Mum to launch into one of her lavish imaginings again. Instead, she replies, "One where we don't have to worry about the roof over our heads being taken away. And we can have dinner as a family . . . occasionally."

That would be nice, I decide. I turn around and glance back at Pete's house, missing Dad. I don't think we've had a single dinner together as a family since I've gotten here. Tonight, he has to stay late to help Pete sort out all the seeds for new crops.

"At least Carla and her Mum don't have to worry about their roof . . . it's free," I say with a sigh. That's one nice thing about living there, I suppose.

"No such thing as a free roof. You're always cuffed to your gratitude," Mum says. "Remember that."

As she drives, I form a handcuff with my fingers and tie it around my other wrist, trying to understand. How can *gratitude* cuff a person?

*

I'm still thinking about it in math the next day.

We're doing fractions, which are easy-breezy compared to what we were doing in China before I left, but today Mrs. Carter divides us into groups of three.

"Lina, Finn," she says. "And Jessica."

Jessica?? My whole body grows hot. I stay frozen, staring ahead, as Finn turns to Jessica. He reads from the sheet. "All right, I think we just have to take turns rolling the dice," he says. "And figure out which fractions are bigger. You wanna go first?"

"Sure," Jessica says, grabbing the dice. She rolls twice. "Two and three." She and Finn write down ⅔ on their papers. Reluctantly, I jot it down on mine, too.

"Lina, do you want to go next?" Finn asks.

I reach for the dice. I roll a three and a four. I write ¾ on my paper and circle it, because it is definitely bigger.

"Uhh, I don't think so!" Jessica says. "Two-

181

thirds is way bigger than three-quarters! Just think, two-thirds of a pizza is like almost the entire pizza!"

I shake my head. I turn the paper over and furiously draw a pizza. I try to shade it in to show her that three-quarters of the pizza is in fact way more.

"Your slices are not even! Look, your pizza's not even perfectly round!" Jessica rolls her eyes. Under her breath, she mutters, "Top emerging artist – as if!"

Glaring at her, I grab another piece of paper. *That's it – it's on!* This time, I draw two perfect pizzas with bubbling cheese. I make the crust look as three-dimensional as I can. But as I'm drawing, Jessica starts drawing too, except hers has way more toppings than mine. Suddenly, I'm in a pizza-off with Jessica!

"You guys!" Finn waves his arms, trying to get our attention. "It's just one math question. We don't have to draw the whole Pizza Hut menu! Can we move on? We still have fifteen more!"

We ignore Finn and keep drawing, adding more and more toppings. I will admit, having not eaten a lot of pizza, I don't know what all the other toppings besides pepperoni are. So I just start adding random ones – bok choy, mandarin oranges, lotus seed, century egg, tofu, bamboo shoots, and shrimp.

"One more minute!" Mrs. Carter calls.

Jessica and I look up and see Finn tossing the dice by himself, scrambling to finish. Jessica and I quickly copy down everything he writes on his paper – there's no time to finish our pizza war.

When Mrs. Carter comes to collect our papers, she looks down at our answers and frowns.

"Three halves is less than one half? Really??" she asks.

"Lina just kept drawing pizzas, Mrs. Carter! She was so unhelpful!" Jessica blurts out. She points at the seventeen pizzas on the desk.

My jaw drops. The gall of Jessica to blame it all on me!

"Actually," Finn starts to say in a tiny voice, "Jessica also drew some."

Jessica shoots him a death stare as she grabs my drawings and shows them to the class. "Ummmm, oranges on pizza? I would never draw that. That's disgusting!"

As my entire class makes gagging noises and fills the room with *ewwwwws* and *grosses*, Mrs. Carter gives me a regretful sigh. "Lina, there is a time and a place for art, and I'm disappointed that you doodled for so long during math."

I nod as Mrs. Carter lectures me, shrinking up like a mandarin orange sitting on a bed of hot, laughing cheese.

"Have patience . . . ," Mrs. Ortiz says. "My first year, I didn't say a word to *anyone* in my class until the end of that year. In fact! —" She holds up a finger.

I wait while she digs through her big leather purse and pulls out her wallet. I think she's about to give me ten dollars because I look so blue, and I start waving, *No no no.* No need for a tip. But then she pulls out a yellowed piece of paper. I lean over curiously, peering at the perfect handwriting. It says:

Ana Ortiz entered Pinebrook Elementary on September 19, 1971. She could speak no English. We have been working with her on a pre-primer level in reading. She does very well on most of her math. We've been working with her on her English for a whole year. It has only been within the last week that she has begun speaking very limited sentences in English — and we're so proud of her! She is being placed in year 2 because students are not retained due to limited English.

Mrs. Henley

I stare and stare at the last sentence, relief engulfing me. Her eyes smile at me. "I keep this in my wallet to remind myself it's okay to take my time. There's no set timeline for anything in life. So don't rush. You'll get there in your own time . . . I promise."

I smile. From one orange-pizza eater to another, her promise means a lot.

Chapter 38

I head straight for the library with my cafeteria brown-bag lunch, hoping to find more books like *Flea Shop* and *Swing It, Sunny.*

Mrs. Hollins beams when I walk inside. She waves me over and shows me her *If You Like This Book . . . Read This Next!* poster – it's almost finished!

"How are you liking *Swing It, Sunny?*" she asks me. I give her an enthusiastic thumbs-up.

She hands me two more book-cover cutouts to add today – *Pie in the Sky* and *The First Rule of Punk.* I take a seat next to Mrs. Hollins at the librarian desk and eat my three-na sandwich. Actually it's a *tuna* sandwich, but Mrs. Corso, the cafeteria server, likes to joke it's a three-na sandwich. I didn't get it until I got to the library and looked up tuna, except I mispelled it *two-na*. That's when I got the joke. I laughed so hard, tuna came out of my nose.

As I'm eating, I'm drawing swirls and stars with my marker on the poster. Mrs. Hollins shares one of her caramel See's candies with me. I close my eyes as the caramel melts in my mouth, thinking of my lao lao. She *loves* caramel.

Mrs. Hollins points to *Pie in the Sky*.

"I love that book," she says. "It's about a boy who moves to Australia when his father dies. And he's trying to start this bakery in honor of him."

Immediately, I think of Carla.

"Can my friend read?" I ask Mrs. Hollins.

As soon as I finish the sentence, I put my hand over my mouth. I look at Mrs. Hollins, studying her face to see if I made any mistakes, but she looks tickled pleased.

"Yes, she certainly can!" Mrs. Hollins gushes. "It's right over in the stacks, under *L*."

I stuff the last of my sandwich in my mouth and make my way over to the stacks, stopping by the water fountain to get a drink. I walk over to *L* and grab *Pie in the Sky*, nearly tripping on a pair of feet. I follow the dirty Vans shoes all the way up to bright blue-and-yellow Rams shorts.

"Finn?" I ask.

Finn quickly scrambles up from lying on the library floor and sits cross-legged on the carpet. He puts a finger over his mouth and tells me to hush.

"We're not supposed to be in here," he says, putting a bookmark inside his graphic novel. "Mrs. Hollins will be mad —"

I shake my head. *No she won't.*

He points to my copy of *Pie in the Sky.* "You like graphic novels too? That's awesome!"

He shows me the one he's reading — *New Kid* by Jerry Craft. I join him on the carpet. Finn hands me *New Kid* and I flip through it, giggling at the image of the First-Day-of-School Zombie Apocalypse. I turn the page to an illustration of Jordan Banks in the cafeteria, holding his food and looking for a place to sit. He's the size of an ant in the picture when everyone else is normal size.

I stare and stare at the picture. That's exactly how I feel walking through the cafeteria every day!

Finn glances over and sees the page I'm looking at.

"You thinking about Jessica?" he asks. "Ignore her. She's just being melodramatic as usual."

I give him a funny look. I didn't know melons could be dramatic.

"*Melodramatic* is someone who's always making everything into a big drama," he says. "Like that whole pizza business – was that really necessary?"

Exactly!

"Don't let her live in your head rent-free," Finn says.

I burst out laughing. That's *totally* what Jessica's been doing. I think about all the time I've spent thinking about the bathroom wall, wondering if the words are still in there, whether anyone's cleaned it off by now, when I can go use that bathroom again. Talk about back rent!

"So, what are you doing with Mrs. Hollins over there?" Finn asks, grabbing a bite of his own sandwich.

"Making poster," I answer. I decide to speak English instead of Chinese with Finn, so he'll actually understand me and not think I was making wontons with bookmarks. "How about you, why you here?"

"I'd just rather read than play sports in the hot sun." Finn shrugs.

My eyes flash with surprise.

"But you shirt." I point.

"Oh, my dad just buys a lot of Rams stuff," Finn

says. "He's what they call a *super*fan."

I'm confused. His dad is an air conditioner?

"A superfan is someone who plans his whole life around the games," Finn tells me. "If a parent-teacher conference falls during an away game, forget it. He once skipped my birthday party because he was too in the zone during a mock draft."

"What's a mock draft?"

"Like a practice draft," he says, and then mumbles under his breath, "Like my parents and their 'trial separation.'"

I scratch my head, not understanding.

He tries to translate in Chinese, but I still don't fully understand. Finally, Finn grabs a piece of paper from his backpack and draws two houses – one with his Mum and one with his dad. He draws himself between the houses, sitting on the grass. With a very big frown on his face.

Whoa.

Finn definitely does not have an invisible thread.

"Part of me wishes they'd just do it already. Get it over with," he says. "The other part worries if they do . . . will I be separated forever?"

He draws a zigzag line down his chest. I put my

finger over the familiar zigzag. I wish I could take a big old glue stick and patch his heart back up. Instead, I tell him a line my grandma used to say to me all the time.

"You not separated. You be double loved."

Finn gives me a smile. The bell rings. I try to return *New Kid* to Finn, but he says, "You wanna borrow it? Meet back here tomorrow at lunch and we can talk about it?"

I nod. I hold up a finger. "I have book for you, too!"

I run over to my backpack by Mrs. Hollins's desk and get out my copy of *Flea Shop*. Mrs. Hollins is in the middle of unpacking books from a new box of orders. I kneel down and help her pick up all the packing peanuts on the floor.

"Thanks!" Mrs. Hollins says. "You can just toss those in the trash."

I gather them all up, squeezing the little white foam pieces in my hand. As I throw them all in the trash and help Mrs. Hollins put the boxes into the recycling bin, she beams at me. "Thanks, Lina, for all your help," she says. She points at the corner of the poster. "I left the last spot for my new student librarian to recommend her favourite book."

It takes me a minute to realise she's talking about *me*. I walk over to the computer to print out a small cover of *Flea Shop*. Proudly, I take the glue stick and paste it to the poster. Then with Mrs. Hollins's special glittery pen, I write my very first English words for all to see.

Great book — Lina Gao.

Chapter 39

Millie's bouncing her knee in the air in a knee-jump dance when we walk over to Pete's later. "When do you have library day?" I ask her, eager for my sister to see my poster.

"Not until next Monday," she says.

"Let me know if you see anything special! On the wall!" I tell her. Millie replies with a dance move. "That a new TikTok dance?" I ask her.

"No, it's Hazel's. She's doing it for the school talent show," Millie says. "I bet they're going to practice it all night at the sleepover."

"Forget her dance. Make up your own!" I suggest.

"But Hazel takes *private* dance lessons. She has a choreographer! I don't even know how to *spell* the word *choreographer*."

"So?" I ask. "You don't need a choreographer."

"You don't know about America. A private choreographer is *next-level*."

Ouch.

"I don't know much about America, you're right. But I know you don't need next-level at seven."

"Yeah I do!"

"No you don't." I shake my head. "You just need talent. Like this."

To prove my point, I start rocking my body and shaking my arms. My sister giggles.

"Stop! What are you doing?" she cries.

The more she freaks out, the more I wave and twirl and bounce and scoop. I look like one of those flimsy balloons behind the Winfield car dealerships Mum drives by to get us to school, but I don't care.

I dance because I want to show my sister this is why we dance – to have fun, not for views. To celebrate. Like me saying my first sentence to Finn – in English! And writing on Mrs. Hollins's poster! And now it's hanging up high in the library! I dance for kicking Jessica out of my head! And for finally making a friend!

Okay, so he's a boy. But he loves to read!

I can feel Finn's copy of *New Kid* bouncing around in my backpack. I can't wait to sit under the shade of Carla's tiny home and spend the afternoon reading. And I *really* can't wait to hear what Finn says about *Flea Shop*!

But when we get to Pete's, he has other plans for me and Millie.

*

"I want all these dishes washed and dried before your mother gets back," he says. "And when you're done with that, the floor needs to be swept and the porch needs a good hosing down."

Millie and I exchange a glance.

"But we have homework!" Millie says.

I nod eagerly.

"Well, this ain't a library. This is a farm. Everyone works." With that, he tosses me and Millie cleaning rags.

For the next hour and a half, Millie and I bust suds, clean floors, and hose down the porch for Pete, while he yells commands at Mrs. Muñoz and Dad out in the field.

"No, don't plant that there!" Pete says. "Is that plastic I see in the compost? Get that out of there!"

Carla rushes over to help her Mum pick through the compost.

Pete mutters under his breath to me and Millie, "Can you believe it? Our Earth is in crisis mode – in 2020 alone, sixteen freshwater fish species went extinct – and people still can't separate their trash."

Pete sure is a walking encyclopedia of science knowledge.

"People. We overfish, overexploit. Do before we think. Use too much of everything – cups, straws, plastic forks – wasting the Earth away!"

He turns to me. "Which is why we need more microregenerative farms, like this one, near urban centers. As the world gets hotter and we have more extreme weather, there will be less water. And food will become a serious problem. Now if we're smart, and we farm smart – I'm talking cover cropping, mulching, composting, and taking care of the soil – we can actually *store* carbon in the soil, reversing the effects of climate change."

My eyebrows shoot up. Even though I didn't understand most of that, I caught the "food will become a serious problem" part.

I think back to Bei Gao Li Village, wondering what all the kids there will do once food becomes even more expensive. A few families have tried farming again, like little Tao's family. But the land has become so barren, it's hard to grow anything except chives.

But maybe they're not using the right methods.

"More! More!" Pete calls to Mrs. Muñoz.

Mrs. Muñoz spreads the compost. "I think that's enough," she says.

"Not if you want that cauliflower to grow strong!" he says. "Pack it in and the worms will do the job. We gotta feed Mother Earth!"

I put my hose down for a second and walk back inside to get my backpack, so I can take notes. Maybe if I mail all of this to little Tao, his family can start growing lush carrots too!

The hallway to the front door is still wet from our mopping, so I cross behind the dining room. As I'm walking down a narrow, dark hallway, past the bathroom, I glance at the pictures hanging up on the wall. I spot a picture of a beautiful woman with long brown braided hair and bright rosy cheeks, sitting on Pete's rocking chair on the patio. Pete stands next to her, in his farmer hat.

Is that a *smile* on his face?

I look closely and see the two wedding rings on their hands.

Pete's married??

Chapter 40

I run out to tell my sister this exciting news. But before I can, Pete gives me an earful about leaving the water hose on.

"You know how much water you're wasting?" he asks. "How many plants, trees, organisms *die* every minute of the day because they don't have enough water? We're in a drought! Get it through your head!"

He comes stomping over to me. I squeeze my eyes shut, trying to stand as still as I can. All the while, I'm wondering, *Who on earth would want to marry "him"?*

"I better not catch you wasting water again," he hisses. "Now go, scat. And stay off my soil! Your foot is the equivalent of an earthquake!"

Millie and I race down the steps, toward Carla and the tiny home.

"His *mouth* is the equivalent of an earthquake!" I say to Millie. "We cleaned his whole house and he didn't even say thank you! What a squash-head!"

Then I remember why I ran outside in the first place.

"Did you know he's married?" I ask Millie.

"Really?" Millie asks.

We tell Carla this information. She's sitting in a beach chair in the shade, next to her tiny home, doing a complicated math calculation on a clipboard. She takes a break from her math lesson and sips her fresh homemade lemonade.

"He *used* to be married," Carla corrects us.

"Did something happen to his wife?" I ask, gazing back at Pete. That would explain why he's so angry.

Carla shakes her head. "Nothing like that. He once told my Mum his ex-wife lives on the East Coast. Virginia Burton. She writes books about farming." She holds up a finger. "I think I have one of her books!"

Millie and I wait as Carla scrambles into the tiny

home and comes out with a big book called *The Basics of Farming*.

Carla hands it to me. I open it up and read the dedication.

To my husband, the maverick, the dreamer, the nurturer . . . whose green thumb makes everything he touches grow.

Huh. There's no mention of squash-head on the list.

I put the book down and open my backpack, suddenly remembering.

"I have book for you, too," I tell Carla, handing her *Pie in the Sky*. "It about a boy who moves to Australia and wants to make pie."

"I love pie!" Carla beams at the book. "My dad used to make the *best* croissants. And he'd fill them with all sorts of different sauces and jams . . . my favourite was raspberry-chocolate. It was tangy and sweet – the raspberry made my tongue tickle while the chocolate hugged it."

At the description of raspberry-chocolate croissants, all our tummies rumble.

"I wish we had a *real* kitchen," Carla sighs. "Then

I could make it — I still have the recipe and we got lots of raspberries!"

"Can you use Pete kitchen?" I ask. But I know, even before finishing the sentence, that there's no way.

Just for the fun of it, though, I check into the Imagination Hotel and pretend to be Pete stress-eating all of Carla's croissants in the middle of the night. Nom. Nom. Nom. Carla starts laughing her head off.

"Stop! You're gonna make me spill my lemonade, and then I'll have to take another cold shower!" Carla cackles.

I gaze over at the outdoor shower. "How does this thing work?" I ask.

"Easy!" Millie says, running over to show me. She's lived here before, so I guess she knows the tricks. "It's called a gravity shower!"

Carla points to the giant bucket on the top of what looks like a bamboo port-a-potty. "You put water in there — well, actually it's *supposed* to collect rainwater, but we're in a drought — and you take a shower with the water from the bucket."

"Cold?" I ask.

"*Very* cold," Carla says. "Especially at night."

I shiver. It reminds me of the time Homer and Bart Simpson went camping and lost their clothes after falling into a frigid, raging river.

Millie opens the bamboo door and starts pretending to be washing herself. That's when an idea pops into my mind.

I turn and tell Carla my idea, and she giggles and nods enthusiastically – she's in.

"What are you guys talking about?" Millie asks.

"Nothing!" I reply to Millie. "Hey, let's keep practice your dance!"

"Dance?" Carla asks, her feet gliding on the dusty ground. "I want to dance!"

Carla and I start throwing our arms in the air, twisting our bodies and snapping our fingers to an imaginary beat.

"You guys aren't even doing it right!" Millie hollers, running over. "It's like this! Watch closely – it's called the crisscross!" She crisscrosses over with her feet, making tiny tornadoes in the dust as she dances. Then she flings her body forward dramatically. "I call this the dolphin!"

"Dolphin! Got it!" I shout.

We follow her example, throwing our bodies

forward, like a pod of dolphins jumping in the ocean. Not even Pete's hollering for us to "knock it off" can stop the three of us criss-crossing, dolphining, and giggling up and down the field.

"Now, I add clock-pow!" Millie instructs. She interlocks her arms so they look like two clock hands and bangs one hand against the other. "Pow!"

Pete starts stomping down the porch steps toward us.

We race across the field, clock-powing through the strawberries as he chases us. By the time my Mum finally arrives, we have the entire routine down by heart. And Pete looks about ready to chuck us out like weeds.

Thankfully, Mum comes with good news.

Chapter 41

"Great news! After *hours* on phone, the general manager of 99 Ranch say he'll take some strawberry and broccoli. And if you have any dill, he take that, too – his Chinese customers love making dill dumplings," Mum says to Pete breathlessly.

"How much he paying?" Pete asks.

Dad walks out to the porch with a calculator and a big notebook.

"Five dollars a basket for strawberry. Fifty cents a head for broccoli. Ten cents a bunch for dill," Mum says, reading from her notebook.

"Five dollars a basket? That's less than the farmers' market!" Pete frowns, shaking his head. "You explain to him that these are organic? No pesticides, no nothing?"

"Yeah, I did. Maybe if we start off at five dollars and he like them, he can go up in price. Besides, you say they not going to last until the next farmers' market!"

Dad punches in the numbers. "We'd still be making a profit," he tells Pete.

Pete sighs heavily under his farmer's hat, weighing his options.

"Tell him we'll start at five dollars," Pete says. "But if he sells all fifty baskets of strawberries, he's going to have to cough up an extra dollar per basket."

Mum does a little squeal. "I'll let him know!" she says. Her eyes dance animatedly, meeting Dad's. "So now that that's settled, can we get that advance on my husband's salary, so I can get back to *my* business?"

"Nothing's settled," Pete reminds her. "You just did the first step. I don't see any cash."

"But –"

"I'm not giving you a penny's advance till you finish the job! That's the deal!" Pete says. He gestures to Dad. "Now help me box up all these strawberries!"

*

That night, while Mum tries to firm up the order with the 99 Ranch manager, Millie and I get back to all our bath bomb customers. We tell them to wait a little longer – there are some issues with getting supplies.

"How do you spell *supplies*?" I ask Millie.

"*S-u-p-l-y-s,*" Millie answers.

I type that into the computer. Now that I've written my first English words on a poster in the library, I'm feeling more confident helping my sister respond to customers. A red squiggly line appears.

"Are you sure?" I ask Millie.

She glances at it. "Oh yeah, maybe it should be two *p*'s," she says. "And change the *y* to an *i-e*. There's this rule, I think!"

I try that. It works!

"What are the other spelling rules?" I ask, curious.

Millie shrugs. "There's a lot. I don't really remember," she says. "And some of the rules are confusing – like *i-e* but not after *c*. But then the word *chief* is *i-e* after *c*."

"So what do you do?"

"You just try stuff!" Millie says, practicing her clock-pow again. I smile. "It's okay to get words wrong – I get 'em wrong all the time!"

"But I thought you got a medal in spelling!" I blurt out. "Doesn't mean I don't make mistakes!" Millie says.

I gaze at my sister, grateful and surprised. I crawl into bed, reaching for my copy of *New Kid* and thinking of her words. She didn't have to say that, but I'm glad she did. It makes me feel a lot better to know that I'm not the only one making mistakes. Even Millie, with her bazillion awards, makes mistakes in English too.

Maybe learning English is like a TikTok dance. I just gotta try, and not worry so much!

I imagine myself bursting into my classroom tomorrow, talking effortlessly like I did today with Finn! But then I picture my classmates' laughing faces, pointing at me and mocking my bizarro grammar, and it's so hard to evict my own fear, no matter how much back rent it owes.

Chapter 42

New Kid is too good! I run into the library before class the next morning, looking for Finn. I can't wait till lunch.

"Lina!" a voice shouts.

I spin around and Finn is holding *Flea Shop* with his fingers tucked in the pages.

"Oh my God, the part when the customer walks in, scratching everywhere, and asks if they sell flea repellant – I was dying!" Finn says.

I grin.

"Oh, what about when her Mum find out she draw on money?" I ask, running over and flipping to the page when Cat gets so bored in the store, she draws mustaches and baseball caps on all the presidents on the bills in their cash register.

Finn pulls out a dollar bill and reveals his own highly doodled George Washington.

I laugh so hard, my belly hurts.

"What about you? How did you like *New Kid*?" he asks.

"I love!" I tell him. I stayed up all night finishing the book. I flip to show him the scenes of Jordan feeling like he's in between two worlds.

Finn nods knowingly.

But my *favourite* scene of all is Jordan Banks having dinner with his grandfather.

"They eating Chinese food!" I tell Finn.

Finn grins and rattles off all the dishes Jordan orders in Chinese – pepper steak, General Tso's chicken, and shrimp lo mein.

His pronunciation of these dishes is perfect. But that's not why I love the scene so much. I love it because like Lao Lao, Jordan's grandpa also just moved to a senior center. And like me, Jordan says that makes him sad.

I stared so long at that panel.

"My grandma also in yang lao yuan. I miss her," I confess to Finn.

"Can you go visit her?" Finn asks. "Or go out for

dim sum with her? I know a great place –!"

I shake my head. Sadly, my grandma is a lot farther away than Jordan Banks's grandpa.

"She on other side of world," I whisper.

He looks down at his copy of *Flea Shop*.

"Just like Cat's grandma . . . ," he says.

I nod. I feel my whole body relax at being understood. A great book says all the words for you that you've been holding in, all sewn up inside.

"Maybe you can Zoom?" Finn suggests.

Again, I shake my head. If only Lao Lao were not so allergic to smartphones . . .

"Okay, how about this, you can *draw* your Zoom and all the things you'd say to her!" he suggests. "And mail it to her!"

I perk up. There's a thought!

"Like a graphic novel?" I ask.

Finn nods excitedly. "Yeah! I'll help you!" he says. "I know all about how to draw graphic novels. I've been learning since I was in third year! My Mum signed me up for this class! I'll teach you! But first" – he glances at his watch – "we have to talk to Mrs. Carter. We need to get *these* books into the Book Tasting! Will you come with me to talk to her?"

I hesitate. It would be *so* much safer to stay right here in the library until the bell rang.

But then I look into Finn's eager eyes. I imagine Cat Wang and Jordan Banks clapping and cheering for me – *Go, Lina! You can do it!* – and I follow Finn out of the library.

Chapter 43

"*Flea Shop* and *New Kid*! Of course! I've read *New Kid* and I loved it, but I haven't read *Flea Shop* yet!" Mrs. Carter says, smiling at our two books. She's wearing a purple dress today with black-and-white photos of female inventors. It's such a cool dress, and I stand at her desk, admiring the pictures.

"It's amazing!" Finn says. "You have to do a Book Tasting on it!"

"All right, I will!" Mrs. Carter grins, flipping to the back of *Flea Shop*. "Oh, the author is Asian American!"

I bounce on my feet, feeling proud.

"How did you like *Flea Shop*, Lina?" "I like," I say in a small voice.

Mrs. Carter sits up eagerly. She leans closer to me

and encourages me to elaborate. "Oh yeah? What did you like?"

"It . . . really . . ." I pause, trying to think of how to put it. The book was like a warm blanket for me. When Cat struggled with English, I felt less alone. When she messed something up with a customer, it made me feel like less of a dope when I got a red squiggly line replying to one of our customers. Most of all, when she worried about her future, I felt more secure in mine. Because she's a big author now. It fills me with hope that I could be someone too.

Even here in this new land, where *i-e* isn't after *c*. Where blue isn't always a colour. Where Mama says we don't have the same options as everyone else.

I stare at Mrs. Carter and Finn, trying to come up with the words.

"You want to tell me in Chinese?" Finn asks gently.

I shake my head. I don't. I want to say these words to them in English. I think of Mrs. Ortiz's words – *Have patience, you'll get there!* I know I can do it. The words are just at the edge of my tongue. But as the other kids start walking into the room, I freeze up like a rusty pipe.

I take my copy of *Flea Shop* and dash back to my seat.

It isn't until Finn walks back, slides down next to me, and says, "You did great! I hope she picks *Flea Shop* next!" that I realise something. I might not have finished my *whole* sentence, but I started it.

And that's something! I pick up my pencil and start making a list in my sketchbook:

People I can speak English to:
- Mum
- Dad
- Millie
- Carla
- Mrs. Muñoz Rosa (neighbour)
- Mrs. Ortiz
- Mrs. Hollins
- Finn
- Mrs. Carter

My list is growing!

Chapter 44

"Lao Lao!" I gush into the phone when Mum comes to pick me and Millie up. We're on our way to Pete's. "I finished two books in English! *Flea Shop* and *New Kid*! And I finally made a friend at school!"

"That's terrific! What's she like?" Lao Lao asks. "Is she nice to her elders, like you?"

"He." I glance in the rearview mirror at Mum. But she's too distracted by the car in front of her, its driver sitting at the red light texting. "*His* name is Finn and he loves reading!"

"You made friends with a boy?" Lao Lao gasps. She makes it sound like I made friends with a fire-breathing dragon.

"So what?" I ask, rolling down my window just

an inch. This conversation is starting to make my throat dry for some reason.

"So, you can't be friends with a boy. I thought we talked about this!" Lao Lao says. "It's improper — especially at your age. You've been watching way too much American TV!"

I frown. I have not! She's probably so bored in her nursing home, she's been binging *Friends* and now she thinks I'm dating a paleontologist with a pet monkey. I cover the phone speaker with my hand so Mum can't hear. "We're just *friends*, Lao Lao. All we do is go to the library and talk about books."

"Who goes to the library and talks?" Mum asks, overhearing.

"No one," I call out, blushing.

"See! You can't even tell your mother! Put her on the phone! I want to talk to her about this!" Lao Lao orders.

I panic and shake my head. What if Mum sides with Lao Lao? I'll lose my one school friend. The only person who gets me, who thinks I'm funny, and not because of the way I speak English!

"Sorry, Lao Lao . . . the reception is really bad here," I blurt out. "We're going to have to call you back."

With that, I get off the phone. For the rest of the car ride, I sit and stew in my guilt that I just hung up on my grandmother. And the very confusing worry . . . what if Lao Lao's right?

Is it improper for a girl to be friends with a boy?

Chapter 45

"Of course it's not improper to be friends with a boy," Carla says to me.

We're walking over to the pond, all the way in the back of the farm. Millie's sprinted ahead, eager to see if the pond's still full.

"But my lao lao so mad," I say.

"She's just old-fashioned. She thinks all boys are one way."

I think back to all the hand-farters in my last classroom. They were like a different species from Finn!

"We're all individuals!" Carla says. "That's what makes us so special. I was friends with a boy once – he lived on our farm in Italy. He's the one who taught me how to milk a goat. And you know something? I miss him. He would talk to the plants every day, teach them to grow without so much water."

"You can *teach* plants?" I ask.

She chuckles and nods. When we get to the pond, the basin's cracked dry. The drought has sucked up every drop of water. Millie sits at the base of a lone oak tree, frowning and throwing rocks in the bare gully. I think about what Pete says about the world being a dust bowl one day.

"I want to go swimming." Millie frowns.

I glance at Carla and we run across the dry pond, moving our arms around, "swimming."

"*For real,*" Millie says. "I'm sick of imagining."

I walk over and sit beside my sister. I know she's thinking about her friends having fun at the sleepover without her.

"What if we play the Eagle and the Chicks?" I ask her in Chinese. "It's an old Chinese game – I'll teach you! You can be the eagle!"

"I don't want to play some stupid Chinese game," Millie mutters, throwing another rock.

"Millie!" I exclaim. That hurt.

My sister gets up and runs back toward the main house, muttering, "I just want to be by myself."

I'm tempted to chase after her and get an apology

out of her, but Carla touches my arm with her hand. "Let her be," she says. "Sometimes you just gotta be sad for a little while."

With that, she reaches up to the first branch of the big oak tree and retrieves my copy of *Pie in the Sky*, hidden away.

"Did you read?" I ask.

Carla nods. "It's so good. You're gonna love it! I dreamed of cake all night long," she says. "Carrot cake with cream cheese topping! Chocolate-raspberry torte! Blueberry cheese-cake!"

Mmmmm. I close my eyes, imagining the sweet, buttery smells wafting through the air.

"And not only that . . . My dad was there too! Baking with me," she says.

I flash my eyes open. "That's great! What he say?"

A calm, nostalgic smile washes over Carla. "He didn't say anything. We just baked . . . side by side, like old times. And he looked good, not sick."

"How he die?" I ask gently.

"Cancer," she says. "You want to hear the terrible thing?"

I nod.

"There *was* a medicine for what he had. But our

insurance wouldn't pay for it. My Mum fought and fought, but they kept saying they needed more tests. Finally, my Mum got tired of waiting and sold our house to try to pay for it. But . . . by then, it was too late."

I put my arms around Carla.

"I'm so sorry," I tell my friend.

I hold Carla as she cries. "I think it ate my Mum up, all that waiting. It's why she's always moving. If she stops for just a minute, the pain will yell louder than Pete."

I gaze out toward the field at Mrs. Muñoz, picking lettuce. I know the steep, narrow gorge of regret well. For years, I was mad at myself for not hugging my Mum's leg so hard, that snowy Beijing day at the airport five years ago, that she couldn't possibly leave me behind no matter how hard she tried.

"I wish I could tell her it's okay, you know?" Carla says, dabbing her eyes. "Thinking about him doesn't have to be a sad thing. Maybe it can be a happy thing . . . like reading this book."

I nod. "I think it can."

"Is it okay if I hang on to this book a little while longer?"

"Of course!" I say. Carla gets up and holds out a hand. She pulls me up and we walk back to the tiny home together.

I think about the big bulletin board in our library, declaring **BOOKS ARE SLIDING DOORS AND MIRRORS**. For so long, I thought I was all alone. Lao Lao was the only door that ever stayed open for me. Her world view was my world view. But now with these books, I'm starting to unlock many more . . . and I realise I have a lot more in common with other people than I thought.

Mum comes running over. "We're all set! The 99 Ranch folks are picking up the order tonight! As soon as it's done, Pete's going to call me and give me the advance."

"That's great!" I grin.

As nice as it is hanging out with Carla, I have missed Mum. She holds out a hand to me.

"C'mon. Let's go on home and start sorting out all the bath bomb orders!" she says.

I skip ahead, then remember Millie! The surprise!

"Wait! Before we go," I say to Mum, "can I do one thing?"

Chapter 46

Millie squeals in the outdoor bamboo shower as Carla and I raise the water bucket. Instead of water, it's filled with Mrs. Hollins's packing peanuts! She let me keep them instead of throwing them all away. It seemed such a shame to waste them, especially since I knew they were not exactly good for the environment. But they sure looked cute . . . almost *exactly* like bath foam!

"Ready for your bubble bath?" I ask.

Millie giggles. "YES!"

I give Carla a nod, and with one big grunt, we pull on the lever. Hundreds of packing peanuts tumble down on Millie as she screams.

I grin from ear to ear as my sister throws the "bath foam" up in the air with her hands. I take a mental snapshot of my sister's joy, to draw it later. But first . . .

"You thinking what I'm thinking?" Carla asks, grinning. "Let's go!" I run.

The two of us jump into Millie's bath! We throw packing peanuts at each other, squealing and smiling. One thing is for sure. There's no *way* those girls at the sleepover are having more fun than this.

Mum sits down on our bed that night. We spent the rest of the day messaging our customers, letting them know we're *almost* ready with their orders and that they can get 15 percent off for referring their friends! Thanks to Mrs. Ortiz and all my reading, I'm getting better and better at replying to the messages.

"I'm proud of you," Mum says of my progress in English. "And I'm even more proud of what you did back at Pete's for your sister. That was *very* nice."

Millie produces a packing peanut in her hand, which she kept as a souvenir. "Best sleepover ever."

I grin. "See, we don't need a real bathtub!" I tell Millie.

I think my statement is going to make Mum happy, but her face falls a little. "I'm sorry I can't give you girls a real bath . . . yet. I'm working on it."

I can tell how much it pains Mum not to be able

to give us everything she wants in her imagination.

I turn to Mum and repeat the line that Mrs. Ortiz told me, in English. "There's no set timeline for anything in life."

Mum's face dissolves into a smile. "Thanks, kiddo," she says.

As she reaches for the light, I take a chance and ask, "Mama, why'd you leave China?"

The leaves outside the window move and the shadows dance on the wall as Mum thinks for a long while. "You really want to know?" she asks.

I nod and sit up.

"I wanted a place where my girls can grow up to be anything they want," she finally says. "Not have anyone put a cap on your imagination. But that's not so easy in China."

Slowly, she starts telling us about her job at Panda Amusement Park.

"I was their chief Imagineer," she says. "I designed the Cloud ride, taking you through all these little cities *inside* the clouds."

"There are cities inside clouds?" I ask Mum.

"That's what I dreamed up! I designed cities no one else could even imagine!"

Her face is full of optimism, like the moon.

"But when I had Millie, something changed. My boss started giving all the projects to my male colleagues. They were worried about how I was going to be able to juggle work obligations with two small children. They just couldn't *imagine* that a mother of two could handle it."

"But, Mama, I thought the one-child policy changed a long time ago," I say. I remember studying about it in school. According to the government, families can have up to three children now.

"Maybe on paper," Mum says. "But in reality, companies always have their own preferences and prejudices. Which fester silently."

I shake my head. It's so wrong.

"That's why your aunt Jing never had kids," Mum says. "But I did. I left China so you girls would never have to compromise your dreams."

My eyes grow heavy with emotion. I always thought my parents were like little Tao's parents, who left him in Bei Gao Li Village for Shanghai so they could make more money. Now I know it's so we could fly.

I'm so glad Mum finally told us the truth. She

peers down at me in the moonlight.

"But you must promise me you'll never put a cap on your *own* imagination," she says.

"I promise, Mama," my sister and I say.

Mum smiles and kisses our foreheads. As she leaves, I clutch my blanket close and say "I love you," in a faint whisper.

Mum doesn't hear it but Millie does.

"Love you too," Millie says.

I look up. It feels so unexpected to hear it from my sister, like discovering a White Rabbit sweet under your pillow.

Millie adds, "And I'm sorry I said the thing about the Chinese game. I didn't mean it."

I reach up and give her soft arm a light poke with my finger, *It's okay.*

Chapter 47

That weekend, the landlord, Mr. Beezley, calls Mum to remind her that the back rent is due. Millie and I hover in the hallway listening.

"You got the money, right?" he asks over the cell speakerphone. "It's due in four weeks!"

I peek over at Mum. Her face turns ash white.

"Yes, we working on it," she says nervously.

"Working on it? Or you have it?" Mr. Beezley asks. "Because the rent moratorium's over. No more free lunch – you gotta pay up or get out."

Dad jumps in. "You'll get your money," he assures him. "Thirty-seven hundred dollars and not a penny less," Mr. Beezley says. "That's what you put me out during this whole mess!"

"But the government, didn't they reimburse –"

"That's none of your business what I get from the government," Mr. Beezley says. "You know how long that'll take? Can't depend on Uncle Sam. Meanwhile, I got expenses. I got mortgages. You think it's easy being a landlord during a pandemic? It's terrible."

"I appreciate everything you going through," Mum says. "But we struggling too. If you just be a little patient."

"My days of being patient are over. Come up with the money or you'll find yourselves out on the street. And good luck getting another landlord to rent to you ever again with an eviction record," Mr. Beezley says, hanging up.

My parents stare at each other. Dad puts his hand on Mum's knee and tells her everything's going to be all right.

Mum sinks to the floor, folding up her yoga mat and blankets. Dad's still wearing his clothes from yesterday. He got home so late from Pete's, he didn't even have time to change. When he sees us, he puts on a smile.

"You girls want some breakfast?" he asks. "I got some ripe avocados that just fell from the tree!"

He walks over to his bag and produces two green dinosaur eggs. That's what they look like to me.

"We don't need avocados," Mum says. "We need money."

"Let's not panic. We still have our security deposit with Beezley. That's twelve hundred dollars right there."

"All right. And how much do we have in our emergency fund?"

"You know we can't touch that," Dad says. "That's for if one of the girls breaks her arm and we have to go to the hospital."

"How *much*?" Mum asks again.

Dad sighs and puts the dinosaur eggs down. "About fifteen hundred dollars," he says. "But our deductible on our insurance is *six thousand dollars!*"

"What's a deductible?" I ask.

Mum tells me to take my sister and go sit outside. When I protest, she says sharply, "NOW!"

Reluctantly, I walk over to the door with Millie. We sit outside on the cold cement steps, listening to the soft murmur of Saturday-morning cartoons from those families that are fortunate enough to have a TV. And cable.

We wave good morning to Rosa walking her terrier. She hears our parents fighting through the window, and Millie and I duck our heads in embarrassment.

"Don't you worry," Rosa says. "My mama and papa fought for sixty-eight years, and you know something? It made their love strong. You girls have breakfast yet? Here, I get you a concha."

Rosa goes back to her apartment. She comes back out with two sweet conchas. We thank her and nibble on our loaves. I'm petrified to move, for fear of missing a word. I'm petrified to listen, too, because it sounds like sharp glass. Every time one of our parents raises their voice, another shard breaks.

"Are they like this a lot?" I ask Millie.

Millie nods slowly.

"Only when we have money problems," she mutters, turning her shoe over to examine the hole in the sole. Millie takes her shoe off and hits it hard against the pavement to get the rocks out. "I hate money."

"Was it better when we were living at Pete's?" I ask Millie.

Millie shakes her head. "No, that was way worse,"

she says. "They fought a *lot* more there."

"Why?"

Millie tells me about the many rules Pete had. "No going out, even on Dad's day off. No friends over. No speaking Chinese!"

"*No* speaking Chinese?" I ask her. I remember Pete hollering about that once, but I half assumed he was kidding.

"Pete said it would ruin my chances of doing well in school," Millie murmurs. She peeks over at me in shame.

In that moment, I recognise the worry on Millie's face. It's the same one I've been carrying around secretly – *Will I ever be American enough? Can I do well in this country?* I reach out and give my sister's head a few gentle pats. I think back to what Mrs. Ortiz said on the very first day I met her – the point of our class is not to erase your other language. "Don't listen to that artichoke," I tell her.

"We didn't. But one time, Pete caught Mum talking to me in Chinese and he made her drive around to all the hiking trails and horse trails and gather up horse poop for his compost. Mum came back stinking furious. She told Dad that's it. We're leaving. But Dad was scared. He said living outside is too expensive. Pete only pays him fifteen hundred dollars a month."

"Fifteen hundred dollars? That can't be right," I tell Millie. Even Lao Lao makes more than that – I know from managing her finances after Lao Ye passed away. She gets a good, healthy pension from the Chinese government each month, even now!

"That's what it is!" Millie insists. "I remember hearing them fight about it."

"But Dad works so much for Pete!" Almost fifteen hours a day, and even on the weekends, since I've been here!

Millie shrugs. She scoots closer to me and puts her head on my shoulder. I lower my head to touch hers, hoping our touching heads can communicate the words caught in my throat. *I can't imagine hearing all that by myself. But now you have me.*

We nibble the rest of our bread, watching the ants at our feet, trying to tune out the thunderous raindrops of Mum and Dad arguing. Together.

Chapter 48

When the ants have carried away the last of our crumbs, the door finally swings open.

"Get dressed, girls," Mum says.

Millie and I scramble up. We brush the crumbs off our pajamas.

"Where we going?" Millie asks.

"To the library," Mum says. "I'm going to research the law – see if it really makes no sense for us to apply for the rent relief thing –"

"We already agreed not to apply!" Dad calls out. "Pete's going to advance us my salary, and we'll make up the rest of the money. You just have to be a little more patient!"

But Mum's already out the door. Millie and I follow, grabbing our hoodies.

The Winfield Public Library is massive. It has two floors, and the windows are so shiny, for a second, I think I'm at the Beijing Airport. And we're landing. My grandmother's at the other side of security. She's walking normally and her hands are totally better! Her face lights up when she sees me and Millie. She's totally forgiven me for hanging up on her. For putting her in a nursing home. For leaving her. She hugs me in her arms and welcomes us home for the summer.

"Lina, I'm going out to the picnic area to practice my dance!" Millie tells me, bringing me back to reality.

"Kay," I mutter back, heading over to the kids' section. While Mum goes to the legal books section, I browse the children's stacks. One book catches my eye. It was the first book I helped Mrs. Hollins put up on the poster – *Fumble*. I pick it up. Unlike the other books I've read, it's not a graphic novel.

I'm a little intimidated by all the text . . . but also a little excited to let my imagination fill in the pictures.

As I sit down on the floor to start reading,

I overhear two loud voices debating.

"No, Mum! I don't have time for SSAT!" a familiar voice protests.

I look over. *Jessica??*

Jessica shoves a big thick book at her Mum. I read the spine. *Secondary School Admission Test,* it says. I use Mrs. Ortiz's decoding methods to figure out *Admission* means to get in. Is Jessica applying to a different school?

It takes every ounce of self-control not to jump up and whoop for joy.

"You're going to *make* time," Jessica's Mum says. "I won't have you staying in that hippie, artsy *public* school the rest of your academic career!"

"We came here because you said I can check out what *I* want," Jessica says, hugging *Drama* by Raina Telgemeier.

"Is that a graphic novel?" Jessica's Mum gasps, and tries to pull the book from her daughter's hands. "What did I say about graphic novels? They're not *real* books!"

Whoa. Now I understand why Jessica's wound up tighter than an erhu. Her Mum is *beyond*!

"Yes they are!" Jessica protests. "All my friends

are reading them! Mrs. Carter's doing a whole unit on them!"

Jessica's Mum rolls her eyes dramatically. "That's another reason why we're switching schools! You should be reading the classics. *To Kill a Mockingbird. Tom Sawyer. Huckleberry Finn.*"

"But I want to read *Drama*!"

"Yeah, I know you *want* to. I *want* to be at the Four Seasons Maui right now, getting my nails done and sipping pineapple juice, but instead I have to go to yet *another* diversity and inclusivity meeting at the District. You think I *want* to listen to the superintendent talk about how we need more representation in the PTA?"

With that, Jessica's Mum snatches Jessica's copy of *Drama* from her hands and reshelves it in the biography aisle.

The student librarian in me scowls.

"You're going to go home, you're going to study the SSAT, you're going to get into an elite private school where you belong. Where my representation and my money are *actually* appreciated!" Jessica's Mum hands the SSAT book to Jessica.

"Are the questions hard? Will you do them with

me?" Jessica asks, looking at the thick book worriedly.

"You know I don't have time for that, with my schedule. I've got to monitor the renovations at the ski house! But I *will* get you that hundred-fifty-dollar-an-hour tutor everyone's raving about. At those rates, she can't afford for you to fail."

As I watch them walk out, I can't help but feel a little bad for Jessica, trailing behind her power-walking, graphic novel-rejecting Mum. Not enough to make me forgive Jessica for all the things she said about me on the bathroom door.

But . . . enough to make me walk over to the biography section and reshelve *Drama*. Just in case she comes back looking for it.

Chapter 49

It takes me a little more work to understand *Fumble*. That's because according to Mrs. Ortiz, it's a "prose" book.

We're sitting in the art center on Monday, going over the book. She teaches me the word *squished*, which is a lot trickier than it looks. Mrs. Ortiz teaches me the pronunciation and I copy her mouth shape. It's pronounced "s-k-wished." Mrs. Ortiz says it's one of the words that does not follow the *oo* rule.

"What's the *oo* rule?" I ask Mrs. Ortiz.

"It's just a pronunciation rule. Whenever you see *u-i* together, you *usually* pronounce it 'oo,'" Mrs. Ortiz says.

She writes down *fr-ui-t* and *j-ui-ce*. I pronounce both of them with the *oo* sound in the middle.

Next she writes down *s-ui-t*, as in *suitcase*.

I stare at the word, thinking of all the suitcases Lao Lao bought right before we both left. There were the three big ones for me, and three big ones for her. It *looked* like we were both going on an adventure. But I knew, as I helped Lao Lao choose the items to take with her to her nursing home, that she wasn't going on an adventure like me. She was going to be all by herself. And this time, she didn't have her Wilson.

"The other *u-i* word that doesn't follow the *oo* rule is this one," Mrs. Ortiz says, writing down the letters *g-u-i-l-t*.

As Mrs. Ortiz teaches the word *guilt* to me, my eyes flood.

"What's wrong?" she asks.

My chin trembles as I struggle to hold on to my feelings. But I know sometimes that when hard feelings form into a ball, no amount of invisible thread could keep them in a second longer.

In my muffled, embarrassed, teary English, I tell Mrs. Ortiz how guilty I feel about leaving my lao lao in China.

"Oh, Lina," Mrs. Ortiz says, putting her pen down

and hugging me. "It's not your fault."

I shake my head. *But it is!* She doesn't understand. "Things hard for her there." I tell her about the nurses and the other residents. And Lao Lao's bonsai tree. And my aunt living so far away. "But things here getting easier for me. I have two friends." I hold up my fingers. "Three if I count you."

Mrs. Ortiz gives me a smile and assures me that she definitely counts.

I rub my eyes and blow my nose and confess, "I feel triple guilty about that."

Mrs. Ortiz waits for me to calm down. Then she teaches me a trick. With her pencil, she circles the *i* in the word *guilt*. "I want you never to forget the *i* in *guilt*," she says. Then she looks into my eyes. "I want you to repeat after me, *I* am important."

I repeat the words, "I am important."

"Yes, you are. You and your hopes and dreams."

Her own eyes grow misty as she continues. "As immigrants, we are burdened with a lot of guilt. For leaving our loved ones. Leaving our home. Sacrificing so much, or watching our parents sacrifice so much. But I want you never to forget the *i* in *guilt*."

She reaches for my hand.

"It's in there for a reason. And it's not any smaller than the other letters. Your dreams matter. *You* matter. Never forget that."

I smile through my tears, holding Mrs. Ortiz's hand. Leave it to Mrs. O to make me feel better *and* teach me a way never to forget how to spell *guilt*!

I've never had a teacher be so nice to me before. In my old school, such treatment was usually reserved for the walking calculators. But here . . . it's for all kids. That makes this place pretty special, I decide.

Chapter 50

I'm sketching Mrs. Ortiz in the library, during lunch, when Finn walks in.

"Whatcha working on?" he asks, sitting down next to me. He pulls out a sandwich from his backpack and takes a bite.

"No nachos?" I ask him, pointing to my own delicious gooey spread. I feel proud of myself for pronouncing *nachos* right – "nachos," not "nakos." It was one of the first words Mrs. Ortiz taught me.

"My Mum doesn't let me get school lunch," Finn says. He peers longingly at the cheesy chips, loaded with onions and beans. "But that looks so good."

"You want?" I ask.

Finn grins and reaches for one of my chips.

I can hear my lao lao's voice in my head. *You're*

sharing food now with a boy?

"Mmm . . . ," Finn says, gobbling up a nacho. His glee when he munches is very cute. I suddenly panic – does this mean I think *Finn's* cute??

I move an inch away, just to be safe, even though I don't *think* he's cute. It's just his enthusiasm for sticky chips that's cute.

"My Mum never lets me eat like this at home. I always have to wait till I'm at my dad's. It's one of the things they're constantly fighting about," Finn tells me between bites.

"My parents fight too," I confess to Finn, thinking back to the big fight they had on Saturday. Mum found a long list of immigration and tenant lawyers at the library, but she and Dad bickered about whether to call any of them. Dad said it would be too expensive, and even taking time off work to go see them would be tough. In the end, Mum agreed to wait for Pete to give us the advance.

"What do your parents fight about?" Finn asks.

"Money," I reply. I brace for his reaction. But Finn just shrugs.

"Oh, my parents totally argue about that," he says. "My Mum thinks my dad spends way too much money on football. Which he does. *But* he's taking me to Vegas next weekend!"

"Wow!"

"Yeah! I'm excited!" Finn exclaims, rubbing his hands together.

"Is important game?" I ask.

"Oh, I don't care about the game. I just want to spend time with my dad," Finn says. "I've got the whole thing planned out – after the game, we're going to go to M&M's Las Vegas! *Twenty-eight thousand square feet* of chocolate decadence. You get to customise your own M&M's!!!"

Finn looks like he's on a sugar high just talking about it, and I laugh.

"Then after that, we're going to go on the Ferris wheel!" he says.

As Finn rattles off more places in Las Vegas, I can't help but feel a stirring of envy. I wish I could go on a fun trip with my dad. Or take another ride to the mountain. I want to add more to our simple high five, but he's always working.

Finn's face tenses. "I just hope his football team wins," he says. "Otherwise, he'll be in a *lousy* mood."

"Why your dad like football so much?" I ask him.

Finn shrugs.

"Beats me. I wish I could understand it," he says. "He's been trying to get me into it since I was four, spending money on private sports coaches. But I just don't care about it. You think that makes me weird?"

I shake my head. I repeat the words Carla said to me. "We're all individuals. That's what makes us so special."

"Thanks," Finn says. "But sometimes . . . I wonder . . . what it would be like, if he looked at me for a second, the way he looks at John Wolford."

"Who's that?"

Finn explains he's the quarterback. "Instead, he got a *nerd* who can't throw."

I don't know what *nerd* means. I decide it's a kind, sensitive boy who misses his dad. The kind of person I'm honored to be friends with. And Lao Lao would be too, if she knew him.

"Hey, Finn, can you really teach me how draw graphic novel?" I ask.

I don't want to hang up on Lao Lao anymore, or squeeze everything I want to tell her into a two-minute phone call. I want to show her my life.

Finn grins, grabbing a piece of paper. "Sure! First rule of writing a graphic novel: Decide what you want your story to be. A happy story? A sad story?"

I chew on my lip, trying to decide.

Finally, I say, "I want my book to be sliding door."

With that, I take a deep breath . . . and tug my invisible thread free. I begin to tell Finn everything.

Chapter 51

Finn is so shocked when I tell him about the bathroom wall. It takes all my English words to convince him not to storm into the girls' bathroom and go look.

"We have to tell someone!" he says. "Trashing you on the bathroom wall, first of all, that's vandalism!"

I shake my head, not knowing what *vandalism* means. Finn says it means when someone destroys school property.

"Not to mention it's terrible and mean, and goes against all our school values!" He thrusts a finger toward the **BE KIND** sign outside.

"That's just sign." I lower my voice to a murmur. I think about my excitement the first day I saw it.

Lately, I've been hurrying past it.

"Fine, don't do it for the sign. Do it for Cat!" Finn jumps up and goes and grabs another copy of *Flea Shop* from the shelf. He flips to the part in the story where Cat finally stands up for herself to the mean girls in her class.

"When I got to this part, I cheered so hard for Cat!" he says.

He peers at me with kind, encouraging eyes. But I am not a character in a novel. This is real life, and Jessica's not just anyone. Her Mum has her own private parking spot at the school!

"I'm not going to do that," I tell him.

"You won't have to do it alone," he says, putting his hand on my arm. "I'll do it with you."

I look down at his hand on my arm as the door swings open. Two boys from our class walk into the library and call out to Finn. They see Finn's hand on my arm, when their eyebrows jump to their mops of blonde hair.

"Bro!" Nate says to Finn. "What are you doing?"

Finn instantly takes his hand off my arm, his face redder than a tomato. He moves his backpack between us.

"Hey, bro," Finn mutters back.

"Finn! Bro! Tell me you're not hiding in here with the foreign exchange student!"

Before Finn can even respond, Nate and Preston start making kissing noises at us and I hide my face in embarrassment, bolting for the staff bathroom.

I stay there, long after the lunch bell has rung, too chicken to reappear. Too mad to go back to class. Too confused to work on my graphic novel.

Now I don't know *what* to include in my book to Lao Lao. Do I write about what just happened? My ears turn purple as I imagine my grandmother's reaction . . .

Told ya to stay away from boys.

Chapter 52

I'm in the bathroom for so long that Mrs. Hollins finally calls the nurse, who calls my Mum.

Mum picks me up from school forty-five minutes later. I manage to convince her I got a bad stomachache from eating all the nachos.

"Oh, you poor thing. Must be all that cheese," Mum says. "I'll make you some congee when we get home from Pete's."

"We're going to Pete's?" I ask.

"To get the advance!" Mum says. "We sold 99 Ranch the vegetables, so now he has to give us the cash, like he promised!"

"Great!" I thrust my arms up in the air at the chance to see Carla again.

As soon as we get to Pete's, I bolt for the tiny

home. I find Carla inside, taking a break from her science class and washing raspberries.

"Hey!" she greets me, handing me a berry. "What are you doing out of school so early?"

I spill my guts to her about what just happened with Finn, squirming as I repeat the words the other boys said.

"Ignore those doofs," she says.

"But they're like his brothers –"

"What!? Where do you get that?"

"They called him bro."

"Oh, that's nothing," Carla says. "Everyone calls everyone bro."

In between mouthfuls of berry, Carla explains that the word *bro* is just a slang term for male friend. It doesn't actually mean brother, or even close friend.

I look at her, confused. "Really?" I ask. "But why Finn say *bro* back?"

"Because he was trying to fit in. Bro culture is *very* powerful. That's why there are so many guys out there buying overpriced baseball caps!"

So that explains it. I reach for a raspberry, relieved. As I feel the tangy juices in my mouth, I think about Finn. I've never seen him in a baseball cap. But he *does* wear head-to-toe Rams gear. But only because he wants to please his dad, which I'm certain he hasn't told any of those bros.

I decide I know more about him than Nate or Preston. But I sure wish they didn't talk to him that way . . . or to me.

I swallow the raspberry and confess to Carla, "Maybe too hard for boy and girl to be friends."

I think about the eucalyptus tree . . . I'd hate to have to go back there again.

"No. It's not too hard. I mean it's hard . . . it's a *terrible* thing what they said," she tells me gently. "But Finn didn't say it –"

"But he trying to fit in with them . . . You said so!" I remind her.

Carla shakes her head. "Yeah, but it doesn't mean he's the same as them. People are individuals, remember? Give Finn a chance. Don't let those guys destroy your friendship." She pops a raspberry in her mouth and tells me proudly, "My Mum and dad were best friends *for years* before they got together."

I give her a small smile. I glance out the window at Mrs. Muñoz and am surprised to see her out by the greenhouse, holding a book.

"Oh, I totally forgot to tell you! My Mum *loves Pie in the Sky* too!" Carla says. "I gave it to her last night and she hasn't been able to stop reading!"

It thrills me beyond words to see Mrs. Muñoz take a break and read. "That's great!"

Carla adds the last of the raspberries to her lemonade pitcher. Before I can ask her if she and her Mum have had a chance to talk about the book, I hear Mum and Pete having some sort of argument on the main house porch. I run over.

"I don't understand! The sale's complete," Mum says. "Why can't I get the advance?"

"One sale. It's not like you got us a long-term *contract* with 99 Ranch," Pete says.

"You didn't say anything about long-term contract!" Mum cries. My dad hears the exasperation in her tone. He jolts over from the greenhouse.

"All you have to do is get on that phone and start buttering up that store manager."

Mum looks absolutely livid when we walk up the steps to the porch. "No. You ask me to sell strawberries. That's what I did. Look – no more strawberries! All gone!"

"It's a start! Now I'm saying . . . go and finish the

job," Pete says. "If they liked the strawberries they got, you should have no problem convincing them to give us a long-term contract."

"Why don't *you* convince them?" Mum asks, pointing at Pete.

Dad walks over to her and tries to calm her down. "Qian, please . . ."

"No! He keeps moving the goalpost!" Mum protests to Dad in Chinese.

Pete raises his hands, as if the sound of Mum and Dad talking in Chinese is hurting his ears. "Please! No Chinese!"

My heartbeat skyrockets. Hearing it up close in person is a whole different experience. I think back to those bros in the library calling me the "foreign exchange student." I think of Cat in *Flea Shop*, finally mustering the courage to push back. And I turn to Pete, my face full of resolve.

"Why?" I ask Pete.

He seems shocked by my outburst in English. "What do you mean why?" he asks. "Because it's my house, I like to know what's going on! I have the right to understand what's being said on my property!"

"I saying to my husband, you keep moving the

goal," Mum tells him in a calm and even voice. "And we running out of time."

"You're not running out of time. You still got almost four weeks," Pete says, deciding for her. "I'll give you a week to wrestle a long-term contract out of 'em. That's plenty of time. And then when it's done, you'll get your money."

Mum's so upset by the conversation, she says we're going. I run back to say goodbye to Carla.

As I chug a glass of lemonade before we hit the road, Carla says something startling to me.

"Pete's never going to pay up," she says. "I've seen him do this a million times. He strings along every vendor with the *promise* to pay . . . the fence guy . . . the seeds supplier . . . the high school kids who go around to restaurants collecting compost for him."

My pupils widen at this information.

"That's his shtick. And the *real* reason he can't get certified by the organic farmers' association."

I walk back to Mum, fuming. If Pete thinks he can just dangle a carrot in front of my Mum and keep her working for him forever, he needs to bury his head in his geraniums. Because she is WAY. TOO. SMART.

Chapter 53

On our way back to school to pick up Millie, I try to tell Mum what Carla said, but she's in a weird trance. She just keeps saying, "Uh-huh," to everything I tell her. It's like she's reading a book while she's driving.

We wait in the pickup lane. I see Finn. We lock eyes for a second.

I immediately hide my head, slouching as far down in the passenger-side seat as my legs will go. Thankfully, Mum's too in her own world to notice. I peek out at Finn and watch him get into his dad's Jeep Wrangler. I search for the expensive baseball hat. Sure enough, it's on his dad's head.

Finn, meanwhile, studies our Honda Civic, with the trunk scraped and one of our back lights duct-taped on. He cranes his neck, as if looking inside for me. I hide my head even farther, mortified.

Millie jumps into the car. "Well, you'll never guess what happened today!" she announces. "Hazel's sleepover was a *disaster*!"

This news temporarily lifts Mum from her trance. "Really?" she asks, pulling out of the parking lot.

I relax and sit back up.

"One of the Starbursts – Hazel thinks it was Emily – stole her AirPods," Millie says. "She *just* got them! And now they're gone!"

"Wait, so they're just missing."

"No, they're stolen. Hazel says that Emily must have stolen them because she's been talking about getting AirPods for the last few weeks."

"But they could be anywhere! She could have lost them at school, or at the park!" I say in Emily's defense.

"You're not getting it! Emily's out! The Starbursts are down one person, and get this . . ." Millie switches to English. In her excitement, she blurts out, "Today at recess, I was dancing and Hazel said it looked pretty fly."

"She said you looked like a fly?" I ask, confused.

"No, *fly*. Like cool! Fire!" she adds.

Okay, now she's just hot-and-colding me.

"She means Millie looks good," Mum chimes in. "But wait a minute, Millie, I thought you were over Hazel and her group."

"I am over them," Millie insists, in a tone that makes me wonder. "But I have to be practical, Mum. Their TikTok account has eight thousand followers. Mine has fifteen."

I look at Mum, hoping she'll put a stop to this madness.

But all she says is "We'll talk about this later."

*

That night, I'm reading *Fumble* in bed, still waiting for "later." Mum's too busy, though, doing the laundry that's been piling up for days while we've been over at Pete's, opening up our mail – most of which is bills – and replying to our customers who are demanding shipping dates.

Most of them are losing patience now and moving on to other sellers. Mum's dream of selling at Target is falling apart. Millie and I try our best to reply to everyone and ask for a couple of more days . . .

even though I know it might not matter, given what Carla told me.

Still . . . we try.

Millie practices her dance moves in front of the mirror as I read.

"Check it out." She takes her head in her hands and does a little twirl with her hair. "I'm calling it Hair Ferris Wheel. What do you think?"

"I *think* you're better off without the Starbursts," I say, putting my book down.

"I'm not gonna be *like* them," Millie says.

"Oh, so you admit it's obnoxious accusing your friend of stealing when you can't find something," I say to Millie.

Millie nods her head gently. "But it's too hard breaking out on my own. Look at this video."

She dashes out to get Mum's phone, then plops down on the floor, next to my bottom bunk. She taps on TikTok and goes to Hazel's Starburst account. She shows me a video of them dancing. They're not even in perfect sync with the music.

"This video has five thousand views," Millie says. She taps on her own account and presses on one of her videos — of her dolphining, clock-powing, practically breaking walls. The view count? Fifteen.

I understand how frustrated my sister feels. It's the way I used to feel in China, when I didn't stand a chance in math because everyone else was getting privately tutored. Like it just wasn't fair.

But this is friendship we're talking about. I turn to a page in *Fumble* and show my sister what Hector says about his friend Logan. Hector is trying to make Logan feel better about not getting on the football team. He tells Logan not to think about his bad throw, because he has a heart of gold.

"*That's* the reason to be friends with someone, not view counts," I tell Millie.

Millie puts Mum's phone down and stares curiously at the book.

"So does Logan get on the team?" she asks.

I smile. "You'll have to read the book to find out." "Why does he want to play football so bad?" Millie asks.

I put the book down for a sec. "You really want to know? Because he wants to impress his dad." I sit up to educate my sister. "His dad is a bro. A bro is someone who wears a lot of hats."

Millie gives me a funny look. "What? That's not

what a bro is."

"It *is*!" I insist.

"What kind of hats does he wear?" Millie asks, picking up the book and turning the pages.

There are no pictures, so we have to imagine. I picture Logan's dad wearing a big cowboy hat like Homer Simpson once wore, with big huge letters that say MANLY on it. I sketch it for Millie.

"Manly?" Millie asks, giggling.

"Logan's dad says playing football makes you manly. That's why Logan wants to get on the football team, so maybe his dad will finally come to see one of his a cappella performances –"

My school Chromebook dings as we're talking.

I hop over to see what's up. There's a chat request from Finn. I glance back at Millie but she's picked up *Fumble* and started reading.

I click it open.

Hey, Finn writes.

Hi, I type back.

I'm sorry about back in the library.

I think for a long while, then type **It's OK.**

Nate and Preston, they're not really my friends, if that's what you're wondering.

I let out a big sigh of relief. I think of what to type . . . smiling, I tease him, **OK bro.**

😨 **Very funny. Bro.**

I chuckle.

Anyway, before we were RUDELY interrupted, u were telling me something important. You should definitely tell someone about that bathroom wall.

I shake my head at the computer. **I don't want to,** I type.

A few seconds pass.

OK. But I'm here if you do.

Thanks, I type back.

The front door opens. "Hey! I'm home!" Dad calls. Millie scrambles out of bed to go see Dad. I quickly type into the chat, **See you at the library tomorrow?**

I wait impatiently as Finn responds. A smile spreads across my face when he finally replies.

100

Chapter 54

Mum's already in her pajamas, making up the mat on the floor. As Dad changes out of his work clothes, he puts a stack of hundreds on the table.

Mum scurries over to the stack of bills. "How'd you get him to pay?"

Millie and I go over too and start counting. Our eyes turn to marbles when we finish – *seven hundred American dollars!*

"What'd you do? Sell him your left kidney?" Mum asks Dad, following him into the bathroom. He splashes his face with water, watching the muddy water slowly go down the drain.

"I renewed my contract with Pete," Dad says.

Mum walks out of the bathroom, dead quiet.

She doesn't even look at the money. She just

sits down on the mat and starts spreading out her blankets. Millie crouches to help her. "Same terms?" Mum asks finally.

"Yes," Dad says, walking out of the bathroom. He takes in Mum's disappointment. "But we got the advance – half my salary! That's a lot! That's what you wanted."

"Not what *I* wanted," Mum corrects. "What *we* wanted. But not like this." She shakes her head. "Did you at least try to negotiate for better hours? Better pay?"

Dad sighs and walks over to the kitchen. He opens the fridge, surveying the empty contents. He finally pours himself some cereal.

"Can we just talk about this later?" he asks, sinking into a kitchen chair. He stares at the cereal spoon, looking like he's willing himself to find the energy to lift it. "I'm so tired."

"Because he works you to death. Look at you! Your back hurts. Your knees need to be iced daily," Mum says, walking over to the fridge and getting Dad three bags of frozen peas. He puts one bag over each knee, and one on his back, and closes his eyes. "You're falling apart working for him."

"So what do you suggest? I quit? What happens to our green card application then?" Dad asks, peeking out from one eye.

At the mention of the green card, the air thins. "Did he say anything about that?" Mum asks, sitting down next to Dad. "Maybe we should go to his lawyer and just make sure –"

"You want to spend three hundred fifty dollars an hour?" Dad picks up the bills. "Because that's what it's going to cost."

Mum fights back the tears in her eyes. "I just wish it were easier." She grabs a dishrag nearby.

Dad's pea bags fall to the floor as he reaches gently for Mum's hand. "Hey, come here."

But Mum moves her hand away an inch.

"You gotta think positive," Dad says. "It's all going to work out."

I stare at my parents' hands on the kitchen table. So close, yet so far away. If there were a seven-hundred-dollar magnet that could bring them together at this moment, I'd buy it.

Chapter 55

Mum kicks into high gear early the next morning, going over to the store to buy all the supplies while Dad drops us off at school.

As he drives, I tell him what Carla said about Pete.

"Is it true he always stiffs his vendors?" I ask Dad. "That why he can't get organically certified?"

Dad shakes his head. "No, that's not why. He can't get organically certified because he'd rather put every penny he makes back into the land, rather than on getting some certificate. I'm not disputing that Pete's cheap. But most farms operate at a loss, and the fact is, Pete's working hard for *us*."

"Why for us, Dad?" I ask.

"Well, sweetheart, so we can *have* a future. A path forward! A way to eat and produce food that doesn't kill the environment . . . and if we can do it even forty miles away from Los Angeles, it gives us hope for the future. We can build up the soil so it can hold more carbon, farm with compost, so compost doesn't end up in a landfill and become methane gas – all that's for us, and it's priceless."

I never thought about it that way before.

"He may be rough around the edges, but his heart's in the right place. He cares more about doing what's right than most folks . . . ," Dad says. "Which is why he gave me the advance."

I chew over Dad's words as Millie and I climb out of the car. Millie beelines for the playground to catch some last swings before class. But I hang back a second. This time, Dad extends his hand.

I grin and high-five him back. I think that's going to be it, but Dad's fingers hold on to mine. He teaches me to make a fist. And he bumps his fist with mine.

"See you later, sunflower!" he says as he drives off.

I glow inside as I skip toward the courtyard, bumping my two fists together as I run – *bump! bump! bump!* I've never bumped fists with anyone before! I feel totally cool, like Otto-the-rocking-bus-driver-on-*The-Simpsons* cool!

I jerk my hands down when Preston and Nate spot me. They walk over to me, both wearing frayed Lakers hats.

"Hey, Lina." They grin. "Looking for Finn?"

I shake my head, walking away from them. But they follow me.

"I'll tell you where he is if you teach me something in Chinese," Preston says.

Nate starts giggling. "Dude, don't," he says.

"No, I'm serious! I want to learn," Preston continues. Then, with an eyebrow waggle, he asks, "How do you say *I look so fine* in Chinese?"

At first, I refuse. But then I get an idea. I open my mouth and pronounce the words as slowly as I can.

"I," I say in Chinese, "am a stinky tofu."

"I am a stinky tofu," Preston repeats proudly.

Loud laughter erupts from behind me. I turn around, and it's Finn, walking up to me. He gives me a high five, paying absolutely no attention to what his friends think.

"Bro, did I get that right?" Preston asks Finn. "I am a stinky tofu!"

Finn gives Preston a thumbs-up. "Perfect! Nailed it!" Finn assures him.

The two of us stand back and watch as Preston goes up to random girls in the courtyard and gleefully declares his odour.

Chapter 56

"So you're not going to believe it," Finn says when we get to class. "We're doing *Flea Shop* next for Book Tasting! Mrs. Carter liked it so much, she's going to read it out loud to us!"

I do a little silent cheer in my seat. "When?" I ask Finn.

"Today!" Finn says.

I resist the urge to bump my own fist.

Jessica overhears us talking and whines, "What's so great about *Flea Shop*? I don't want to read about fleas!"

Mrs. Carter holds out the book to show Jessica. "It's not about fleas. It's about a flea market *shop*. *And* it's a graphic novel."

Jessica peers curiously at the cover when she

hears that.

I bounce in my seat excitedly as Mrs. Carter passes out the copies – one for each table. But before she can start reading, there's a knock on the door. It's Mrs. Ortiz.

"Lina? You ready?" she asks.

I hand our table copy of *Flea Shop* to Finn with a regretful sigh. For once, I'm sad about leaving my regular class. I wish I could stay and see the rest of my class slip into my shoes . . . just for a minute.

*

Mrs. Ortiz must have sensed my disappointment, because she offers to play a game with me today.

"It's called Nonsense Speech," she says. "Basically, you and I will take turns making a speech on a bunch of nonsense topics."

We're in the art room again, and all the chairs and tables have been moved aside. Mrs. Ortiz and I are sitting on the carpet.

"You want to try?" she asks.

Normally a speech would scare me, but a nonsense speech . . . it's pretty hard to mess that up! I nod eagerly.

"Okay . . . first topic." She reaches into her big red felt hat. It looks like the hat in *The Cat in the Hat,* which is a book that she and I have also read together. I peek over at the tiny scraps of paper inside. She pulls one out. *"How do you wrestle an alligator?"*

She demonstrates for me that wrestling is pulling and tugging in a fight. I giggle and clear my voice.

"How to wrestle alligator. Number one, wear long trousers. Number two, put lots of soap on your hand, not very tasty. Also easy to slip out if get inside alligator's mouth."

Mrs. Ortiz cracks up. I grin, delighted to make her laugh. I keep going.

"Number three, put strong underwear over a lligator's eyes and mouth."

Now Mrs. Ortiz is practically on the floor.

"Finally, bring phone to take selfie."

I conclude my speech and Mrs. Ortiz claps wildly. I beam, proud of myself. That was the longest speech I've ever made!

"Now my turn!" Mrs. Ortiz announces. She pulls another topic from the red hat – hers is *Why did the chicken cross the road?*

She makes a hilarious speech about a rooster named Bob who got into a fight with another rooster named Gary over what song to crow at the crack of dawn. Bob wanted to sing *do-doodle-do*, and Gary wanted to sing *cockadoodle-do*. They couldn't agree, so Bob went across the street.

I bust a rib laughing. This game is fun!

My turn. I grab another piece of paper from the bag. This time, the words say What would you bring to a dessert island?

"Not a deserted island," Mrs. Ortiz clarifies, putting her finger under the word *dessert* so I learn the difference in the spelling. "Two *s*'s, for *extra sweet*."

I think long and hard.

"My sketchpad and colour pencils," I start. "My parents. My sister – and I leave Mum's phone at home so she just dance for fun. Not for views."

"Great idea!" Mrs. Ortiz says.

"I'd bring my friends Carla and Finn . . . My books." I smile at Mrs. Ortiz. "And my lao lao, of course."

I imagine the two of us sitting on lily pads made of caramel.

Mrs. Ortiz puts a hand to her chest. "I love that."

"I'd tell her everything. No invisible thread on the island!"

"Invisible thread?"

I reach up with my hand and make the sewing gesture around my mouth. "In China, gotta be careful what you say."

Mrs. Ortiz reaches for my hand, then looks me in the eye. "I want you to know it's different in America. You are free to say and write what you believe here. It's how we make progress."

I nod.

I am feeling the thread less and less every day, thanks to her and my growing confidence. I tell Mrs. Ortiz I'm working on a graphic novel for my grandma.

"Oh, that's wonderful! Have you started yet?" she asks. "Can I see?"

I shake my head shyly. I haven't officially started yet. Every time I think of it, it's a little daunting.

But Mrs. Ortiz tells me not to be intimidated. "You don't have to write the whole thing in one go. You can do a little bit every day. Baby steps. Just like learning English."

She gets out a brand-new blank sketchbook from

her bag and hands it to me. I turn to the first page in the sketchbook, thinking of Lao Lao back in the nursing home and how much I want her to know about all the other people I'm bringing to my dessert island. *Baby steps.*

I start dividing up the page into panels.

Chapter 57

I draw in the car on the way home. Mum waits at the school exit light impatiently, eager to get us home.

"I've already made forty bath bombs," she says. "Lina, you start customizing them. Millie, you and I and Carla are going to keep the assembly line going."

"Carla?" I ask eagerly.

"I spoke to her Mum and she's thrilled to help!" Mum says. "We're going to pick her up on the way home!"

Yesssss! I throw my arms up.

*

Ten minutes later, Carla gets into the car. Talk about a real scientist! She's got her safety goggles on and a white lab coat! With her clipboard in hand

and her hair up in a pony, she slides into the car.

"Let's do this thing!" Carla says.

"All right, Dr. Muñoz!" I tease her.

With our new resident head of chemistry, we're ready to get down to business.

The afternoon flies by as we mix, pack, dry, and customise. Carla comes up with a creative way to pack the dry bombs so that a rainbow releases when you put one in the water. Mum lets us test it out, and it looks so cool, I wish I were a tiny spoon, enjoying a bath in the sink.

We make bath bombs for puppies, birthday parties, Bar Mitzvahs, and graduations. We make bath bombs for anniversaries and divorcearies. It's so fun painting so many messages for people, and I teach Carla and Millie how to paint on the bath bombs too.

When Mum says it's time for Carla to go home, Carla and I both look disappointed. Carla says she'll be back tomorrow. I walk my friend to our Honda so Mum can drive her back.

"Thanks so much for helping us," I say to Carla.

Carla gives me a hug. She reaches into her lab coat and pulls out my copy of *Pie in the Sky*. "Thank you for this. My Mum finished it last night."

"What she think?" I ask.

Carla lingers by the side of the car.

"She loved it. We finally talked about my dad," Carla says. "She asked me if there was still a hole in my heart as big as the pie in the sky."

"And?" I ask Carla.

"I told her there isn't, because Dad lives there now," Carla says, patting her chest. "And I want him to have the softest, happiest place to live."

I smile at Carla. What a wonderful, beautiful sentence in English. I try to remember the light of this perfect moment so I can draw it in my graphic novel.

"She hugged me and said she's not quite there yet, but she's working on it," Carla tells me as she gets into the car. "And that's something."

"It really something." As I wave to Carla, I hug *Pie in the Sky* to my chest, thinking about the hole in my own heart, hoping my graphic novel . . . when I finally show it to Lao Lao . . . will patch it up.

Chapter 58

I show Finn the first ten panels of my graphic novel at the library the next day! I can't believe I've already finished ten panels! I brace for his reaction as he looks at the illustrations of me arriving at LAX, thinking my life was going to be like Lisa Simpson's in *The Simpsons*. Only to find myself knee-deep in baking soda, trying to keep up with bath bomb orders in our tiny apartment, while Pete yells at Mum and Dad to sell more carrots!

"That is amazing!" Finn gushes, chuckling.

"Really?" I ask.

Mrs. Hollins walks over and Finn ecstatically shows her my work. Again, I hide my head, preparing for the prickly embarrassment of showing too much of myself. But Mrs. Hollins laughs too and tells me,

"This is even better than *Flea Shop*!"

I blush hard and shake my head. *Nothing* is better than *Flea Shop*. Still, I'm pretty flattered.

"Keep going! I want to read more!" Mrs. Hollins says.

I smile and tell her I'll try. I pull out *Pie in the Sky* from my backpack and return it to her. Then I pull out *Fumble* and hand it to Finn.

"This for you."

"Really? I can bring it to Vegas!" He turns the book around and reads the back. When he sees that it's about football, he starts giving it back to me. "I'm not really into sports books."

"Just read it," I urge him. "Trust me. I'm student librarian."

Finn tosses it into his backpack. "Fine. I'll give it a shot, I guess."

I laugh, realizing he's made a sports joke. I'm understanding more and more jokes these days!

*

By Friday, I'm almost at forty panels! The book is starting to be a real book!

When I get to the panel about the bathroom stall,

I take a deep gulp of air. As I wait for Mum to pick me and Millie up, I stare at the pages, trying to decide whether to draw it or not. I know I want to be honest with Lao Lao, but do I want to be *that* honest? It will upset her so much if she knows.

But then, as Mum's car gets in the long pickup lane, I think of all the letters Mum sent to me. Pictures in front of nice houses that we didn't even live in. And I decide I don't want that for my book. I don't want a bunch of fake panels, of me fake smiling. I want the truth.

There is freedom in truth.

Yes, there is pain.

But there is also joy.

The joy of not being afraid to talk about it . . . the courage to not erase it.

As Mum pulls up to the front, I quickly sketch the bare bones of the bathroom stall, then pack my pencils and my sketchbook. Millie beats me to Mum's car.

"Guess what?" she tells Mum. "I told Hazel about our new rainbow bath bombs and she wants to buy twenty of them, for her birthday spa weekend tomorrow! Can we make them for her?"

"Of course!" Mum says.

"Wait, she's buying them direct from you?" I ask. "You told her we make them?"

"Course not!" Millie shakes her head. "I told her they're *super* hard to get online! But I know a way to get them fast – and I'll bring them to her house! So she texted her Mum, and her Mum said that's fine. They're paying us two hundred dollars cash!"

Mum does a little squeal when she hears that. "That's two hundred dollars we don't have to share with Etsy! Good work, baby!" Mum leans over and kisses my sister on the head.

I smile. I have to admit . . . two hundred dollars is a lot. Millie did good.

As Mum steps on the gas, I lean over and ask my sister whether that means she's invited to the birthday spa weekend.

Millie shrugs.

"She didn't say. Whatever. It doesn't matter," she says.

I raise an eyebrow at Millie, studying her, as she clutches Hazel's Mum's number and address tight in her hand.

Chapter 59

What exactly is a birthday spa weekend?" Carla asks, packing the bath bombs in the mould as we work that afternoon.

I glance at Mum, grinning. She looks totally ready to check into the Imagination Hotel too. It's been a while.

"It's a weekend where you arrive and someone spray you with rose water," Mum starts in English.

"And they give you slippers," I add.

"Made of Jell-O," Millie chimes in, looking up from her mixing bucket.

"And you jump into a swimming pool of sparkling fizzy drinks." Carla grins, getting the hang of this game.

"The bubbles massage your toes," Millie adds.

"And tickle your hair!" I say. "When you get out, they give you towel —"

"Made of marshmallows," Mum concludes.

We sit back and imagine this dream weekend as the sweet aromatic essential oils of our bath bombs waft up our noses. I peek over at my sister, so lost in her imagination that she drops the bath bomb in her hand.

Mum's eyelids flip open and the reality of our factory comes crashing down on us as we all check out of the Imagination Hotel and get back to work.

No one sighs louder than Millie.

Mum reaches over with her baking soda finger and presses lightly on Millie's nose. "You'll have a weekend like that soon, sweetie."

Millie nods, wiping the white powder off her nose as she continues mixing. Carla scoops out another bath bomb and packs it in the mould.

"So where's her house, anyway?" Mum asks.

Millie looks around, searching for the piece of paper with Hazel's address. She looks everywhere, the floor, her hoodie pockets, her jeans. But she can't find it. She starts panicking.

"What's wrong?" I ask her.

"I can't find the piece of paper! The one with Hazel's address on it," she says. "It was right here! In my hoodie pocket!" She stares down at her giant mixing bucket. "You don't think it fell into . . ."

We all stare at Millie's mixing bucket. I get up and go help my sister stir and search through the ingredients, trying to locate the piece of paper. But it's not in there.

I follow Millie's eyes over to the bath bombs already moulded, sitting to dry.

Uh-oh.

"Maybe they'll think it's a surprise?" Millie asks nervously. "Yeah!" Carla agrees. "A fun mystery! Could be cool!"

With a grimace through her teeth, Mum shakes her head. "That's not the kind of surprise we want to give customers," she says, reaching over for all five of Carla's freshly made bath bombs and chucking them out.

As she's about to discard them, I make a desperate plea to save them!

"We can use them!" I tell Mum. "Let's save them for *us* later"

Mum gives me a faint smile as she puts the bath

bombs into a drawer. I look over at Millie, who's already on her Chromebook, messaging Hazel for her address.

As I get back to painting with my mica, Mum thinks out loud. "You know it *would* be pretty cool if we could put a *real* surprise in the bath bombs."

I think of the puppy party we just made all those orders for. "Like a dog toy?" I ask.

"Or a *toy* toy!" Mum beams, fireworks going off in her head.

Leave it to my Imagineer Mum to turn a mistake into an exciting new product line! I can almost hear the *ka-ching* sound!

Chapter 60

Later that night, when we drop off Carla, Mrs. Muñoz is in the main house, sweeping the floor. Pete's in the living room, deep in concentration as he goes over the books. I can hear him punching on his calculator.

"Hey, sweetie!" Mrs. Muñoz greets Carla, putting the broom down. "How was your afternoon?"

"So fun!" Carla says, showing off one of the bath bombs we made. Mum let her keep one as a thank-you present. Carla's excited about adding it to the giant water bucket when she takes another outside shower.

"Oh, that smells so good," Mrs. Muñoz says, closing her eyes and breathing in the gentle lavender scent.

Excitedly, Carla tells her Mum all about our plan to put toys inside the bath bombs. She asks her Mum if she can come over and help us tomorrow, too.

"Of course!" Mrs. Muñoz says. "So long as you help *me* make some treats tonight."

Mrs. Muñoz points to a brown grocery bag sitting on the kitchen counter. Curiously, Carla walks over. Millie leans over as she watches Carla pull out ingredients.

"Almond flour . . . butter . . . chocolate chips . . . Are we making cookies?" Carla asks.

"Actually, I thought we'd try making some raspberry-chocolate croissants," Mrs. Muñoz replies with a shy smile.

"Like Dad used to make?" Carla asks.

Mum puts an arm around my shoulder, watching this sweet exchange.

Mrs. Muñoz nods, tucking a strand of Carla's hair behind her ear and smiling. "I've already got the dough started. You think you still remember the rest of the recipe?"

"Four tablespoons almond flour, one-quarter cup powdered sugar, raspberries, and chocolate!" Carla recites. "But where are we going to bake it?"

Pete walks into the kitchen with his gigantic ledger, banging the counter with his cane to get our attention. "All right, folks. Party's over, this isn't an auto shop waiting room. Some of us have work to do." He lifts his big book. "So unless you're here to do the dishes –"

"Actually, I thought I'd make you dinner . . . ," Mrs. Muñoz says. "We have a lot of vegetables left over from the farmers' market."

"Dinner?" Pete asks.

Mrs. Muñoz nods earnestly. She lists all the things she can make with the ripe vegetables – squash soup, crisp green bean salad, and steamed artichokes.

Mum jumps in with a few dishes of her own. "Stir-fried broccoli! And stewed aubergine!"

"No stir-fry. I don't want any of those fumes. But . . ." Pete glances at his fortress of canned chickpeas on the counter. "Squash soup sounds nice. I guess I can take a break from eating carrots and hummus."

"Squash soup it is!" Mrs. Muñoz says. "And for dessert – raspberry-and-chocolate croissants!"

Carla and Millie do a happy dance – dolphin, clock-pow, YEAH!

*

While Carla helps her mother cook, and Mum and Millie go to the back to help Dad wrap up in the greenhouse, I venture over to Pete's library.

He sure has a lot of books in his study. It's a beautiful room off to the side of the house, which it seems he rarely uses. Most days, he plants himself on his favourite wicker chair on the back porch, reigning over everyone in the field with his eagle eye.

Tonight, the fire roars from the study's brick fireplace, beckoning me.

I walk inside and gaze at the books. They span an entire wall, and there's even a ladder for the books that are hard to reach at the top.

I study the authors' names on the leather-bound spines, looking for Virginia Burton.

I find one copy immediately. I read the title, *Gardening in the Desert*. I look inside for the dedication.

To my darling husband, Pete, who once told me only life knows how to heal life. You're so right. Working on this book has healed me in so many ways . . . I hope it brings light to you, too, my love.

I run my finger along the words, trying to understand what she means. *Heal her from what?* I wonder.

I thumb through the rest of the book, hoping to find a letter or something. But there's only dense text on gardening. I put the book back. I scan the shelves for another Virginia Burton book and find a paperback next to a bunch of mystery novels. This one is called *Mixed Cropping*.

Again, I turn to the dedication.

To P.B. – the original mixed cropper, who loves to grow everything together so that the plants can dance under the sun. It is my distinct pleasure in life to dance with you.

I look at the date of publication. Thirty-five years ago. Clearly, they were madly in love. Virginia's fondness for Pete was as bright and lush as the zinnias outside. So what happened?

"Dinner's ready!" Mrs. Muñoz calls.

"All right, all right, I'm coming," Pete says, pounding down the stairs with his cane.

I put the book back and walk out to join Pete,

hoping the buttery smells of pureed squash and freshly baked croissants will soften his edges and he'll let us look inside his sliding door . . . if only for one night.

Chapter 61

Carla sits next to her mother, passing around the green beans. I look around the table at the great bounty of food that my dad and Mrs. Muñoz lovingly grew.

"Now this *really* is farm-to-table," Mum says, reaching for Dad's hand.

As the two of them hold hands, I poke Millie, who smiles too. It's so wonderful to see my parents at the same dinner table for once . . . and in love. Pete awkwardly holds up a glass.

"I know I don't say this often," Pete says. "But it takes a village to make a farm work, and well . . . you're all my village. In one way or another."

It's as close to a thank-you as I've ever heard from Pete, and Dad holds up his glass.

"Hear, hear," Dad says. "It's an honor, sir."

Mrs. Muñoz ladles out the squash soup. "So how did you get into farming?" she asks Pete.

"That would have to be my ex-wife, Virginia," he says, slurping a hearty spoonful of soup. His face glows as he talks about her. "She absolutely loved gardening. We got this land for dirt cheap, during one of the worst droughts in California. You should have seen this place – nothing but plant pollen and burnt powder, as far as the eye could see."

Pete grabs a soft breadstick and points it to us as he talks.

"I was working on the farm of this guy Axel, at the time, up in Goleta. A total brute. The way that man tilled his soil, day in day out, cutting up all the roots, the beehives, the worms. He didn't care." Pete shakes his head. "So when this land came along, I took it. I thought . . . if we can heal this place, then my God maybe the world does have a chance."

Hearing Pete talk – not yell, but actually talk – calmly and passionately about his farm – I have to say, it is quite inspiring. I can see why Dad chose to follow him all these years.

I look over at Carla, who's polished off all her dinner in record time and is now staring at the raspberry-chocolate croissants.

"We absolutely have a chance," Dad agrees. "I've seen it with my own eyes here. What the soil can do if we put life into it. Anything can grow."

Pete's smile fades a little. "Not anything . . ."

"I have to admit that of all the farms we've worked on, this one has the most varied and bountiful harvests," Mrs. Muñoz says, reaching for the croissant tray. She hands one to Carla and offers me and my sister one.

The buttery flakes break against my fingers as I take a bite. Even though I'm not quite done with my dinner yet, I can't resist. My eyes close as the chocolate dances with the raspberry on my tongue. It tastes absolutely heavenly.

Mrs. Muñoz passes one each to my parents and to Pete.

Pete puts his aside and continues talking about farming.

"You know the secret?" he asks. "Some crops, like beans, they restore the soil. Others, like tomatoes, suck out the nutrients. By rotating and mixing them, with flowers and shrubs, I create what's called agroforestry."

Dad turns to me and explains in Chinese, "Agroforestry is planting based on what each crop can and cannot do for the soil. It allows the soil to thrive."

I nod and look up, half expecting Pete to scold us for speaking Chinese, but he lets it slide tonight.

Instead, he gets up and goes to his study. He returns with Virginia's book on mixed cropping.

"It's all right here, if you want to read about it." He shows it to Mrs. Muñoz.

Mrs. Muñoz admires the book, staring at the photo of Virginia Burton gardening on Pete's farm. In the picture, she's wearing overalls and a yellow plaid shirt, her lush hair shining in the sun. She looks stunning.

Mum leans over. "She's beautiful," she comments.

Pete blushes. "She's a major writer now," he says.

He takes back the book from Mrs. Muñoz while gazing at the picture of Virginia Burton.

"She had the sharpest mind of any farmer. If something wouldn't grow, she'd try a million ways to get it to grow. This one time, she even played music for the crops." He chuckles at the memory, pointing out to the field. "There'd be jazz on that side for the lettuce, and classical on that side for the asparagus!"

His face blooms at the memory.

"I'd say to her, Gin, you running a farm or a concert?" he recalls.

I smile. It's clear how much he adored her.

"Who came up with the idea to plant trees on the farm to attract beneficials?" Mrs. Muñoz asks.

Carla turns to me and explains, "Beneficials are insects that help – like bees and ladybugs. And praying mantises!"

"She did! I was skeptical at first, but she was right. The beneficials are absolutely essential to keeping a healthy farm," Pete says. "When she saw it was working, she got so excited. She went around trying to teach other farms. She wanted to do farm tours, educational camps. Pass it on to the next generation, which is how she started writing."

Thinking of the next generation, I wonder out loud, speaking between mouthfuls of croissant: "Did you guys have any kid?"

Pete's face instantly tightens. All his joy shrivels up. Uh-oh. I can tell from his deep frown that I've stepped on a tender crack. His mouth purses into a sour pit again as he slams his book shut and grabs his cane.

"I'm turning in," he announces.

"I'm sorry, Pete!" I apologise, getting up. Did I offend him with my nosiness? The crumbs from my croissant rain on my plate.

But Pete just keeps stomping toward the stairs, calling out as he walks, "Thanks for dinner. But let's not make this a habit. This is a farm, not a restaurant!"

"Yes, sir!" Dad calls back.

As Dad helps Mrs. Muñoz tidy up the kitchen, I go up to Carla and apologise for ruining her Mum's amazing dinner. I shouldn't have asked about his kids. But his strong reaction makes me even more curious now . . .

"Same," Carla says, reaching for another croissant. Her third of the evening. "I wonder what happened. I wish he hadn't charged off like that. I was actually starting to like him, especially when he was talking about his wife."

"Me too."

She holds her raspberry-chocolate croissant high in the air. Together, we admire the golden edges, baked to perfection.

"Does it taste as good as your dad's?" I ask her.

She thinks for a long while. "They taste different. Dad's were more sweet. These are more tangy – maybe because of the raspberries."

"Maybe."

Hand in hand, we walk out to the back porch and sit under the stars.

"I used to think different was bad," Carla says, putting her head on my shoulder. "But now I think, maybe different can be good, too."

"I think it can," I say, gazing at the stars.

Chapter 62

In a low voice, Dad tells me in the car that Pete's wife had a miscarriage.

"What's a miscarriage?" I ask, trying not to wake Millie, asleep next to me.

"It means when his wife was pregnant, the baby didn't make it," Mum says.

I gasp.

"She lost it right on the farm. She was ten weeks pregnant," Dad says. "Baby girl."

"What happened?"

"They don't know. One day, the baby just stopped growing."

I put my hand to my stomach, trying to imagine the devastation, especially on someone like Pete. I think back to Virginia's dedication in one of her books – *To my husband, whose green thumb makes everything he touches grow*. No wonder he's all chopped up inside.

"That's why he doesn't want to talk about it," Dad says. "Everyone grieves in their own way. And his is through work. In honor of his daughter."

I nod, understanding a little more about Dad's prickly boss than before I went to dinner. I still don't like the way he speaks to Mrs. Muñoz and my parents, but now I see the mulch of grief wrapped around each frown.

*

Bright and early the next day, we go right back to Pete's.

He's forgotten all about Mrs. Muñoz's delicious food and has gone right back to bossing her around. Carla couldn't get into our car fast enough.

We head over to the 99 Cents store to pick out cheap toys for the new bath bombs. Millie, Carla, and I load up on little dinosaurs and cute kitties to put in the middle of our moulds. Mum gives us five dollars so we can each pick out something for ourselves. Carla buys a key chain with a green thumb on it for her Mum.

"For when we get our own place," she says.

"Really?" I ask her excitedly. "You and your Mum thinking move out?"

"Not yet . . . but I think she's almost there," Carla says. "Last night's dinner just reminded her of everything we're missing. It was so much fun."

"You get eat any leftover croissants in the morning?" I ask Carla.

"They were *all gone*. Would you believe it?" she asks, doing a killer impression of Pete stuffing himself.

I laugh, and quickly get out my sketchbook so I can draw her hilarious impression. I show her my graphic novel – I'm almost at twenty pages now!

"That's amazing!" Carla says. "When are you going to send it to your grandma?"

"Soon." I smile, reaching for a beautiful card and envelope.

To our delight, the ninety-nine-cent toys fit perfectly inside our moulds! Working as fast as we can, we make one after another, imagining the joy on the customers' faces as the bath bombs melt and our adorable toy kittens join the baths! We carry on working as Mum preps dinner. We're having chicken and mushroom stir-fry tonight. As

Mum chops up the parsley, I put my mica paint and brush down and walk over to the kitchen.

"Smells great," I tell her.

"It was your favourite dish when you were little," she tells me. I'm so flattered she remembered that I hesitate to tell her anything about the dish I don't like.

But then I glance down at the little green leaves.

"You don't need to put parsley in it, though," I say softly. "I like it without it."

"Really?" Mum asks.

I nod shyly.

She stops chopping and puts the little green leaves down. "I like it without too." Wiping her hands, she touches my nose with a gentle finger. "The true flavours come out more."

With that, she holds up a mushroom for me to smell. As I'm breathing in the rich aroma, Dad walks in with a surprise of his own.

"Look what I got from a yard sale!" he exclaims. He holds up a giant box – it's an inflatable hot tub!

"WHAT?!" Millie and I exclaim, rushing over to help him with the box.

"Only ten dollars! I can't believe I finally found one! I was driving home today and I saw it. The guy said we just need to blow it up!" Dad says. "Now you guys can finally test out your products!"

"We can finally take a bath!" Millie jumps up and down. She does her elaborate high-five sequence with Dad. This time I don't even get jealous. I wait patiently for them to finish, then do my own with Dad – my fist bump is perfectly timed this time!

As Carla and I start pulling the hot tub out of the box, Mum points at the clock.

"It's six p.m.! Millie, what time you tell Hazel you going to be at her house to give her the order?" Mum asks Millie in English.

"Six thirty," Millie says.

Mum grabs the bombs from the table – all perfectly wrapped and boxed – and her keys. "We gotta go!" she tells Millie. Carla and I jump up too.

On the way out, Mum kisses Dad and whispers in Chinese, "Can I just say? That was very, very sweet. How long have you been on the hunt for a tub?"

Dad shrugs. "Oh, just since you sold your first bath bomb . . ."

Mum hugs him, her eyes twinkling. I can tell the purchase means more to Mum than all the orders in the world.

Chapter 63

In the car ride over to Hazel's, Carla and Millie toss out suggestions for which bath bomb of ours we should try first in the hot tub!

"The vanilla-rose one!" Millie says.

"Oooh! How about the lavender-violet one?" Carla suggests.

"And afterward, we can do a face mask! I saw a YouTube video that you can do a homemade one with yogurt and honey!"

"Like in *Mrs. Doubtfire*?" I ask excitedly. That's another one of my favourite American movies.

"Sounds like a plan for *great* sleepover," Mum says, winking at Millie.

Millie's face glows with excitement. As Carla borrows Mum's phone to tell her Mum our plan and ask her for permission to spend the night, we pass the tall gates of Hazel's house.

Our jaws drop to the floor of our Honda as we drive up the long private road to her massive mansion. It looks like something straight out of *Keeping Up with the Kardashians*, with an in-ground trampoline, basketball courts, tennis courts, and the biggest pool I've ever seen.

This is her house??

*

Hazel walks out in her fuzzy slippers and cashmere pajamas.

"Hey," she greets Millie.

"Hi!" Millie hands her the bath bombs. "Happy birthday!"

"Thanks. It's actually my half birthday," Hazel replies with a yawn. She lingers for a second, then awkwardly pulls out two hundred-dollar bills. She hands them to Millie.

Millie stares at the cash, in disbelief and glee. "Thanks!"

Hazel glances back at the house. The music is thumping from inside, and I can hear the laughter and giggles from the other half-birthday guests. "Do you want to stay?" Hazel finally asks Millie.

Millie is *dead*. She's so floored, she can't even talk. But then she gazes over at me and Carla. Her eyes flit between us and Hazel's lush pool, which is about eight thousand times the size of our little box hot tub. And I'm thinking that's it, our sleepover's down to two.

But then Millie says in the smallest of voices, "Actually, I have plans."

Hazel raises a sharp eyebrow.

"But I'll see you at school on Monday?"

"Kay." Hazel shrugs, turning back to her house.

As we head back to the car, I wrap my arms around my sister, never more proud of her. As far as surprises in glittering bath bombs go, Millie's choice warms my heart.

Chapter 64

That night, after a wonderful dinner of (parsley-free) stir-fry chicken and rice, Dad uses his superfarmer strength to blow enough air into the hot tub to get it fully inflated.

We put the hot tub outside, in the small alley right behind our apartment. There, surrounded by underwear hanging off our neighbours' windows, Millie, Carla, and I climb inside in our bathing suits. Carla borrows one of Mum's.

Millie is delicately holding the bath bomb we all chose together – a citrus rainbow one with gold mica balloons!

"Here comes the water!" Mum says. "Hold still!"

Mum pours the pitcher of warm water in the hot tub, then hollers at Dad to get us some more.

There's no outdoor hose, on account of the landlord not wanting us to "steal" water, so we have to use pitchers. As Dad comes running over with another pitcher, my sister squeals.

Carefully, Millie puts in the bath bomb. We watch as the fizzy foam starts bubbling in front of us, and a rainbow spreads so wide, it hugs the three of us. A proud smile stretches across our faces as we finally experience the fruit of all our labor.

"Thanks for staying, Millie," I tell my sister.

"I wasn't going to let you test out our bath bombs without me!" she says, swirling up the foam with her finger.

"You probably could have tested 'em out at the party, too," I remind her.

My sister beams, then scoops up a big handful of rainbow foam. "Yeah, but I wouldn't be able to do this!"

Millie takes the foam and puts it on top of Mum's head. Mum shrieks, laughing hard. We hold our wet arms out to her.

"Get in here!" we urge.

As Mum climbs in, Dad snaps a picture of us with his phone. I reach out with my hand for a frothy high five and fist bump. Tonight, Dad adds two more moves — a handshake followed by two finger snaps. I giggle as he takes my slippery hand and splashes water with his snapping fingers.

*

I'm breathlessly recapping our amazing sleepover to Lao Lao the next day and how Dad even dunked his head in after "shaving" with the foamy lather, when she tells me she's had a fall.

"WHAT??" I ask.

"Oh, don't worry, I'm all right. Luckily, the nurse was right there to catch me," Lao Lao says.

I hold Mum's phone tight in my hands. Still, the worry fogs my eyes. I look around for Mum, then remember she and Millie went to drop off Carla. "How did it happen?" I ask Lao Lao.

"I was in the cafeteria, getting a pear, like I normally do. As I was reaching over, I lost my balance. If it weren't for the staff grabbing my hand, I would have broken my hip."

I put a hand over my heart. "Oh, Lao Lao."

"I guess my foamy hot tub days are over," she says with a deep sigh.

I shake my head into the phone, refusing to accept that. "No they're *not*." I'm going to personally bring Lao Lao a bath bomb. We're going to check into one of those fancy hotels in Beijing. She has to sit in the foamy hot tub too and let the beautiful rainbow run over her fingers!

"I'm getting too old. But I'll tell ya, they really do watch you like a hawk in this place. The second anything happens, boom — they're right there with a medical team."

I let out a small smile. Could it be that Lao Lao finally sees *something* good in her new home?

"Have you made any friends?" I ask.

"No. Have *you* at school? Besides that boy?" she asks back. I knew she was going to bring Finn up again. I briefly consider changing the subject. But then I tell her, as proudly as I can, "No . . . Finn's still my friend. He's helping me work on something for you . . . something that'll cheer you up. You'll see!"

"Tell me later. I'm getting a little tired now. I'm going to take a nap —"

"Oh, Lao Lao! Before you hang up! What's the address for Bei Gao Li Village? I want to write to

Little Tao and tell him some American farming techniques!"

"That's nice of you," she says, giving me the address. I jot it down in my sketchbook. "Say hi to him for me, will ya? I don't know if I'm ever going to make it back."

"You *will*, Lao Lao," I promise, again feeling a tug at my heart. Anxiously, I start leading Lao Lao toward the Imagination Hotel, painting a picture of the two of us traveling to Bei Gao Li together steaming baozi and hugging little Tao! And then Lao Lao getting on a plane and coming back to America with me!

But the phone reception goes bad before I can finish. "Your voice is breaking up. I'll talk to you later. Miss you," she says, hanging up.

When I get off the phone, I stare at my graphic novel, the deep and painful worry lodged in my throat . . . What if Lao Lao has another fall? What if her time in the waiting room comes to an abrupt end before I'm even close to ready?

My Chromebook dings as I pick up my pencil.

I walk over to the table and see INCOMING CHAT VIDEO CALL REQUEST from Finn.

Video call?? I thought he was in Vegas!

I press accept.

"Hey!" Finn's face appears. He's in a giant hotel room. Rams gear is spread out all over the floor and bed. There are dishes and potato chip bags and Coke bottles everywhere.

"How's Vegas?" I ask him.

"Stinks," Finn says. "The Rams lost, so of course my dad doesn't feel like doing *anything*. Not the M&M factory, not the Ferris wheel, not even going to see the erupting volcano at the Mirage. He's just holed up in his room!"

Finn takes me across the hotel suite on his phone to show me. The door to his dad's bedroom is closed. Finn knocks, but his dad does not stir.

Finn walks over to the minibar fridge, across the room, and gets out a pack of Skittles. He throws it at his dad's door, but his dad still does not stir. Finn frowns. "This was supposed to be a fun weekend," he mutters into the camera.

"I'm sorry," I tell him.

He picks up my copy of *Fumble*.

"It's just like in this book," he says, holding it up. "I'm so sick of trying to live up to his sports mania.

Feeling like I'm not *man* enough because I don't care about the Rams. What kind of forty-seven-year-old locks themselves in a room when their team loses . . . and doesn't come out for the entire weekend!?"

As Finn talks, I see the door behind him opening. His dad's awake! He's coming out! I try to wave and get Finn's attention, but he continues spilling his guts.

"Someone can come in here and kidnap me, he'll never know. He'll literally be the first person in the world to lose his son because he was too upset over a football game! A football game that has nothing to do with him! It's not like he's *on* the team! Maybe he thinks he is, but I have news for him – he's *not*! It's so embarrassing!"

"Who are you calling embarrassing?" Finn's dad asks, red-faced.

Finn turns around and faces his dad.

"You, Dad!" Finn says. "Did you know I had nothing to eat last night? You were passed out cold, and I didn't know what to do. I wanted to go downstairs, but I didn't want to leave you."

"Why didn't you just order room service?" Finn's

dad asks.

"I finally did! I was so mad I ordered the truffle pizza. I thought it was going to be a normal pizza, but it had flakes of *feet* on it – it smelled so bad!" Finn blurts out, pointing to a greasy uneaten pizza on a silver tray on the coffee table.

I shudder. *Feet pizza?* Okay, that sounds even worse than my orange pizza.

Finn's dad's face burns as he replies sarcastically, "Oh, I'm so sorry you had to eat truffle pizza in a suite at the Bellagio. How mortifying."

Finn blinks the hurt from his eyes as he hugs *Fumble*. He fires back at his dad, "Yeah, it *was* mortifying. Because I thought this was gonna be *our* weekend. That's why I came! Not to see the Rams!"

"You think that's lost on me?" Finn's dad shouts. "I know you have zero interest in the game – you never have!"

Finn takes in his dad's disappointment.

"You know how lonely that feels? To have your boy be the *only* boy who doesn't like sports?"

Finn shakes his head. "I'm sick of you putting your toxic masculinity expectations on me!"

"Toxic masculinity?" Finn's dad laughs. "That's

rich. Where'd you get that? From this?"

He grabs *Fumble* from Finn's hand. To our horror, he drops it on top of the greasy feet pizza.

"THAT'S A LIBRABY BOOK!" I scream.

Tense seconds go by. Neither of them says anything.

Finally, Finn whispers, "Please, can I have my book back?"

Finn holds out a trembling hand. For a hopeful second, I think Finn's dad will realise the error of his ways and break down. He will walk over and hug Finn and tell him he's so sorry. That Finn's enough, just the way he is. I hold my breath waiting for this pivotal scene, drawing it in my head.

But the seconds tick by and Finn's dad does not pick up the book.

Instead, he mutters, "Clean up this mess. This is the last time I'm taking you to Las Vegas."

Chapter 65

I race toward campus looking for Finn the next day. But he's not in the library, nor is he in class.

"You looking for Finn?" Mrs. Carter asks. "His Mum just emailed – he's out sick."

All morning I stare at his empty desk next to mine.

At recess, I send him three messages on my Chromebook. But he doesn't reply to any of them. I finally slip a piece of paper into his desk as I'm walking out to Mrs. Ortiz's class.

I wanted to give it to Finn in person. It's the graphic novel version of the weekend Finn *should* have had: Finn and Dad going to the M&M factory together, riding the Ferris wheel, and going to see the erupting volcano.

Just because he didn't get to do it doesn't mean he

doesn't deserve it. I hope he knows that.

*

Mrs. Ortiz reaches for a tissue as she double-checks my spelling on my graphic novel. I finally worked up the courage to show her the first thirty pages.

"It's exquisite!" she says.

I don't know what *exquisite* means, but the look on her face is pure joy.

"Oh, Lina, you've so perfectly captured all the emotions of going to a new country . . . and the guilt of leaving family behind," she says. "I love the mother, the sister, the bath bombs, even the cranky farmer!"

Her face falls serious.

"But I have to ask, the bathroom wall . . . ," she says tenderly. "Is that something that you experienced here at school?"

I nod slowly.

Mrs. Ortiz shakes her head, speechless. "I'm so sorry," she says, offering me a hug.

Wrapped in Mrs. Ortiz's warm arms, I think about how powerful it feels to have what I've lived through acknowledged and recognised, and no longer have to keep it all in and suffer all by myself. To open my door, just for a second, so the world can slide through.

"I will be having a word with the administration about that wall, you can be certain of that," she says. "Thank you for speaking up and writing this important, engrossing piece of art."

"Are there lot of spelling mistakes?" I ask her.

Mrs. Ortiz shakes her head and returns my draft to me with just a few minor corrections.

"You did a superb job," she says. "In fact . . . how do you feel about rejoining your class tomorrow? I think you're ready."

"Tomorrow?" I think about Jessica and immediately shrivel up into an eraser. "I'm not ready!"

But Mrs. Ortiz reaches out a warm hand. "Hey . . . it's okay," she says. "I was scared too, when I transitioned out of ELL. But think of it as the next chapter in a really good book. Don't you want to find out what happens?"

Well, I do really want to talk to Finn . . . if he's there tomorrow. And hear Mrs. Carter read *Flea Shop* out loud. I put my fingers to my lips. *But am I ready to talk to my whole class?*

"Your readers are waiting," Mrs. Ortiz says with a smile. "I know I am. You want to give it a try tomorrow?"

It fills me with gratitude that Mrs. O believes in me with all her heart. I think back to what I was like when I first came to her class. Mrs. Ortiz gave me so much more than just English. She gave me the confidence that I can make it in this country, if I just try hard.

Slowly, I nod.

Chapter 66

Finn finally messages me back later that day. Millie and Carla are out with Mum mailing off a big shipment of bath bombs.

Thanks for the drawing, he writes.

I put my mica paint down and type in the chat, confused. **How you get it?** I write. **You not at school today.**

My Mum came by to get all my homework. And she saw it. We ended up having a good talk about everything. And I feel a lot better now.

Oh good. What she say?

That that was not an appropriate way for Dad to respond.

How is your dad?

He's back at his place. But . . . he did order

me another copy of Fumble. So at least I'm not gonna get in trouble with Mrs. Hollins.

That's good! I was worried about having to tell Mrs. Hollins her beloved book now smells like feet pizza. **Guess what? I go back to regular class tomorrow.**

Great! Finn texts. **Just in time! We're reading the part in Flea Shop where Cat uses the antique letter opener to make a peanut butter sandwich. And then gets peanut butter all over her parents' mail! And has to lick it off!**

I burst out laughing. **I love that part.**

Me too. Hey Lina?

What?

You think it's weird that I still miss him? Finn asks. **Even though I'm still mad at him?**

No, I type. I think of my own years of being furious at my parents for leaving me behind yet missing them so much it hurt. Two sides of a bath bomb, I tell Finn.

😆, Finn says.

I smile.

Thanks for being there this weekend. Not there there, but you know. On the phone.

See you at school tomorrow? I ask.

I close my Chromebook. I get up and am walking to the living room to get more bath bombs, when suddenly I hear loud, impatient pounding on the door.

Instead of Mum, Carla, and my sister, I find a tall, burly, gum-chewing man with a thick beard, in a tan jacket and sunglasses, standing in our doorway.

"Where's your mother?" he asks.

"Mailing something," I say to him. "Who are you?"

"I'm the landlord, Alvin Beezley," he says. Walking inside, he nearly squishes a row of bath bombs with his big shoes.

I'm wondering whether to call Mum, when she walks through the courtyard with Millie and Carla. "What can I help you with?" Mum asks.

"Just came by to remind you, your back rent's due in less than three weeks," Mr. Beezley says.

"I know, we working as hard as we can!" Mum tells Mr. Beezley. She tells him about our bath bomb business, showing him the care and attention and toys we're putting in each of our products. "We're on track to coming up with the last thousand dollars," Mum says.

"It's thirty-seven hundred dollars, not a thousand dollars," Mr. Beezley reminds her.

"I know, but we figure with security deposit —"

"Wait a minute, you can't use the security deposit to pay for your back rent," Mr. Beezley says.

"Why not?" she asks.

"Because! The security deposit's for damages . . . and from the looks of this place, you're going to need it!" Mr. Beezley says, pointing to the blemish on the carpet from all the mica powder. "Look at this place! The stains on my carpet!"

The blood drains from Mum's face. She drops to the floor, scrubbing the carpet with her fingers. "No stain! I don't see any stain!"

But the harder she digs her nails into the carpet, the more she rubs in the powder.

Frantically, she begs Mrs. Beezley, "Please. You got to count the security deposit. Without it, we not going to make it! My husband and I already try everything —"

"Save your excuses. The next time I'm here, you better have all thirty-seven hundred dollars. Or y'all be looking at the tent city over by the landfill."

I suck in a breath, thinking of all the women and

children kneeling outside the tents. Mr. Beezley gives me and my sister a long hard look as he crushes three more bath bombs on his way out.

*

Mum scrunches into a ball so tight after he leaves, she practically looks mouldable.

"We're not going to make it," she mutters in a trance, shaking her head. "It's too much money. It's impossible!"

Millie and I try to zap her out of it. "Course we can!"

"Not without the security deposit! How are we going to come up with twenty-two hundred dollars in three weeks?" She rocks her body. It hurts me so much to see her this way.

Mum grabs for her phone. "We should leave now . . . before he starts the eviction process."

"Now??" I practically jump in horror.

"Where would we go?" Millie asks.

"Maybe you can stay with us . . . in the tiny home!" Carla suggests. "Millie and Lina and I could share a bed."

Even as she says this, her voice drifts. It'd be an impossible squeeze.

"We can still make it work," I say to Mum. "If we just sell enough bath bombs —"

Carla starts madly mixing the ingredients.

But Mum shakes her head firmly. "I thought we were just a thousand dollars away from the goal. Now we're twenty-two hundred dollars away from the goal. It's humanly *impossible* for us to make that many bath bombs in three weeks! We can't."

I kneel down beside her. "But, Mum! What about the first Asian American bath line at Target?" I remind her. "You can't give up on your dream that easy!"

"It's a fool's errand!" Mum says. "It's just too hard!"

Hearing her say this stirs something in me. I want to shake her. Tears spill out of my eyes as I tell her what I've been keeping bottled up inside. "You know what's too hard?" I say in Chinese. "Staying in China while all you guys were here. Seeing Millie grow up with you guys, while I waited by the mailbox!

Putting on my best dress to take pictures, hoping you'd send for me . . ." My voice breaks slightly. "*That's* too hard. But I kept fighting and believing. And that's what you have to do too, Mama, if you want your dream. You have to be willing to do everything for it. Like me, coming here."

Mum takes in my words, shocked, the tears gushing down her cheeks. "Oh, honey . . ."

Millie runs toward us with her baking powder hands. The three of us hug in a cloud of baking powder dust.

"I'm so sorry," Mum says. I feel Mum's wet apology in my hair and all I can do is nod, buoyed by the hope that finally . . . she knows.

Dabbing her eyes, Mum promises not to give up on her dream. Not to give up on our home.

It feels so good to hear Mum say these words. Through the blur of my tears, I reach over to her, and I take a chance. "I love you, Mama," I say shyly.

The words feel right. Not fake on my tongue, or hollow like the hallway walls.

"I love you too," she says back.

Her love coats my empty tummy as I smile back at her.

Chapter 67

I take a deep breath before walking into class the next day. Today is the first day of my new chapter.

A chapter I will rock!

I will pull my invisible thread out and toss it once and for all by speaking in class! And I will feel proud, because I belong there!

I see Finn sitting at our desk, waving me over. I smile.

"Hey!" he says. I take a seat. He slides over a piece of paper. I open it up carefully. It's a drawing of him sitting in front of the Bellagio fountain, eating a pizza with a giant foot on top and reading. I laugh.

Mrs. Carter clears her throat softly at us, giving us a look to put our doodles away.

"Welcome back, Finn, and, Lina, I'm so glad

you can join us," Mrs. Carter says. "I think we're all dying to find out exactly what happens to Cat. Just to refresh your memory, she's just experienced something very unpleasant at school. Where did this unkindness take place?"

I catch Jessica rolling her eyes behind me. But a few hands wave wildly from the back.

Mrs. Carter calls on Eleanor.

"On the PE field! Natasha was mad at Cat because she missed a baseball catch, yelling at her to open her eyes bigger! Then when the PE teacher wasn't looking, she pulled her eyes up at Cat!"

"Come *on*," Jessica protests. "She could have been trying to get the sweat out of her eyes! It was like a hundred degrees!"

My whole class starts talking all at once.

"That's impossible! She was clearly pulling her eyes! Look at the panel!" Priscilla objects.

"*And* she yelled at Cat to open her eyes bigger – that's racism!" Bobby says.

As more and more classmates weigh in, Jessica doubles down. "They were in the *middle of a game!* You think Natasha really has time to be racist when they're tied and down to the last inning?"

Finn turns to Jessica, furious. "So Cat couldn't have possibly gotten hurt, because they're *tied*???"

Jessica starts panicking. "Look at that field – it's humongous! Look at where Cat's standing and where Natasha's standing. Is it possible that Cat *thought* she saw something, but actually it was totally innocent?"

I feel the fire building inside me. A thousand degrees of hot, burning questions bubble like lava, like *Is what you wrote about me on the bathroom wall "totally innocent"?*

But my slow tongue cannot compete with my classmates' much faster ones.

"She used both hands, though! Who gets sweat out of *both* eyes with both hands at the same time?" someone asks.

"And what does time have to do with it? It's not like people aren't racist because they have a train to catch!" Evan says.

"I'm glad you're all fired up," Mrs. Carter says. "This is exactly why I want you to read books – to see the world through someone else's eyes. I can tell you as a Black person, I have had moments just like this . . . where I've wondered, did this really happen? *How* could this happen to me? It's so easy to brush these experiences under the rug. But I am so proud of Catherine Wang for shedding light on them, so that we all learn and grow. Sometimes an experience that seems impossible to us is actually the lived experience of many other people. And by understanding that, we *all* become more empathic human beings."

I look around the classroom. Priscilla and Eleanor are eagerly nodding. Many of my classmates are already reading on, too deeply engrossed by the story to respond. Preston and Nate, Finn's bros, are fighting over who gets to hold the book.

"All right, then let's begin. Chapter seventeen . . . ," Mrs. Carter says.

As Mrs. Carter reads in her smooth, soothing voice, I settle in. I can feel the sighs of Jessica from behind me. And while it irritates me that she actually tried to *dispute* that Cat got made fun of by her classmates, it surprised me just as much that so many of my classmates jumped to Cat's defense!

Mrs. Ortiz was right. You never know until you turn the page. And my new chapter, so far, has me on the edge of my seat.

Chapter 68

Mum's late picking us up. Millie tells me her good news as we wait.

"I made a new friend!" she says. "Her name is Mallory! She just moved here from New York City and guess what? She likes to dance too!"

Millie dances out the last part, moving her hips as she says "dance too."

"That's great!" I exclaim. "Did you show your dolphin clock-pow?"

Millie shakes her head, blushing.

"She's from New York City. She's not gonna want to do dolphin."

"I don't know you'd be surprised!" I encourage my sister. I think back to language arts this morning. All this time, I was so sure everyone in my class was gleefully contributing to the bathroom wall about me. But after this morning, I don't think so.

Mum's car finally pulls up.

"Guess what I did this morning? I wrote a business plan!" Mum says.

"Cool!" I say, jumping into the car. "What's that?"

Mum hands me and Millie the papers as she drives. The title reads **JML BATH BOMBS: SEEKING PARTNERS FOR A ONE-OF-A-KIND PRODUCT THAT TRANSPORTS YOU AS YOU RELAX.** In her plan, Mum's listed all of our products, the profit margin, and the levels for investment and potential profit return.

Leave it to Mum to put her Imagineer boss hat on and turbo this side hustle!

"Wow, Mum, this is fantastic!" I say.

"I thought about what you said. You're right! I'm not giving up until I've talked to every toy shop in Winfield and presented them with my plan. If just one of them wants to be our partner, we'll make our goal!"

I clap my hands, so game for this plan.

"In that case, you're going to need a few more graphics," I tell Mum with a smile.

"*And* a cool TikTok," Millie adds with a grin.

*

Back at the apartment, while Millie puts together the fun TikTok, I draw cute graphics for the plan.

I sketch smiling kids covered in foam, and frothy puppies swimming in bathtubs. I draw out our long line of expanding products – bath bombs of all shapes and sizes, custom bombs with messages, bombs with toys and surprises!

Finally, I work on an illustration of Mum – a woman who came over from China, full of hopes and dreams, who despite all the hardships and challenges refuses to imagine anything less than what she and her daughters deserve.

When I show Mum the illustration, she pulls me in for a hug. Seeing the look of pride stretch across her warrior face . . . I know it's worth coming all the way across the world for.

"Thank you for seeing your mama," Mum says.

As she kisses me on the top of my forehead, we make a plan to start distributing the business plans tomorrow!

Chapter 69

At school the next day, I wriggle impatiently in my seat. I can't wait to go from store to store after school today, telling folks about the plan. Maybe Mum's business will grow into a *real* store — just like Cat's in *Flea Shop*!

As Mrs. Carter reaches for her copy, my classmates and I sit eagerly at the edge of our seats. But Mrs. Carter barely gets through the first sentence when our classroom door flies open.

In walks Mrs. Scott, Jessica's Mum, with Principal Bennett.

"Can we have a word with you?" Mrs. Scott asks Mrs. Carter.

Uh-oh. The stern tone of Jessica's Mum's voice lets us know Mrs. Carter's in trouble. I wonder if it has anything to do with our little "debate" in class yesterday.

Mrs. Carter looks just as puzzled. "Sure," she says, putting down her copy of the book. She smooths out her red flowerprint dress and tells us to read silently until she's back.

But no one is reading. We all turn to Jessica, who shrugs like she doesn't know what's up but sits there looking all smug. Oh, she totally knows. We move our chairs closer to the open windows, craning our necks to listen.

"I heard about what happened yesterday," Mrs. Scott says to Mrs. Carter. "That was humiliating for Jessica, and completely unacceptable."

"I'm sorry, what's unacceptable?" Mrs. Carter asks.

"For her to get singled out and *piled on* like that. She was distraught when she came home. Did you know that she refused to come out of her room — not for SSAT class? Not even for a trip to Sephora?"

"I don't know what to say . . . ," Mrs. Carter says, looking over at Principal Bennett, who stands next to Mrs. Scott, looking very unhappy to have to be there. But standing silently by. "Why would you pick such a divisive book in the first place?" Jessica's

Mum asks.

"Divisive?" Mrs. Carter's eyebrows jump. "It's a book about a Chinese American girl who runs a flea market shop. I'm sorry . . . what's divisive about that?"

Principal Bennett steps in. "Mrs. Scott has . . . concerns. About the relevance of this text to our students."

"Can't you see? It's not relatable. It's not appropriate!" Jessica's Mum cries.

My cheeks roast, hearing that. *Flea Shop* is the most relatable thing I've ever read. As for appropriate, if she thinks *Flea Shop*'s not appropriate, I hate to think of what she thinks about *my life*.

"Jacob, can we talk about this in private some other time?" Mrs. Carter asks, appealing to Principal Bennett. "I have a class to teach."

"No, we will talk about it right here, right now," Mrs. Scott insists. "Because I won't have my daughter exposed to another minute of that isolating trash."

"Isolating trash? I have never seen kids more excited about a book before! They are riveted. They come to school every day begging to know what happens next. I have kids in the class who want to take the book home –"

"And do I need to remind you *how* it is you have copies for every kid in the class?" Mrs. Scott cuts in, pointing a finger at our class. "That didn't just happen. *I* made that happen. I expected you to pick a book like *Stuart Little* or *Huckleberry Finn*, not some *immigrant* book!"

"Well, immigration happens to be a part of the Common Core. And our nation," Mrs. Carter says flatly.

Finn lets out a hoot next to me. *Go, Mrs. Carter!* he mouths. I exchange a small smile with him, even as the worry mounts.

"That's up to me to teach my kids, as their parent. It's not the school's place to teach immigration," Mrs. Scott reasons. "I want you to stop the read-aloud and hand back all your copies of *Flea Shop*."

"That's not the way things work –" Mrs. Carter starts to say.

But Principal Bennett says with a heavy sigh, "Marion, I'm so sorry. But until there's a review on this book, we have to pause the read-aloud."

There's a collective gasp from inside our class as we bang on our desks in protest.

"WHAT!?" we shriek.

"That's ridiculous!" Finn says.

Mrs. Carter pleads with Principal Bennett. "Can't I at least get through the chapter? The kids are dying to find out what happens to Cat, who, by the way, is sitting in her principal's office, telling him about something unkind that happened to her. Hoping he'll do the right thing."

She holds Principal Bennett's gaze until he looks away.

"I'm afraid my hands are tied," he finally says.

I stare at his perfectly untied hands, fighting the tears in my eyes.

Chapter 70

We fly into the library later during lunch. "They can't just do that!" Finn roars, begging Mrs. Hollins with his eyes. "They can't just *ban* a reading and yank the books away! Midsentence!"

I dig my nails into my palms. It's enraging, what just happened. After Mrs. Carter walked back inside, she collected our books, promising each and every one of us that this wasn't over. Still, the books were gone.

I shake my head, disturbed on so many levels. As a student librarian. As an Asian American. As a new immigrant, whose life mirrors those of the characters Mrs. Scott called "isolating trash."

"I am so sorry. I'll tell you the same thing I told Mrs. Carter when she emailed me this morning –

345

it's unacceptable," Mrs. Hollins says, shaking with just as much fury.

Mrs. Hollins tells us that this kind of book banning has been happening in schools all over the nation, though she never expected it would happen at Winfield.

"It's flat-out censorship. And the only way to stop it is to speak up!"

"But how? Where?" Finn asks.

"Come to the school board meeting," Mrs. Hollins says. "There's going to be an emergency one in a few days. Tell them how much you love this book. They'll want to hear from the kids – the community. Tell them why this matters."

Finn nods, fired up. But I swallow hard. *Me? Speak at a board meeting?*

I'm too chicken to even speak up in class. I still haven't uttered a single word to the rest of my classmates since the first day of school. And we all know how *that* turned out.

"It's going to take *every single one of us* to protect our freedom to read," Mrs. Hollins says.

As Mrs. Hollins hands me her own personal copy of *Flea Shop*, I realise she's doing this for me. To protect *my* right to see myself in books.

A girl whose life is "not relatable."

Whose very presence is "divisive."

But yet a girl who has every right to read, same as everyone else, and to speak without an invisible thread stitched across half her lips.

I think of the fire in my mother's warrior eyes. And what she once reminded me.

You're the daughter of first-generation immigrants. Your blood is made of iron will and determination. Your backbone is built from the sacrifices and impossible decisions of all those who walked before you.

And I promise Mrs. Hollins I will show up at the meeting.

Chapter 71

"You can't show up at the board meeting," Mum says when I tell her what happened later that day. Millie's in our room stapling business plans. Mum had gone to FedEx to print them all out on nice paper.

"Why not?" I ask.

"First of all, we're not even supposed to be at the school – we don't live in Winfield! We just permitted in," Mum says.

"But the school needs me!" I protest. "Mrs. Hollins and Mrs. Carter and Mrs. Ortiz! And all the other kids who want to find out what happens!"

"And what's everyone else in the town going to think?" Mum asks. She picks up one of the business plans and points to the papers. "We're trying to get businesses to invest in our plan . . . Is this the best time to be making trouble?"

The question temporarily knocks me off my axis. I think of Lao Lao and the warning she gave me every morning – *watch your words, lest they label you a bad apple.* But I shake my head firmly at Mum.

"We're not making trouble!" I tell her.

Still, Mum chews her nail. "People will talk. These school board meetings are a big deal in a small town like Winfield. Everyone goes and then talks about it on Facebook! They take sides. I just don't want us to get caught up in the middle of this culture war, when we have so much on the line."

I fall quiet. I know Mum's thinking about our green cards. How we can't afford to rock the boat with anyone in Winfield. On the other hand, I know if I don't at least *show up*, that boat's never going to include someone like me again. I must look pretty sad, because Mum puts down her business plans.

"Are you *sure* you want to do this?" she asks with a sigh.

I nod. "Mum, you told me never to let anyone put a cap on my imagination."

Mum touches my cheek gently.

"Yes, baby, I did."

"Well, that's what they're trying to do here," I tell her. "Believe me, I don't really want to go either. It would be so much easier if I just stayed invisible." I take a deep breath. "But I don't want to be invisible *my whole life*. And that's what this board meeting is all about."

Mum takes a long, deep breath. Then, ever so slowly, she reaches for my hand. "Well, in that case You won't have to go alone."

*

For the next two days, while we go around pitching businesses in Winfield in the afternoons, I practice for my big board meeting at night.

Mum says it's going to be at the community center, which is this very nice clubhouse down by the lake. She says that each person who wants to speak will have two minutes. It's important to not dawdle because the two minutes will go by like *that*.

I do not believe the two minutes will go like that.

I believe the two minutes will be like two long years in space, trying to figure out how to land my spaceship safely back on Earth.

As I'm fretting over what to say, Millie appoints herself my stylist.

She picks out a white dress for me to wear. It's by far my nicest dress. I try it on, shocked it still fits.

"It looks great!" Millie says.

I gaze at my reflection in the mirror, my face falling slightly.

"What's wrong?" Millie asks.

"I wore this at Lao Ye's funeral," I say.

Millie starts digging inside the closet again. She shows me *her* funeral dress for Lao Ye. I stare at her black wrap dress.

"You guys had a funeral too?" I ask.

Millie nods.

"At the park. Mum put pictures on the grass," Millie says. "She cried her eyes out. Even the clouds were sad."

I'm so surprised to hear this. It fills me with so much peace that my family was able to pay their respects to Lao Ye, in their own way.

I hug my sister, running a hand through her silky hair.

"So do you like the dress? If you don't like it, I can find something else," Millie offers.

I shake my head. "No, it's perfect," I tell her. I gaze out the window, up at the clouds. I hope my grandfather is watching me from heaven.

I hope he'll give me the courage to use my voice tomorrow.

I remind myself that fear and courage are two sides of the same bath bomb.

This time tomorrow, I hope my courage side lathers.

Chapter 72

The community center is packed when Mum, Dad, Millie, and I arrive at 5 p.m. on Saturday. Thanks to Mrs. Hollins's emails, half of Winfield is at the meeting. I spot Finn right away, sitting with his Mum. He waves at me and gives me a thumbs-up sign.

I let out a small smile, then plunge my gaze to the floor when I spot Jessica and her parents. They are definitely *not* giving me a thumbs-up sign.

I follow my parents and Millie over to a row off by the side and sit under the frigid air-conditioning.

The school board chairperson, Dr. Dan Peters, calls the meeting to order.

"Good evening," Dr. Peters says. "Thank you for coming out to this special school board meeting. We're here to discuss the urgent issue of whether to allow the children of Winfield Elementary to keep reading a graphic novel called *Flea Shop*, in light of recent parent complaints. Now, Mrs. Hollins, will you give us a description of *Flea Shop*?"

"Certainly." Mrs. Hollins stands up. She walks to the front of the room and takes the mic. I watch as she unfolds a small piece of paper and reads the description of *Flea Shop*. "Published in 2018, *Flea Shop* follows Cat Wang, a ten-year-old immigrant girl, who helps her parents manage a flea market shop in the town of Anaheim, California. It's about Cat's experiences in the shop, as well as at school, as she navigates being a new kid in a new country."

"Thank you, Mrs. Hollins."

"Oh, and I might add, it's based on the real *lived* experience of the author, a Chinese American immigrant."

"Well noted. Will one of the parents who take issue with this book please let us understand where you're coming from with your objection?"

Jessica's Mum stands and walks over to the mic. "Thank you. I'm Jessica Scott, a longtime advocate of literacy and parent of two children in this school. Anyone who knows me knows how much I love books. I am a staunch believer in access to books, which is why I give so generously, year after year, to make sure our schools can afford books for all our kids. But this book . . . this book is simply not for this community."

"Can you elaborate?"

"There are scenes in here where Cat is convinced some of her classmates treat her differently because she's a person of colour."

They do treat her differently, I want to say, *literally, by mocking her right in front of her face.*

"Now, I understand that that may be her interpretation. But that's not *my* interpretation of the world. As a parent, I encourage my kids not to see colour. When I look at the world, I see people. Experiences. Tastes. Interests. Places you like to go on vacation. I see *individuals*. And that's the world view I want my kids to have. Bottom line, that's what this is about. It's about my right, as a parent, to have a say in the world view that my kids get taught."

Mrs. Scott thanks the board. As she walks back to her seat, I see many parents nodding. But just as many frowning. The next speaker up is Mrs. Carter.

"Unlike Mrs. Scott, I view my job as not to push

a specific world view, but to prepare children for the future. The future is made up of people from all walks of life, all ethnicities, and, yes, all different colours." Mrs. Carter glances at Mrs. Scott. "This is a fact. We need simply to go to the Census Bureau to see this fact. Books like *Flea Shop* are so incredibly valuable because they allow children to step into the shoes of another person from a different culture and understand what they're going through. I think of reading as giving kids a toolbox for the future."

She turns to face all the people in the audience. "So I ask all of you in this room, do you want your children to have as many varied and powerful tools in their future toolbox as they can . . . or to just give them one wrench?"

When Mrs. Carter puts it like that, the room falls so quiet, you could hear a hairpin drop. Sometimes the truth is so powerful, it takes up all the air in the room.

Then a hand raises. I look over and to my surprise, it's Carla's Mum. She told us she was working today, so I didn't think she was going to come. But as Carla waves at me from the side of the room and her Mum makes her way over to the mic, I lean all the way forward.

"Good evening. I am not a parent in the school district. I am a homeschooling Mum. I chose to homeschool my daughter because I thought I had all the tools. But recently, I realised . . . there are some tools I can't give her, because I don't know that she needs them . . . until she does. Conversations we can't have, because neither of us can find the words. Until we read them. Books are an important bridge."

She takes a long, deep breath and looks over at Mrs. Scott. "Believe me, I know how you feel. I know the fear of being powerless in a world you can't control. A world you don't, at times, understand." Mrs. Muñoz pauses. "Three years ago, I lost my husband. For the last three years, I've been running. I thought that by avoiding certain hard topics with my daughter, I was shielding her. Now I realise it takes courage to admit I don't have all the answers – none of us do. But if I'm afraid to have the conversations, if I'm afraid to read a children's book . . . what possible hope do I have of giving her the courage to deal with life?"

A few parents stand up and clap, including Finn's Mum. As Carla's Mum goes back to her seat, I spy a

Rams baseball hat moving across the opposite aisle. For a second, I think it's Finn, but the man is much taller. I realise it's his dad!

Finn and I exchange a worried glance as his dad takes the mic.

"Hi, I'm Joe Wright, Finn's dad. I just wanted to add my two cents in here. Growing up, I didn't read a lot of books. I played football instead, and I'm proud to have gotten a full scholarship to USC for sports, which allowed me to get out of Inglewood. It changed my life. But my son there . . . Finn . . . he loves books. Recently, we were in Vegas, and he brought this book *Fumble* to the Rams game – they lost, unfortunately –"

There's a collective wave of sighs and headshaking at this unfortunate result.

"Not a fun weekend. I took it pretty hard, and Finn was frustrated with me. We got into an argument and – I'm not proud of this, but – I threw his book *Fumble* in the pizza."

I look over at Finn, shrinking in his seat. Nate and Preston are deeply engrossed, as is Jessica's dad, who's nodding so furiously, his neck's gotta hurt.

"When your kid disagrees with the way you see

the world, nothing hurts more. That's God's honest truth. You feel like you've failed as a parent – how did I not raise someone who gets me? What did I do wrong?"

Finn's dad takes a long breath.

"The answer is, nothing. Because kids are not clones. Do I wish that my son and I could talk our heads off about football all day long? Absolutely," he admits. Then a small smile forms. "But I also raised a reader. When I got home, you know what I did? I ordered a new copy of *Fumble* to replace his copy that I threw in the pizza – *and* I ordered myself a copy. And you know what? I kinda like the kid in the story. The kid can't play football to save his life, but he's funny. And he cares about his family. And I do too."

Finn's Mum smiles. I can see Finn blinking furiously under his glasses – he's so moved.

"So I thank you, his school, for having books like *Fumble* and *Flea Shop* on your shelves. Thank you for making this place *bigger*. So that the kids who go here . . . don't just get exposed to one tiny slice of life. And the adults don't either."

Finn jumps up and claps for his dad, as do I.

Fired up by Finn's dad's speech, I reach for my own notes scribbled on a piece of paper. Mum gives my hand a squeeze. I stand up slowly and make my way over to the mic as my classmates' jaws drop.

Whispers engulf the room as people gossip.

Who's she?

Isn't she the new girl?

I thought she doesn't speak English. What's she going to say?

My heart thumps in my chest as I grab the mic. Staring out at so many strangers, each and every one of whom speaks English better than me, I feel my knees wobble. But adrenaline pushes me forward as I remind myself that I have worked too hard and waited too long for this moment.

And I rip out my invisible thread.

Chapter 73

"Hi. I am Lina," I tell the school board members. "I go to fifth year at Winfield Elementary School. This my first year in America."

I look over at Finn, who gives me two thumbs up – *keep going!!!*

"I used think America is like *Simpsons*," I start to say. "But then I arrive, and it is very different than *Simpsons*. My parents work a lot harder than Homer and Marge."

I get a big laugh from the audience. My heart skips a beat. They think I'm funny!

"And my sister and I are not like Bart or Lisa. Instead, we worry many things, like will Mum sell enough bath bomb for rent? Will Dad come home for dinner instead of work, work, work? Will we see our grandmother again?" I glance at the audience and see a few people with their hand over their heart.

Looking down at my notes, I swallow hard.

"Will the other girls stop writing about me on bathroom wall?" I ask in my timid voice. I keep my gaze steady on the board members, not daring to peek over at Jessica. Not even as the room erupts in whispers and the temperature climbs. I push on with my speech.

"I don't know answers. But I know I am not alone in these questions. Cat Wang also have same questions. She make me feel less alone," I tell the board. "This why I need this book. Because my life more like *Flea Shop* than *Simpsons*. For me, this book is mirror. For other kids, it is sliding door." I turn to the audience. "A door to see real life."

With a trembling hand, I put the mic back.

An amazing thing happens when I turn around. I see Mum and Dad standing up for me, clapping wildly. Dad snaps a pic of me on his phone. He looks like he's about to burst into tears. One by one, my classmates start standing up too! The claps sweep across the room, like an ocean wave. My sister does a little dolphin from her seat, and I giggle.

I look over at Mrs. Hollins, clapping so thunderously loud, it makes my student librarian heart swell. Mrs. Ortiz makes a heart gesture with her hands and cheers for me from her seat as Mrs. Carter dabs her eyes.

I beam back at all the love and support in the room. I try to understand what this feeling is pounding in my heart. That's when I realise it's the feeling of finally being seen. Never in my entire life have I truly felt it before, until now.

"Thank you for your comments," Dr. Peters says. "We will take some time to consider all these meaningful and important testimonies as we decide on this matter. Thank you for your time this evening, and, Lina, I hope you know . . ."

I turn around.

"We are honored to have you in our school," he says. "Thank you for speaking up."

My throat chokes with emotion as I nod back.

Chapter 74

Mum sweeps me into her arms and hugs me tight when we get home. We're standing outside Rosa's taco truck, getting celebratory tacos, while Dad and Millie run to the store to get some Fanta.

"I'm so proud of you!" Mum says.

I breathe in her pride, smiling.

"Were you nervous? How did you feel?"

I tell Mum, "I felt firebomb proud!"

"Firebomb proud? We're going to have to name a bath bomb after that!" Mum grins.

Rosa says it'll be about ten minutes for all our tacos, and Mum and I go to wait by the stairs.

"You think they're going to allow it?" I ask Mum anxiously. "*Flea Shop*?"

"I hope so," Mum says, tucking a strand of my hair

behind my ear. "After all those powerful testimonies, including yours. I'm so glad you used your voice."

"Me too." It felt amazing to finally chuck my invisible thread.

Under the canopy of stars, Mum asks, "Why didn't you tell me about the bathroom stall at school?"

I look down and shrug.

"Because it was embarrassing," I whisper. Biting my lip, I finally muster the courage to tell Mum the words etched on the bathroom wall and on the wall of my heart.

Mum puts her arms around me. "I'm so sorry. You should have told me."

"It's okay – at least I can use the bathroom in the library," I quickly say. As I describe Mrs. Hollins's lovely staff bathroom, Mum shakes her head.

"That's not the point . . . I'm your mama," Mum says. She gently bumps her shoulder into mine. "You know what that means?" Her eyes twinkle. I shake my head. "It means we should always be able to talk. Not just about the highlights, but about the things that make your stomach squeeze tight."

I look down at my own tummy, all wound up, stiffer than a pinecone. Well, in that case . . .

"Mum?" I ask. "Why'd you leave me in China?"

Mum doesn't say anything for a long time. "I wanted things to be perfect here before I sent for you," she finally whispers.

"Perfect?" I shake my head, my lips quivering. "You think China was perfect?" I tell my Mum what my classmates back home called me. Names much worse than what's written on the bathroom wall. "I don't need perfect. I need *you*."

Mum's eyes flood with tears. "Oh, sweetie, I know. And it broke my heart every day, knowing I left my baby on the other side of the world." She hides her face in her hands. "But I wanted one of my daughters to know me as Qian, who didn't have to worry about the roof over their heads. Who could give you a stable home . . . a stable life."

"But then why'd you bring Millie?" I ask.

"Millie was two when she left. She has nothing to compare this life to. But you . . . you'd know to compare. To miss and want all the things," Mum says. "I didn't want to fail you. And it racked me with guilt."

"Is that why there aren't any pictures of me on the wall?" I ask gently.

Mum nods. I finally understand . . . all this time, Mum's been in her own never-ending waiting room of guilt.

I put my arms around Mama, and I hold her.

"I'm so sorry," Mum says. "For not being a better mother, for not being a better daughter, for missing Lao Ye's funeral . . . all of it. But I was *trying*. You have to believe me."

I reach for her hands and give her an important spelling lesson under the velvet sky.

"I used to feel guilty too," I tell Mum. "But then I learned that *guilt* is spelled with an *i*. And that *I* is just as important."

Mum dabs her tears and kisses my forehead. I snuggle up against her sweatshirt and we both gaze up at the stars, my hand warm in Mum's.

Chapter 75

At school on Monday, I get a hero's welcome. I spot at least five kids carrying around *Flea Shop*. They must have bought it at the bookstore in town. That's the thing about banning books – it only makes kids more curious.

Principal Bennett sees me walking to class and waves at me. In his arms he's carrying fifteen copies of *Flea Shop*. I rush over to help him.

"The school board voted last night to allow the read-aloud!" he says to me.

I almost drop the books when I hear him. *Is he serious??*

"They were very moved by your speech," he says. "Thank you, Lina, for speaking up. And I just want to let you know, the maintenance team is repainting the bathroom walls as we speak. If you see anything like that ever again, please let me know."

I tell him I will.

My classmates are overjoyed to hear the news that we can keep doing our read-aloud. Finn high-fives me, telling me I kicked butt on Saturday. Mrs. Carter begins our language arts lesson by writing a word up on the board.

FReadom

"Does anyone know what this means?" she asks, underlining the word *Read* in *FReadom*.

"Does it have to do with freedom?" Bobby guesses.

"It certainly does."

"But, Mrs. Carter, that's misspelled!" Eleanor says, raising her hand.

Mrs. Carter chuckles and tells us with a wink, "Sometimes we can bend spelling rules to make new words. That's what's great about this country – it's constantly a work in progress. You know what that means?" she asks us.

We shake our heads.

"It means we have the capacity to reflect. And adapt. And that our freedom is only as strong as our people. If we care about our right to read, we have to actively protect it. You've seen how easily books can get challenged. But you've also seen what happens when you speak up." Mrs. Carter smiles. "I want to thank every single person who showed up at the school board meeting on Saturday, most of all Lina."

She leads my classmates in another round of applause. I sneak a glance at Jessica, who doesn't clap or say a word. She just sits at her desk drawing ice cubes. Maybe she's working on a new pizza topping.

"And now, without further ado, let's continue with our read-aloud!" Mrs. Carter says.

"Woot! Woot!" Finn calls out.

The whole class cheers.

*

Mum picks me and Millie up after school. We climb in next to the stack of business plans, ready to hit up the next batch of stores, but Mum turns to us excitedly.

"Guess what?" she asks. "I have good news!"

"Me too!" I tell her breathlessly about *Flea Shop* getting un-banned. "And we got to keep reading and guess what? Five people wanted to sit next to me at lunch!"

"So where'd you sit?" Mum asks.

"I went to the library, as usual. I *am* still the student librarian," I say proudly.

Millie jumps in.

"Guess who told me you're pretty cool for what you said at the board meeting?" she asks.

"Hazel?" I ask.

"No! Mallory!" she says. "*And* she saw me dolphining at the meeting – she thought *that* was awesome too!"

I laugh.

"Of course it is! And she's not the only one who heard Lina's speech," Mum says. "This morning, I got a call from Cindy's Ice Cream. They'd *love* to partner with us. They're willing to give us an initial investment of . . . you ready? A WHOPPING three thousand dollars!"

Millie and I let out a scream.

"I don't get it! They're an ice cream store!" I add.

"They love our concept. And *if* we can somehow make the bath bombs smell like their ice cream, they think it'll be a win-win!"

I giggle. "I know just the girl who can help us!" I tell Mum.

Carla's going to lose her mind!

As Mum steps on the gas and takes a sharp right for the motorway, I ask, "Wait, where are we going? Pete's is that way!" "We're going to stop to see a lawyer first," she says. "Now that we're getting serious investors on board, we'll want to form a real company! Plus, I want to know exactly where we stand with our green card application. I don't ever want you girls to have to feel invisible again."

As Mum drives toward Los Angeles, my sister and I squeeze our hands together, praying to the green card gods.

Chapter 76

Sitting in the lawyer's office in downtown LA, I sketch Mum in my head while she talks to Mr. Thurman, her eyes animated and hopeful as she tells him all about her new business and her plans.

"That sounds wonderful," Mr. Thurman says. "I'll just need some basic information from you to get started with forming a company. I'll need two forms of government ID to start."

Mum starts pulling out her driver's license and passport. She tells Mr. Thurman, "We're getting our green card any moment. My husband's employer, Pete, applied for us two years ago."

"Oh, I'd be happy to help you check on the status of that," Mr. Thurman offers. "We also do a lot of work in immigration law."

Mum glances at us and nods eagerly. "Yes. We'd love to check on the status. Anything we can do to hurry the process up?"

"What did you say your Social Security number was?" he asks, punching his computer keys.

Mum tells him both hers and Dad's.

He tries one, then the other. Both times, he frowns. "Neither is showing up," he says. "But let me just make sure –"

He picks up the phone. Mum reaches for my hand as we wait, squeezing it so tight, my knuckles become white.

Mr. Thurman exchanges words with someone, and waits. Then he asks, "Are you sure?" and hangs up.

"I'm sorry," he says. "It doesn't appear that there's an application in progress for you. Did your husband's employer ever ask him to sign anything?"

Mum says she doesn't know. She doesn't think so. She reaches for her phone, her eyes terror-struck, like she's just seen a ghost.

"You'd better come home," she says to Dad when he answers. "We've got a problem."

*

Dad shakes his head in the car on our way over to Pete's. When he got home, he couldn't believe what the lawyer had told us. "There's gotta be a mistake," he says. "I specifically remember having long discussions with Pete about the application process and how it's going to go. I even *drove* him to his lawyer's!"

"But did you ever sign anything?" Mum asks.

Dad takes a long pause. Millie and I look at each other. *I'm guessing that's a no.*

"I thought maybe his lawyer was taking care of it? Maybe we don't need to sign until the end? I don't know how these things work!"

"Unbelievable," Mum says, eyeing the farmhouse as we park.

She jumps out of the car. Dad runs after her, saying, "Let me handle this. *I'll* talk to him."

"Why are you still protecting him?" Mum erupts at Dad. "Do you know what it feels like to walk to the mailbox every day, for *years*, hoping today's the day I'll get a letter from the INS? Today's the day I'll finally be able to stop walking on eggshells? Know that I'm *safe*, that they can't kick me out? Stop *imagining* my dreams and start pursuing them?"

Her voice shakes.

Dad tries to calm Mum down, but Mum won't have it. She's sick and tired of putting her dreams on hold for some man's word.

The door swings open and Pete comes stomping out, demanding, "What's all this jabber?"

Dad stands tall, facing him.

"We went to a lawyer," Dad says. "He said there's no green card application for us."

"That's what you bolted out of here for? To go talk to a lawyer? I told you, I'm taking care of it."

"Then where's the paperwork?" Mum asks, stepping up. "Show us."

Pete's grip around his cane tightens. "I won't be talked to this way. Not in my own house!"

"Please . . . just tell us the truth," Dad urges him.

Pete lifts his cane and, to our disbelief, starts turning back to the house. He's leaving! Millie jumps into action, sandwiching herself between him and the door.

"But, sir, we had an agreement," Dad says.

In his frustration, Pete blurts out, "I said I'd consider it!"

"That's *not* what you said," Dad says, his cracked

lips practically bleeding as he pushes out the words. "When were you going to tell me?"

Pete uses his cane to try to push past Millie and get inside.

"Answer my dad!" Millie says, glaring at him. "You made me stop speaking Chinese! And pick peas till my fingerprints melted. You made my mama go around picking up horse poop. And she couldn't even take a shower because you refused to let her fill enough water for the bucket. She was stinky! The least you can do is *answer us*!"

But Pete doesn't answer. Instead, he turns and walks down the steps to his garden, like we're invisible. In that moment, my dad finally sees him for who he is. Not a world-saving farmer. But a coward. A coward who duped my trusting parents.

Chapter 77

Mum sleeps with Millie that night, curled up into a ball on the living room mat, exhausted from the injustices of life. I put a blanket over them.

Dad sits at the kitchen table. He looks at me and gives me a sad smile. "You wanna go for a drive?"

I nod right away.

I grab a jacket and follow him to the car, closing the door gently to the sounds of Mum and Millie snoring.

We ride in the silence. Dad takes the 101 freeway north. I assume we're going to the mountain peak again, and I settle in for a long ride. The wind blasts in from his window. I sneak glances at Dad as he drives. His face looks longer than the soybean vine.

"I'm so sorry, Dad," I say to him.

"Don't be sorry," he says. "We'll figure it out."

I look down at my hands, feeling not so sure. Now what do we do? We finally have enough for back rent, but can we even stay in this country?

"Hey . . . ," Dad says, reaching for my hand. "Let me tell you a story."

I look over.

"When I first came here, a graduate student in my biology department told me that the American dream is like a crop. You get out of it what you put in. But once in a while, a drought comes along, and there's nothing you can do."

I gaze up at the cloudless sky, a thousand sparkling stars sprinkled like confetti across the silk canvas.

Dad holds up a finger. "But the fact that you were able to turn the tide at your school . . . that gives me hope."

I let out a small smile as Dad gets off the freeway.

"The fact that you are able to read what you want, say what you want, and imagine a better future . . . *that's* why we keep going. That's what makes it all worth it." Dad pats my hand. "I know you're worried, sunflower. But we'll get that green card. Maybe not today . . . maybe not tomorrow, but one day. And when we do, we'll look back on all this, and it'll just be a brief drought."

I close my eyes as he pulls into a parking lot and imagine the sweet smell of first rain.

When I open my eyes, I look out at the midnight-blue waves and gasp. The beach! We finally made it to the beach!

I run out and jump on the sand. Dad laughs and takes a pic of me with his phone while I chase the crashing waves, forgetting all about the bleak news of the day. All I think about is that I'm here, finally here, on the other side of the coast. I stretch my arm out to my grandmother across the roaring sea. Then I kneel on the sand, and I whisper an apology.

"Lao Lao? Can you hear me? I'm sorry I left you," I tell the waves. My salty tears mix with the ocean mist in my mouth. "But I'm happy here. And I don't know when our American dream . . . our crop's gonna finally be ready, but I want to stick around to watch it grow."

I take a fistful of sand and toss it to the ocean, as an offering. As the waves carry my words out to sea, I hope Lao Lao will tuck them in her seashell. And stick around too.

Chapter 78

Wrapped in Dad's big work jacket, I snuggle up next to him in the car, listening to the gentle lapping of the waves as the velvet sky turns to amber. At dawn, I flutter open my eyelids to see dolphins frolicking in the water.

"Look! There's another one!" I wake Dad up, pointing.

Dad chuckles as he puts his seat up and rubs his eyes. "You think they have to worry about their green card?" he jokes.

"No . . . but they have to worry about finding fish," I reply, which is a *lot* harder as the climate changes. I think about everything Pete taught me about our planet in crisis mode. "Hey, Dad?" I ask. "Is it weird that I still learned a lot from Pete?"

I quickly add, "I mean, I'm still really mad at him."

"No," Dad says. "He's a brilliant farmer. And a terrible employer."

He pauses, looking long and hard at the waves before adding, "He can be both. People are complicated."

"But why?" I ask.

"We'll never really know," he admits. "But I think we can remember the good parts of Pete while still being angry at what he did."

I nod, knowing this mixed feeling well.

"You think we have time to make one last stop at his house, before school? To get my things?" Dad asks.

I nod and reach for the seat belt.

*

Dad stands in Pete's driveway, mustering up the strength to go knock on his door one last time. I walk up the steps with him, resisting the urge to call out, "Carla!" I'll chat with her online later and tell her what happened.

Dad knocks. Pete takes his time answering. Finally, the door swings open. Pete's still in yesterday's clothes. He looks like he hasn't slept a wink either.

"Hi," Dad says. "I just came by to get my things. And my last paycheck —"

"I have it here for you," Pete says. He opens the door and we walk in. Carla and her Mum are inside, packing up Dad's work boots and gloves and putting them in a box. Mrs. Muñoz stuffs the box with as many strawberries and avocados as she can. Carla looks totally devastated for us.

As Pete hands Dad his last cheque, Dad asks, "Can I just understand why? Was it something I did?"

We all look over at Pete, who sits down at the kitchen table.

"Truth is, I wanted to apply for you, I really did," Pete says. "Even went and talked to the lawyer about it. But he told me that in order to get it approved, I'd have to start paying you at the prevailing wage of a farm manager. And I couldn't afford that."

The gravity of this news sinks Dad into a chair too.

"So it was all over money?" Dad asks.

"It was over fear," Pete says. "I didn't want to lose you." He looks over at Dad with his wet, glassy eyes. "This farm's all I've got. I can't let it die." As he looks down at his wrinkled hands, his voice breaks.

"There's life in this soil." Pete starts heaving in his chair, his chest rising and falling with his grief. "I miss my baby so much every day. You gotta understand, I had no choice."

"No," Dad says. "You don't get to do that. You don't get to put this on your daughter. That's not fair to me or to her." Pete pulls himself together and looks into Dad's eyes.

"You're right," he finally says. "I'm sorry I lied to you. If you want me to make this right, fine, I'll go and sign the documents with the lawyer today, if you'll just stay with me awhile longer."

He holds his hand out to Dad.

Dad stares at it. Tense seconds pass. But Dad doesn't take it. Instead, he turns to Mrs. Muñoz and thanks her for packing his box.

"Goodbye, Pete," Dad says. "It's been an honor working for you. But I think I'll find my own path now. I hope you find the peace you're looking for too."

My heart soars with pride as Dad walks away. It's the one time I've ever seen him leave a hand hanging.

Chapter 79

TWO WEEKS LATER

"Hurry!" Mum says. "We're going to be late!"

I rush down the hallway, slowing for just a second to admire the new pictures hanging on the wall. I smile at the one of us splashing in the inflatable hot tub, and me chasing the waves at the beach. My favourite is the picture of me speaking up at the board meeting. Every time I walk by it, my heart swells with pride.

As Mum grabs her bag and Dad takes his keys, looking dapper in his white shirt and khakis, I look around for Millie. Is she still digging through her closet for the perfect pair of tights? I hear a giggle in the corner. I look over and see Millie reading my graphic novel on my computer. Mum insisted I scan it in before sending it to Lao Lao, just in case it got lost in the mail.

"Read that later, we have to go! The open house starts in fifteen minutes!" Dad says, patting his belly. "I hear there's going to be *free* cookies."

"And ice cream!" Mum reminds us. Her new partner, Cindy's Ice Cream, is going to have an ice cream truck there!

"Just five more minutes! It's so good," Millie begs, not wanting to take her eyes from my graphic novel. Her reaction is a very nice – no, a very *BUBBLE* – way to make me feel special. There's a knock at the door. Mum opens it. It's Mr. Beezley, coming to collect his rent. Before he can utter a single word, Mum hands him the back rent check.

The expression on his face as he looks down and sees the full amount is priceless. Never in a million pandemics did he think we could pull it off!

"What'd you do, rob a bank or something?" he asks.

"Oh no. I just start a company, created a killer product line, entered into joint venture, and market it like fire on Etsy. What did *you* do these last six weeks?" Mum answers, giving him some serious side-eye.

That shuts Mr. Beezley up.

As he skulks away with our cheque, Mum turns to me, Millie, and Dad. "Ready to roll?" she asks.

"Ready, boss!" Dad replies.

*

The school is all lit up with sparkling lights when we arrive. I spot Mrs. Hollins next to the **OPEN HOUSE** sign, talking to Mrs. Carter and Mrs. Ortiz.

I wave enthusiastically at them. I'm so glad Dad's no longer working for Pete, so he can come tonight and meet my fabulous teachers. As I lead my parents over, Millie spots Mallory and dashes off. I smile as the two of them practice dolphining and clock-powing under my old friend, the tall eucalyptus tree.

Mrs. Hollins, Mrs. Carter, and Mrs. Ortiz gush to my parents about my great progress as a student.

"Thank you for teaching her," Mum says. "She's so lucky to have you."

"The pleasure's all ours," Mrs. Ortiz says. "Have you seen her graphic novel?"

"I have!" Mum says proudly, stroking my hair with her hand. "It's like opening a window into her heart."

My chin trembles slightly as I turn to Mum. All I've ever wanted is to have a direct path to her heart. And now I've got one. I reach out my arms and hug her. "Love you," I whisper, right then and there, even though in all the American movies I've watched, no one has ever said *I love you* at an open house.

But I don't care. I'm living my own American movie, I decide.

Mum hugs me back and says, "Love you too," into my hair.

"Oh Lord, you two are gonna make me cry," Mrs. Carter says, dabbing at her eyes.

Luckily, Finn and his dad walk up. As we let them have a turn talking to the teachers, Finn sneaks me a packet of Jelly Bellys.

"How was San Francisco?" I ask him. They just got back from another weekend trip. This time, instead of taking him to a Rams game, his dad took him to the Jelly Belly factory in the Bay Area!

"You gotta see the factory – it was amazing! Even bigger than M&M's Las Vegas!"

I grin, glad to hear it. As Dad spots Mrs. Muñoz and Carla, I tell Finn I'll catch up with him later. I told Carla about the open house, talking up the fact that there would be free cookies. I'm so glad she came! We walk over to them.

"How are things?" Dad asks Mrs. Muñoz. "I miss you!" "Miss you too," Mrs. Muñoz says. "It's not the same working on the farm without you."

"Hang in there. You just have ten more days left, right?" Dad asks.

Carla does a little happy cheer. I'm so glad Mrs. Muñoz decided to find a new *paying* job – at a flower shop in Winfield! That's not all – Carla and her Mum are officially moving out of the tiny home next weekend and into a small studio apartment, not far from our house!

"Thanks again for agreeing to help us move next weekend," Mrs. Muñoz says. "I know it's not easy for you to come back and see Pete."

Dad bats away the concern.

"What about you? How's the job search going?" Mrs Muñoz asks.

"It's going. There's a new professor at my university. I'm hoping he might be looking for some help with his lab . . . and if that doesn't work, I'll try my luck with the other farms." Dad's voice trails off and he gives a nervous smile.

"You'll land somewhere," Mrs. Muñoz offers.

"I have no doubt," Mum says. "And until you find the right place, you can help me at JML!" She tells Mrs. Muñoz that according to her new lawyer, if her company does well, he might be able to help us apply for a green card – under the extraordinary ability in business category! Mum chews her lip as she adds, "It's a pretty hard category to qualify under, though."

"If anyone can do it, it's you," Dad says, leaning over and giving Mum a kiss. "I'd love nothing better than to help my *extraordinarily* talented wife. If you'll have me."

"Course I'll have you, silly," Mum says.

I smile at the beautiful sight of the two of them, playfully bumping shoulders under the shimmering lights.

"What about you, Carla?" I ask. "Are you still homeschool after your Mum work at the flower shop?"

"Actually . . . I was thinking," Mrs. Muñoz says. "Maybe it's time for Carla to go back to school. Do you think she might be able to get a permit too, since I'll be working in Winfield?"

I scream at the thought of Carla coming to my school. Carla starts jumping up and down! We grab onto each other's arms and giggle with glee.

"AHHHHH!!!" I shout. "It's gonna be amazing!"

"I can't wait!" Carla says.

Excitedly, Mum walks Mrs. Muñoz through the process of getting a permit. She tells Mrs. Muñoz what documents to bring to the school office tomorrow and whom to speak to. As she's talking, her phone rings. Mum hands it to me to answer.

I look down at the number – it's Lao Lao!

"Lina!" Lao Lao's warm voice greets me. "Or should I say esteemed author who happens to be my granddaughter?"

"You got my graphic novel?" I ask her, squealing.

"Came in the mail yesterday, and I devoured it in one gulp," Lao Lao tells me. "Lina, this is really something! I'm so proud of you."

I put Lao Lao on speaker so Mum can hear.

"I loved all the scenes with you and Millie at the farm with your new friend. And that boy Finn, at school. What a sweet boy. Handsome, too!"

"Lao Lao!" I exclaim, blushing. I look around for Finn, but thankfully he's still talking to Mrs. Carter and can't hear.

"I especially like the scene with you and your mama on the staircase, after you got home from the school board meeting. It was so emotional. Tell your mama she's a great daughter and I'm proud of her, too," Lao Lao says.

Mum's eyes grow misty as she listens to Lao Lao's words. "Next time, send me a couple copies, will ya? Some of my friends want to borrow it."

"Friends?" I ask, holding my breath.

"Oh yeah! I finally made some pals here. Li Ran, Ning, and Wei," Lao Lao tells me. "Speaking of them, I've got to get to mah jong. I'll call you again in a few days – Wei has a smartphone. We can even do video chat. It's free!"

I throw my arms up at the possibility of finally being able to "see" my grandma again!

"I'd love that, Lao Lao!" I say. "Miss you!"

Millie runs over and squeezes in. She tells Lao Lao she misses her too, and asks if she can help knit some gloves for her friend Mallory for the talent show – they've decided to enter together as a dance group!

"You got it, Twinkle Toes!" Lao Lao promises.

No sooner do we hang
Bennett calls for everyone
mic in one hand and an envelope

"All right, parents and students
you could join us. Now, the momen
been waiting for . . . we're thrilled to anno
year's special book fair author speaker!"

I scan the courtyard for Finn. He's still standi
with Mrs. Hollins. He looks over at me and crosses
his fingers.

"We had a lot of great suggestions from teachers
and parents. But we decided to let the kids vote this
year. And by popular vote, the speaker they most
want to invite is" – Principal Bennett does a little
drumroll with his mic as he tears the envelope
open – "Catherine Wang!"

My hands fly to my cheeks. My student librarian heart is about to burst! Millie throws her arms
around me as Finn comes racing over and so many
of my classmates cheer triumphantly!

"Mama, did you hear?" I ask.

"I heard!" Mum chuckles at my floored, ecstatic
face, while Dad high-fives, fist-bumps, shakes,
snaps, and hugs me! *Finally!* Dad and I have five

..y, I could do a
..s. Instead, I thank
..art. I can't wait to see
special gestures..nally be able to ask her
I gaze ..en whispering to her book at
Hair ..riting *Flea Shop*? Did her heart
..way mine did when I first showed
..phic novel? Does she still have that
..anut butter letter opener? Most of all,
I want to thank her, for making me feel seen. It is
the most powerful feeling in the world.

"You know what this calls for?" Mum asks,
slipping a fivedollar bill each into my and Millie's
hand. "Ice cream!"

We race each other over to Cindy's Ice Cream
truck, me, Millie, Carla, and Finn. The four of us
giggle and shriek as we run, and for a second, I feel
like we're playing the Eagle and the Chicks again
with Lao Lao in the crisp Beijing breeze. I stop
running for a second and put my hand over my
heart, so Lao Lao can feel it too. Then I hurry after
all my friends.

There's one person standing in line when we get

there. It's Jessica.

I settle in for a long wait, thinking she's going to give some insanely long order, just to annoy me. But instead, she looks at me and asks, "You wanna go first?"

I put a hand to my chest, shocked. "Me?" I ask. "Sure?"

She nods and steps aside.

I gaze at the ice cream board, trying to decide what to order. There are so many delicious but hard-to-pronounce flavours. Once again, I feel the anxiety of getting the pronunciation wrong, but this time I clock-pow my fear.

"Rocky road," I proudly announce. I hand over my money and move over in line.

"Same," Jessica says, reaching for a five-dollar bill tucked inside her book. I notice she's holding a copy of *Drama* in her hands.

"You know what you should read after that?" I say to her. "*Sunny Side Up.*"

"Really?" she asks. "What's it about?"

"About a girl who go live with her grandfather for summer," I tell her. "It's really good."

"I'd love to live with my grandparents for the

summer," Jessica confesses. She lingers for a second before adding, "I'm sorry for what I wrote about you . . . on the bathroom wall."

I blush with surprise. Then I offer her a truce, pointing to her book.

"No more drama?" I ask her. Jessica smiles. "I'd like that."

We eat our ice creams. When the last drop has been licked from our spoons, my sister and I run toward the playground and jump on the swings. We don't know what the future will bring, what crops or droughts await our next chapter, but we kick our legs as high as we can, our hearts brimming with hope, under the glowing moon.

Author's Note

I was six years old when my parents and I moved to America. Like Lina, I was *terrified* that if I made a mistake and mispronounced something in English, I'd be the laughing stock of the entire class.

I vowed not to say anything in school. For an entire year, I sat at my desk, completely silent. I was deeply worried about my future in this country. Was I ever going to find my voice? I stared enviously at the other kids chatting away, while I couldn't push even a single word out. At times, it truly felt like I had an invisible string tying my lips shut.

My ESL teacher was not deterred. She guided me, patiently and methodically, word after word, one after another. I'll never forget when she traced my hand and taught me the word "hand." Slowly, I felt the string loosening, until one day, on the very last week of school, I said my first sentence!

My entire class was shocked. My teacher was shocked. I was shocked.

On the basis of this one sentence, I was promoted to the second grade! For my first report card in America, I did not receive any grades. Instead, all I received was this note:

Yang entered Sherrouse February 19, 1991. She could speak no English. We have been working with her on her English and on a pre-primer level in reading. She does very well on most of her math. It has only been within the last week that she has been speaking very limited sentences in English.

She is being placed in Grade 2 because students are not retained because of limited English.

Mrs. Janice Hanchey

For years, I carried this note in my pocket. I thought, maybe, just maybe, I have a chance in this country too! At the start of second grade, I started going to the library every day. Soon after, my parents and I got a job managing a motel. It gave me an incredible opportunity to practice English (I loved talking to all the customers!), but it was also wildly different from the way all the kids lived in the books

I was reading. None of them lived in motels or looked like me. None of them had parents who worried about getting their green cards or how to pay back rent.

Over time, I started to internalise that difference as something wrong. Something shameful. Something I ought to never tell anybody else about.

So I kept my life a secret. I told myself I could never have a play date, or even a single birthday party, because then my classmates would find out! That's how obsessed I was with keeping my life a secret. That's the price of never seeing yourself represented on the page.

Years later, I became a Mum and I thought to myself, what am I doing? I can't go through my entire life not telling anyone how I grew up, not even my own children! So in the summer of 2015, I sat down to write a children's book for my son. A book that told the honest truth, the ups and downs, the joys and heartbreaks, and yes, the humor – because there was a lot of humor – of my roller coaster childhood living in a motel. That book was called *Front Desk*.

Never in my wildest dreams did I ever think it

would go on to become one of the 30 Most Influential Children's Books of All Time (Book Riot).

Never in my wildest dreams did I think that I'd have children coming up to me at book signings, hugging me, crying, telling me how much my book means to them. That for the first time in their lives, they saw themselves represented on the page!

Nor did I ever expect, in 2021, to hear that my book was getting banned in school districts. My heart dropped to the pit of my stomach when I first found out. A parent reached out begging me to help, because his son's teacher was in the middle of reading *Front Desk* as a class read aloud, and another parent complained. As a result, the read-aloud had to be stopped.

The reason? My book was "divisive."

I can't describe the avalanche of emotions I felt that day. My heart broke for all the students in the class, who weren't allowed to finish the chapter they were on. I ached for young me, who wondered for decades whether her immigrant life was worthy of telling a single friend. I cried for all the progress we've made bringing more representation in books, progress that can easily be rolled up like a carpet if we don't actively safeguard access to books.

So I took to social media and I used my voice. I've been speaking out ever since. I am proud to support the freedom to read, far and wide, as loud as I can, to speak out against book banning, whenever and wherever it happens. My greatest hope in writing this book is to show just how essential books are as sliding doors and mirrors.

Because children need and deserve to see themselves represented in books.

Because no child should have to carry the same crushing weight of wondering if their life is "normal" that I did as a kid.

Because our future depends on it.

Acknowledgments

My heartfelt thanks to my incredible team, starting with my amazing editor Krista Vitola, without whom this book would not be possible. Thank you for always reading my work with such tender care, giving me honest feedback, and trusting me with rewrites. :) I could not be more proud of the work we do together! To my entire Simon & Schuster team – Justin Chandra, Tara Shanahan, Antonella Colon, Beth Parker, Michelle Leo, Nicole Benevento, Caleigh Flegg, Alyza Liu, Kendra Levin, Sarah Creech, Hilary Zarycky, Bridget Madsen, and Chava Wolin – thanks so much for supporting me and my books. I feel so honored to be a part of such a passionate and collaborative team!

To my literary agent, Tina Dubois, thanks for

believing in me and cheering on Lina with every draft! It is the honor of my lifetime being able to work on books with you. To my family at Curtis Brown Translation, Enrichetta Frezzato, Isobel Gahan, and Roxane Edouard, thank you for bringing my stories to the world! Much love to my film agent, Sylvie Rabineau; every day is an adventure and I'm so glad I have you by my side!

All my gratitude to my UK family at Knights Of: Eishar Brar, Aimee Felone, Sophie McDonnell, Natelle Quek, Sabina Maharajan, Ella Chapman, George Charles, Elizabeth Oladoyin and Sam Suthurst – thank you for publishing and championing my books across the pond!

Much gratitude to my lawyer Paul Sennott, for helping me navigate not just my deals, but also, my career! Thank you to Joel McKuin as well, for his wise counsel. A huge thank-you to Shelby Renjifo, my brilliant assistant and friend. Thank you for all your assistance with research on farming practices for this book! It's such a pleasure working with you!

Big thanks to my dear friends Anna Cummins and Marcus Eriksen, for their first-hand insight on organic farming. My heartfelt thanks as well to my dear friends Lindsey Moore, Jennie Urman, and Paul Cummins. So grateful to my author friends Stacy McAnulty, Gene Yang, Stuart Gibbs, Jeff Kinney, Jerry Craft, John Schumacher, Varian Johnson, Victoria Piontek, Mae Respicio, Mike Jung, and Alex Gino for their endless support.

Shout-out to some of my favourite indie booksellers – Brein Lopez! MarySheila McMahon! Cathy Berner! Angie Tally! Chris Abouzeid! Thank you to all the amazing folks hand-selling my books; I truly believe that indie bookstores are the cornerstones of our community. Many thanks as well to Christie Hinrichs and Rebecca Miller for connecting me with schools all over the world so I can share my story!

Most of all, thank you to all the teachers and librarians who give me hope for the future: keep shining, keep inspiring, and keep making a difference in so many young people's lives! This book's for you!

Last but not least, to my family: my husband, Stephen, and my kids, Eliot, Tilden, and Nina, who have all experienced periods of separation from either me or my husband during the pandemic, as our family navigated an intercontinental move. I love you guys. I hope this book is a mirror for you . . . and a sliding door to my heart.

More by Kelly Yang . . .

Kelly Yang

Author

Kelly Yang's family immigrated from China when she was a young girl, and she grew up in California, in circumstances very similar to those of Mia Tang. She eventually left the motels and went to college at the age of thirteen, and is a graduate of UC Berkeley and Harvard Law School. She was one of the youngest women to graduate from Harvard Law School.

Upon graduation, she gave up law to pursue her dream of writing and teaching kids writing. She is the founder of The Kelly Yang Project, a leading writing and debating program for children in Asia and the United States. She is also a columnist for the *South China Morning Post* and has been published in the *New York Times*, the *Washington Post*, and the *Atlantic*. Kelly is the mother of three children and splits her time between Hong Kong and San Francisco.